IDENTIFYING MARKS

"If you think this act you're putting on will distract me from recognizing you, you're mistaken. I recognized you immediately. I know who you are."

Banning's eyes flicked open. "Really? Who am I? *Wade?*"

Thea gasped. "You really are a bastard!"

"And it seems you're really not the *lady* you pretend to be."

Ignoring his deliberate affront, Thea responded, "You're wasting your time if you think you're fooling me. Just for the record, I know you're not Wade. You look like him, but that's where the resemblance ends. Your personality is sadly lacking—but most importantly, Wade was a *lawman.*" Pausing, she then spat, "And you're a *thief!*"

To Meet Again

Elaine Barbieri

LEISURE BOOKS NEW YORK CITY

A LEISURE BOOK®

September 2001

Published by

Dorchester Publishing Co., Inc.
276 Fifth Avenue
New York, NY 10001

ISBN 0-8439-4908-2

The name "Leisure Books" and the stylized "L" with design are trademarks of Dorchester Publishing Co., Inc.

Printed in the United States of America.

Visit us on the web at www.dorchesterpub.com.

To Evan Marshall,
my agent and my friend.
You're the greatest!

To Meet Again

Prologue

1880

"Do you, Wade Randolph Preston, take Thea
Elizabeth Radcliffe to be your lawfully wedded wife . . ."

Reverend Martin's deep voice rang with familiar authority in the small Georgia church,
yet the dreamlike quality of the moment persisted as Thea stared up into the eyes of the
man she loved.

". . . to have and to hold from this day forward . . ."

She had waited all her life for this moment—since she was eight years old and first
set eyes on the lanky, fourteen-year-old son

11

of a nearby rancher; since she saw his reluctant smile flash, and decided then and there that she would marry him one day.

". . . in sickness and in health . . ."

But she was no longer a child, and Wade wasn't a lanky adolescent anymore. He was a man—a tall, handsome man with a smile that still melted her heart—and she was his woman.

". . . until death do you part?"

Wade's dark eyes held hers. "I do."

I love you, Wade.

"Do you, Thea Elizabeth Radcliffe, take Wade Randolph Preston to be your lawfully wedded—"

Gunshots broke the silence of the small church. The sounds reverberated in Thea's mind as Wade's powerful frame jerked with the impact of the bullets that struck him—as she stood frozen with incredulity, and he sank toward the floor.

There were screams from the pews, startled shouts and the sound of running feet. The slamming of the church doors.

Inured to all, Thea kneeled beside Wade. Her sense of unreality expanding, she cradled him in her arms. No, this couldn't be happening. Wade couldn't be lying on the hard church floor, his blood staining the pristine white of her wedding gown. He couldn't be struggling to breathe, his lips forming words that went unspoken. He couldn't be looking up at her, pain creasing his face as she leaned closer, imploring him to tell her this wasn't real.

"Thea . . ."

Unreality vanished when Wade gasped her name. In its place came excruciating desolation as Thea cupped his cheek with her hand and pressed her trembling lips to his.

"Don't cry."

She wasn't crying, was she?

"I . . . love you, Thea."

"You'll be all right, Wade. You have to be."

"No."

Thea's breath caught on a sob.

". . . can't stand to see you cry."

"Wade, please—"

Wade's breath rattled in his chest and his eyelids drooped. Making a supreme effort, he grasped her hand. His dark eyes suddenly acutely clear, he rasped, "Don't . . . don't cry. We'll meet again."

Shouts. Sobs. Racing footsteps.

The frenzy of the moment continued as Wade went lifelessly still.

Chapter One

1882

She must be crazy.

The stagecoach bumped and swayed along the dusty trail as Thea covertly studied the assortment of characters occupying the seats around her. She had never before seen the like of the fellow dozing across from her. Bearded, wearing soiled, fringed buckskins, his shoulder-length hair hanging in unruly strands from beneath an equally soiled, broad-brimmed hat, he looked like a character from a poorly written dime novel—and he smelled perfectly awful.

The fellow seated beside him, also dozing,

wasn't much better. She had never seen a handlebar mustache as broad and sweeping as his.

Seated on either side of her, their wide-spread thighs claiming far more of the seat than they were entitled to, sat two nonde-script, unshaven Westerners who had spent the last hour snoring in an uneven chorus that was driving her wild.

What was she doing here?

Are you sure you want to do this, Thea?

The question softly posed by Maribelle Car-ter a week earlier echoed in Thea's mind. The dear woman had taken her under her wing after her mother had died when she was twelve. Grief-stricken, Samuel Radcliffe had protested vociferously, saying Thea didn't need anybody but him. Maribelle had been there for her again when her father failed to wake up one sunny morning only five years later. Maribelle—and Wade.

Thea, Wyoming isn't even civilized!

It was civilized enough to accept Aunt Vic-toria as a doctor after Georgia turned its nose up at her.

That's what I mean.

And that's the kind of thinking that forced Aunt Victoria to leave.

You hardly know the woman. You haven't seen her since you were a child.

She's my mother's sister.

She's a stranger to you.

She's my only family.

But Georgia is your home!

I'm leaving at the end of the week.

Famous last words.

She'd been too stubborn to admit that Maribelle was right. Aunt Victoria *was* a virtual stranger to her. All she clearly remembered about the woman was that Aunt Victoria's hair was the same brilliant red-gold as her mother's and her own, and that as a child, she'd been unable to understand why Aunt Victoria's eyes were brown instead of the same translucent gray as her mother's and hers. She also remembered that her mother had been proud of her younger sister and the hard work she had put into becoming a doctor, and that when Georgia refused to recognize Aunt Victoria as a medical practitioner, her mother had supported her aunt's decision to move west.

Aunt Victoria had never come back to Georgia, even for a visit, but she had maintained contact by letter. Thea had felt her aunt's sorrow in the letter she wrote after her mother died, and she had felt her aunt's true

17

sadness after her father died, too. Aunt Victoria had asked her to come out to Wyoming then. Thea had refused, giving a single word in explanation: Wade.

Choking snorts from the brawny cowpoke beside her interrupted Thea's thoughts. Frowning when the fellow's snoring resumed, Thea turned to stare out at the inhospitable Wyoming wilderness, which seemed little more than a vast panorama of rolling grassland, distant mountains, bumpy roads to nowhere and choking dust that obscured the sun.

Are you sure you want to do this, Thea?

She had been so sure.

Or had she?

Thea blinked back tears. Two years had passed since the day when gunshots rocked that small Georgia church, bringing her brilliant hopes for the future to an abrupt end.

Thea's jaw twitched with an anger that she knew would never be resolved. Bart Snipes had been caught two days after he shot Wade, purportedly to avenge his brother's death. Showing no remorse, he had left the courtroom shouting, "An eye for an eye!" Snipes had taken the life of a decent lawman for the life of a thieving bank robber who had already killed two men before Wade had been forced to bring him down.

But no amount of anger or grief could change reality when Wade was buried in the same small cemetery where her parents lay side by side.

She had suffered all the platitudes.

Life goes on.

The pain will fade.

You can't mourn forever.

You have your whole life ahead of you. You'll find someone else someday.

Wrong.

Life went on, but the pain didn't fade. She had stopped mourning, but memories continued to torment her, revisiting her at every familiar corner she turned. Yes, she had her whole life ahead of her, but she began to realize that she couldn't face it in Georgia, where Wade's image remained so strong.

Aunt Victoria's letter had been providential.

Maribelle's protest had been immediate.

But you don't know anything about doctoring!

Aunt Victoria's the doctor. She said she needs help—my help.

Why doesn't she get someone in Wyoming to help her?

Maybe because she needs me, her only sister's daughter.

That's crazy!

No, it isn't.

It's too far away!

She only hoped it would be far enough.

Thea sighed. She had hoped a lot of things when she set out. What she had gotten instead were endless days of uncomfortable travel—the last leg of her journey being this backbreaking stagecoach ride plagued by heat, dust-laden air and the odor of her fellow passengers.

Wyoming isn't even civilized!

Weary, Thea closed her eyes as Maribelle's words came back to haunt her.

Gunshots on the trail behind the stage snapped Thea's eyes open. Startled awake and immediately alert, her fellow passengers leaned out the windows to survey the situation behind them. The buckskin-clad fellow jerked back inside when bullets struck dangerously close, exclaiming, "Dammit, we're bein' held up!"

Images of a wedding gown stained with blood flashed before Thea's eyes, and she shuddered. Surprising her, the man seated at her right turned toward her as the stage began sliding to a hasty halt. His craggy face creased with concern, he said, "Don't you worry, ma'am. There's no way Buck or me will let anything happen to a nice young lady like you."

A nod from the fellow on her left confirmed his friend's comment as a voice rang out sharply beyond the stagecoach door.

"Throw your guns out the window!"

The passengers complied.

"All right, everybody out—now!"

Thea looked up at the armed robbers as her brawny seatmate swung her to the ground. There were four of them, their faces concealed by neckerchiefs that allowed only a glimpse of their hard eyes as one man leveled his gun in their direction and the others moved into action.

The strongbox hit the ground with a thud. Thea looked up to see one of the thieves climbing down from the top of the coach while another man shot open the lock and scooped the contents into a sack, and another gathered the passengers' discarded guns and threw them into a pouch attached to his saddle.

Her seatmate protested, "You ain't takin' our guns, are you?"

The answer was obvious.

Taking an angry step when another of the

robbers unharnessed the horses, the driver grated, "I don't give a damn about the strongbox, but leave us the horses. We ain't got no water. We'll be stranded out here if you take them."

"Shut up!" Turning viciously toward him, the short gunman spat, "The strongbox and the horses ain't all we're taking. Empty your pockets—now!"

"Son of a—"

"Watch your mouth, old man, or them words might be your last."

A familiar sense of incredulity held her motionless while Thea watched her fellow passengers empty their pockets. Somehow unable to move, she did not react until a voice sounded softly beside her.

"You, too, sweetheart. Give me your purse."

Thea jerked toward the familiar voice, her heart suddenly pounding. She caught her breath at first sight of the dark eyes looking down at her from the man's partially concealed face.

It . . . it couldn't be.

"Get her jewelry, too. I got a woman who'll take a real fancy to that brooch she's wearing."

His gaze hardening in response to the gunman's order, the thief beside her grated, "You heard him. Give me that brooch."

That voice. Those eyes. It couldn't be!

Gasping as the fellow snatched the purse from her arm, then tore the brooch from her bodice, Thea swayed weakly. She was hardly aware of the supportive arm her seatmate slipped around her or his plea on her behalf. "Leave her be, will you? Can't you see she's scared half to death?"

No, she wasn't afraid. She just wanted—

But the robber wasn't waiting for a response. His job accomplished, he joined the others retreating to their horses.

Thea took an unsteady step toward them as they remounted.

"Stay where you are!"

The short gunman's warning shout halted her. She stood motionless as the thieves turned their mounts and thundered off into the wilderness, dragging the team of horses behind them.

Chapter Two

Squinting against the glare of the sun, Thea stripped the dry linens from the line and turned back toward the small frame house that was now her home in Willowby, Wyoming. Three weeks had passed since the day gunshots had rebounded on the dusty trail behind the stagecoach. The robbery had left her and her fellow passengers stranded in the wilderness with no means of protection or transportation.

Thea frowned, unaware of an observer watching her approach from the rear doorway of the house. She reviewed the incredible events again in her mind.

The stagecoach robbery had been quick

and efficient, as if the thieves were well versed at their job. Left standing in the dust with a horseless stagecoach their only means of conveyance, her fellow travelers and she had started walking.

Shame briefly flushed Thea's cheeks. She had been silently critical of her fellow passengers, yet those same men whom she had disdained had proved to be true gentlemen in their treatment of her, displaying courtesy and concern despite their own physical discomfort. When she began to falter after long, thirsty hours, Harvey Jones, the buckskin-clad fellow she had particularly scorned, had actually carried her until the sheriff's posse found them and delivered them all to town.

She supposed she would never forget finally reaching Willowby at sundown of that endless day. Sharing a member of the posse's saddle, she had arrived hot and dirty, with blistered feet and sunburned skin. Nor would she forget that despite his own exhaustion, her brawny seatmate, Jerry Tack, had hopped off his horse to lift her down onto the hard-packed dirt street; or that her fellow passengers had remained at her side, a weary wall of comfort while she had stood shaken and uncertain in the gathering crowd of unfamiliar faces.

She had recognized Aunt Victoria the second she saw her pushing her way through the crowd. It could have been no one else. Hair that had once been a startling red was now tempered with strands of gray; clear skin that had once been faultlessly smooth and meticulously protected from the sun now showed signs of the harsh Wyoming climate and the passing years; her once fashionable clothing had yielded to a simple shirtwaist and skirt, and incongruous cowboy boots—yet Aunt Victoria's smile was the same, so similar to her mother's that it brought tears to her eyes.

Extending sincere thanks to Thea's fellow passengers and an invitation for them to visit, Aunt Victoria had ushered Thea to her small house, where she had provided food, water to bathe, soothing consolation and a bed with linens that smelled of sunshine.

The days following had turned into weeks as Thea began acclimating herself to her new life. It had been immediately obvious that Aunt Victoria's invitation to join her had not merely been a matter of courtesy. Traveling long miles as she did to treat her patients, her aunt was in dire need of help, and Thea was glad to be needed—yet she continued to feel unsettled.

Aunt Victoria had not pressed her to speak

of her ordeal that first day, and Thea had been silently grateful. She had known it would be impossible to explain why the dark eyes of that one stagecoach robber haunted her; or how the sound of that same man's voice had set her heart pounding.

"What's wrong, Thea?"

Thea jumped when her aunt addressed her. Entering the kitchen, she forced a smile. "Nothing's wrong. Why do you ask?"

Aunt Victoria searched her face for silent moments. Soberly removing the laundry basket from Thea's hands, her aunt placed it on the table and turned back toward her. "I have something to say that's difficult for me, my dear. I've hesitated far too long already, and it needs to be said."

At Thea's obvious concern, Aunt Victoria explained, "You've been a tremendous help to me, Thea. It's only been three weeks since you arrived, yet with your help, I've been able to do so much more for my patients than before. But I owe you an apology. I needed help here very badly. That fact, and my yearning to have my sister's daughter with me became so strong that I didn't stop to consider the danger I was putting you in when I invited you to come out here. That was unforgivable of me. I want you to know that as much as I

wanted you here, if that thought had even occurred to me, I wouldn't have asked you to
come."

"Please don't say that, Aunt Victoria," Thea
said sincerely. "There was no way anyone
could've anticipated that the stagecoach I arrived on would be robbed."

"Maybe not, but I shouldn't have allowed
you to come out here alone. I should have
traveled back East to accompany you."

"*You* traveled here alone when you weren't
much older than I am right now. Besides, I
wasn't really alone." Thea forced a smile. "My
fellow passengers took good care of me. With
their help, I arrived safe and sound . . . and a
little wiser then I was before. I've put the
whole episode behind me."

"Have you, dear?" Aunt Victoria scrutinized her more closely, then shook her head.
"I don't think so, and I think I know what's
been bothering you."

Thea's heart jumped. How could her aunt
possibly know?

Her eyes misting unexpectedly, Aunt Victoria took an unsteady breath. "It was your
mother's brooch that those thieves stole from
you, wasn't it?"

Her mother's brooch.

"You haven't said a word about it, but Jerry

29

Tack told me you were wearing a brooch that caught the eye of one of the thieves. Jerry said one of them ripped it right off your dress. He described the brooch to me."

Her brooch, the cameo that had been her father's wedding gift to her mother. Thea's throat thickened. She had shed many tears in the silence of her new room, knowing the brooch was gone forever, but the full impact of losing that treasured keepsake had been forced from her mind by the memory of dark eyes that would allow her no rest.

"I'm so sorry, Thea. I know that brooch was important to you. I wish there was some way I could get it back for you."

"It wasn't your fault."

"Yes, it was."

Thea was suddenly ashamed. Her aunt was suffering needless guilt. It was time to face the truth. No matter how startlingly familiar the dark eyes of that stagecoach robber had seemed when he had stood beside her—those eyes hadn't been Wade's eyes. Nor had it been Wade's voice she had heard when the fellow spoke, as she had somehow managed to convince herself. Wade was dead. He had died in her arms, and no amount of fantasizing or wishful thinking could bring him back.

Taking her aunt's hand, Thea whispered,

"I'm the one who should apologize, Aunt Victoria. I came here to escape the past; yet, somehow, I've been clinging to it more firmly than I did back home. As for the brooch, it's gone. It's neither your fault nor mine that it was stolen, and there's nothing either one of us can do about it. What's important is that I'm here where I belong now, and this is where I'm going to stay."

Her smile tremulously bright, Aunt Victoria replied, "You're so much like your mother at times, it's almost painful, Thea. The day I left Margaret behind without knowing if I'd ever see her again was one of the saddest days of my life. She and I always said that if we—"

A startling pounding on the front door interrupted Aunt Victoria's sentiments. She turned sharply as the door burst open to reveal two men supporting an unconscious third man between them.

Thea went still at the sight of them.

The first fellow grated, "Didn't mean to bust in on you, Doc, but this fella just rode into town and fell off his horse in front of the saloon. His head's bleedin' like he might've gotten throwed and cracked his head open on a rock or somethin', and he's soaking wet like he might've been lying out in that rain last night."

31

Thea struggled to catch her breath as Aunt Victoria waved the men in. She heard her aunt speaking as if from a distance. "Take him into the back room and stretch him out on the table, Jake," the older woman directed. "I'll see what I can do for him."

Unable to move, Thea watched as the injured man was dragged toward the rear room and out of her sight. She heard the first cowpoke grunt with relief, then say, "He's a big fella, Doc. He's damned heavy. You want us to hang around a bit in case you need us?"

"That might be good." Aunt Victoria sounded distracted. "While you're waiting, you can help yourselves to some of the stew that's on the stove."

The men mumbled their gratitude. They moved toward the kitchen, passing Thea with polite nods that she was too numb to return.

Inwardly trembling, Thea willed herself to take one step, then another and another, until she stood in the doorway of the rear room at last. Rigid, she stared down at the fellow stretched out on the examination table. He lay silent and still, his eyes closed. Blood clotted on an open wound on the side of his head, and his face was blanched of color.

The man was unconscious, inert, but he was alive.

The man was Wade.

* * *

"Who are you?"

The hoarse question resounded strangely in Quinn's mind as he opened his eyes to an unfamiliar room. The question had been posed by a blurred female image that hovered over him as he struggled to clear his vision.

Where was he?

Was he awake, or was he dreaming?

The last thing he clearly remembered was riding at breakneck speed in an attempt to get back to the cabin before Max and Ernie returned. It had been urgent that he did, for a reason he couldn't seem to recall.

Pain knifed through his temple, erasing that thought, and Quinn groaned. He closed his eyes as disjointed images flashed through his mind:

His horse was stumbling.

The powerful animal was going down.

A burst of pain.

The damp ground was beneath him.

He struggled to remount.

He was too weak . . .

"Answer me! I know you're awake. Who are you?"

The desperation in the woman's voice forced Quinn's eyes open. Her image remained blurred as he scanned his surroundings. The room had an unreal quality. Its furnishings were austere, and it was a startling white in color that was magnified to almost painful brightness by the broad beams of sunlight slanting through the window beside his bed.

The woman leaned closer.

"Is it . . . is it you, Wade?"

His vision clearing, Quinn saw delicate features, clear pale skin, great gray eyes looking down questioningly into his and hair the color of fire.

Her breath was warm on his cheek as she whispered almost fearfully, "Oh, God . . . Please tell me, is it you, Wade?"

Wade?

His mind abruptly clearing, Quinn mumbled a curse. It was *her*. Of all the damned luck! He had to get out of here.

Thrusting the woman roughly out of his line of vision, Quinn ordered, "Get out of my way!"

His attempt to sit up was aborted by the sudden, paralyzing pain that knifed through his head, knocking him back against the pillow, and Quinn gasped aloud. He opened his eyes a narrow slit when a harsh female voice ordered from the doorway, "Lie still."

Approaching his bed, an older woman continued sharply, "You're not going anywhere yet. In case you're not quite sure what happened to you, all I can tell you is that from the looks of it, your horse threw you and you hit your head. You made it into town on your own, and two fellows carried you here."

The older woman leaned closer. "My name is Dr. Sills, and the only thing I can add to what I've just said is that you're lucky you're alive after riding with a head wound that severe. I stitched up the cut, but that isn't the worst of it. You have a concussion. You've been unconscious for almost twenty-four hours. You're going to be groggy for a few days, maybe even seeing double for a while, too. If you take it easy and give things a chance to settle, you'll probably be all right—but if you try getting up before I say you're ready, you probably won't make it to the door."

The woman squinted down at him. "In case I haven't made myself perfectly clear, I'm telling you that if you go down again, the chances are you won't get up."

That was plain enough.

Quinn raised a hand to his throbbing head. The effort exhausted him and he closed his eyes as the female doctor spoke again.

"You're in my dispensary now. You can

stay here until you're back on your feet."

Quinn peered out through slitted eyelids at the woman leaning over him, then at the young, red-haired female who stared at him with strange intensity.

She had recognized him.

"What's your name?" the woman doctor asked again. "You weren't carrying any identification, and we should know who you are, just in case."

In case. He didn't like the sound of that.

"Can you hear me? What's your name?"

He took a shallow breath, consciousness fading.

"Your name . . ."

"Quinn . . . Quinn Banning."

"Well, Quinn, I—"

Darkness.

"He's unconscious again."

Suddenly aware of her niece's silence, Victoria turned toward Thea. Thea's posture was rigid and her complexion was chalk white.

"Are you all right, Thea?"

"Y . . . yes."

Victoria was suddenly disgusted with her own insensitivity. Too many years spent in this harsh country had hardened her. She had seen it all since coming to the western frontier as a young, inexperienced doctor. During that time, she'd treated every manner of patient, from innocent newborns to the most hardened of Western characters. She had consoled the helpless and helped the hopeless. She had looked death in the face without flinching. She had met a man she had loved and had hoped to grow old with, and she had barely survived when he did not. Through it all she had cried silent tears and maintained a resolute determination not to back down. Now, almost fourteen years later, she was inured to almost any circumstance. But Thea hadn't had time to grow hard, and Quinn Banning's roughness had obviously frightened her.

Victoria studied the wounded man a moment longer. Jake had been right; Banning was a big man. He was intimidating even in his weakened state.

Frowning, Victoria looked back at Thea, then inquired softly, "He pushed you. Did he hurt you?"

"Pushed me?" Appearing momentarily surprised by the question, Thea shook her head. "No. I'm fine."

"You look pale, dear. Maybe it would be best if you went outside for a breath of air. I can take care of everything here. If you like, you could check at the post office to see if that book I ordered has come in yet."

"I'm fine, Aunt Victoria."

"You don't look fine."

Appearing to reconsider, Thea took a shaky breath. "Maybe you're right. I suppose I could use some fresh air."

Thea left the room, and Victoria turned back toward the bed. She was going to have a talk with Mr. Quinn Banning as soon as he was alert enough to comprehend what she had to say.

And when she spoke, she'd make sure he listened.

Was she dreaming?

Her step quickening as she neared the front door, Thea stepped out into the yard, then halted abruptly to take deep, gulping breaths of air.

Aunt Victoria's patient had said his name was Quinn Banning—but he had said those words in *Wade's* voice, in a tone so familiar that it had sent chills racing down her spine. He had stared back at her from *Wade's* face: He had the same black hair and brows; the same strong, cleanly cut features; the same eyes, so dark and deep that they appeared fathomless. He had formed his few, harsh words with *Wade's* lips—the full, warm lips that she knew so well.

Deep, painful longing shuddered through Thea.

But Wade had died in her arms . . . hadn't he?

And this man had said his name was Quinn Banning.

If that was true, it was also true that this man was a dangerous criminal.

Thea stared at the unfamiliar terrain around her with sudden panic. Was she truly awake, or was she dreaming?

Chapter Three

"I don't know, maybe I made a mistake. Maybe it was selfish of me to ask Thea to come out here. She's accustomed to a more civilized way of life. I'm afraid the bad experience she had when the stagecoach was robbed may have permanently tainted her perception of Wyoming."

Voicing that uncertainty aloud for the first time, Victoria looked up soberly at Larry Hale, who stood a few feet away in her silent kitchen. She had met the intrepid cowman and his wife, Molly, the first day she arrived in Willowby fourteen years earlier, during the couple's first year of marriage. Her first reaction to them was surprise at their seem-

41

ingly disparate personalities—Molly so vivacious and outgoing, and Larry quiet, observing much and saying little. They seemed just as mismatched physically: Molly was small, blond and petite, almost delicate in stature; and Larry was tall, tightly muscled and whipcord tough in demeanor. It hadn't taken her long to realize, however, that there was a softness behind Larry's often inscrutable gaze, and that Molly and he were a perfect match, two sides of the same coin, a man and a woman who loved each other without reservation.

She had weathered the storms of Molly and Larry's union along with them: four sad miscarriages that had left Molly unable to bear a child; a fire that destroyed the ranch house they had lovingly built and then just as lovingly rebuilt; a year of winter storms that almost destroyed their herd; Larry's bout with pneumonia, which he barely survived; and countless other emergencies, both great and small, that forged a tight and lasting bond of friendship between them. She had gradually come to rely on their moral support and the sympathetic ears they lent to her confidences. Their advice had seldom failed her, and there were no two people she trusted more.

Victoria waited for a response to her whispered confidence. Larry's stance was familiar. Leaning a broad shoulder against the kitchen door frame, his arms folded across his chest, he maintained a deceptively casual posture that belied the silent deliberation behind his gaze. That same deceptively casual stance had been his response to many confidences she had conferred on him over the years. She knew only too well that with it came a silent strength that had pulled her through more difficulties than she could name—the worst a long winter of uncertainty that had ended with the eventual discovery of her beloved Luke's body. She also knew that had it not been for Molly and Larry's support, she might not have survived.

That knowledge had made even more heart-rending the news she had been forced to tell her dear friend on a summer night three years earlier: the prognosis that Molly would not live out the month.

In the time since, she had come to value Larry's counsel and silent strength more than ever. His rare smile was a comfort to her unlike any other, and his arrival at her kitchen door at this particular moment seemed somehow heaven-sent.

Victoria glanced toward the hallway when

Larry did not immediately respond. Satisfied that she could not be overheard in the rear room, where Thea had gone to deliver their difficult patient his noon meal, she continued, "I'm so worried about Thea. She's been a great help to me since she came, but she's been unnaturally preoccupied. I've tried to convince myself that she just needs time to adapt to her new life, but I'm afraid the problem is more than a simple matter of adjustment. I think something is troubling her very deeply."

Victoria paused again, then continued in a rush. "She's Margaret's only child and my only living relative, Larry. I don't want to lose her, but neither do I want her to stay here for my benefit if she's unhappy."

Speaking at last, Larry replied, "Did you ask her what's bothering her?"

Almost indignant at the question, Victoria replied, "Of course I did!"

"What did she say?"

"She said nothing's bothering her."

"Well, maybe you should accept her answer."

"She's not telling me the truth!"

"She's saying all she's ready to say."

"You don't understand. She's trying to spare me."

Larry's squinting gaze held hers. "I understand, and you would, too, if you weren't blinded by love. Whatever it is that's bothering Thea, she's not ready to talk about it yet. She has a right to that privacy."

"But I'm worried about her."

"It's a little late to become that young woman's mother, Victoria." When Victoria stiffened at that comment, Larry added more softly, "Thea's a grown woman. She didn't have to accept your invitation to come out here, but she did, and that was her decision. If she stays or not will have to be her decision, too."

"*If* . . ." Victoria's throat choked suddenly tight. Startled at the sudden heat of tears under her eyelids, she grated, "You're right, I know you are, but it's strange. I didn't realize how much I missed my sister until I saw Thea again. Margaret and I were so close. We made a promise never to let anything come between us. Margaret kept that promise. She stood up for me when I told her I wanted to be a doctor. She believed in me when no one else did. She supported my decision to come out here when everyone else said I was making a mistake—and I know now that if she hadn't, I might not have had the courage to come. I planned countless times to go back and visit her over the years, then disappointed her at the last minute every time, for reasons that I can't even recall now. She never told me she was sick; and the truth is, it didn't occur to me for a moment that Margaret wouldn't always be there for me when I needed her. Then she was gone and it was too late. I didn't even have the chance to say good-bye."

Victoria took a shaky breath. "I'll never forgive myself for that, Larry. When Thea wrote and told me about Wade's death, I deliberately waited in order to give her time before I invited her out here to join me. I didn't want her making any rash decisions. Then, when she accepted my invitation, I felt I'd been given a second chance. But something's wrong. It's been wrong since the day she arrived. I can feel it, but I can't seem to do anything to counteract it, and I feel like I'm failing Margaret again."

Shifting his lean frame from the doorway, Larry slid a comforting arm around Victoria's shoulders and tilted her face up to his. She was soothed by the familiar lines of concern on his lean face as he replied simply, "You didn't let your sister down. You came here because you were needed. Your sister understood that. You *stayed* here because you were needed, and your sister understood that, too. That's why she didn't tell you she was sick."

"But I might've been able to help her."

"You did help her. You helped her by proving that her faith in you was justified. She was proud of you. She had to be. It was her decision not to tell you about her illness—*her* decision, just like Thea's decisions are her own."

"So you're telling me it's not my place to interfere—that I can't help Thea."

"I didn't say that. You're helping her by being here for her when she needs you, just the way you've helped so many others in Willowby. Thea knows you care. She'll come to you when she's ready to talk, but until then, there's not much more you can do but wait while she works things out for herself."

Victoria stared up at Larry for a silent moment, blinking back tears. Succumbing to impulse, she raised herself on tiptoe to press a quick kiss on his cheek, then whispered, "I don't know what I'd have done without your friendship all these years. I only wish that I could've—"

Interrupted by the sound of an angry exchange coming from the rear room of the house, Victoria frowned. They were arguing again.

Turning toward the hall with a mumbled word of apology, she took a step, only to have Larry draw her back.

"Let Thea handle it."

"This Quinn Banning fellow is a hard case, Larry. I've never had a more difficult patient, and I don't want Thea to feel—"

"She's a grown woman, Victoria."

"But—"

"Let her handle it."

"I told you, I'm not hungry!"

It was Wade's voice, all right, but the tone was one that Wade had never used with her, and she was sick of it!

Thea stared at the big man glaring at her from his sickbed, then responded coolly, "You have to eat."

Placing the tray on the nightstand beside her disagreeable patient's bed, she returned his glare. Three days had passed since Quinn Banning had been delivered semiconscious to her aunt's door, and he had been impossibly rude and unappreciative from the moment he'd said his first coherent word. His disposition appeared to worsen with each passing hour, until it was now a mystery to her how she could have allowed herself to believe, even for a moment, that he could be Wade.

Thea forcibly hardened herself against features that had once melted her heart. Banning's face was so breathtakingly similar to Wade's that she needed to steel herself against its effect on her—that was still true—but close scrutiny faded its impact. The dark color of his eyes and the sweeping length of his black, straight lashes were the same, but Banning's gaze was hard and cold, devoid of the warmth that had made Wade's eyes come alive. His strong profile and the chiseled contours of his cheeks were incredibly similar, but they reflected not a spark of the humanity that was intrinsic to Wade's personality. The curve of his lips was devastatingly familiar—but that curve appeared somehow incapable of forming a smile. And his voice—yes—it was as deep and stirring as Wade's, but the words it spoke were harsh and humorless—without a trace of gentleness.

Quinn Banning, for all his physical resemblance to Wade, was as callous and lacking in human kindness as Wade had been warm and giving. Put simply, Banning was an insensitive bastard.

China crashed loudly to the floor as Banning unexpectedly thrust the tray of food from the nightstand with the flat of his hand, grating, "I said, I'm not hungry."

Thea did not respond.

"I'm tired. Get out."

"When I'm ready."

"What do I have to do to make you *ready?*"

"Acting like a spoiled child won't do it."

"Oh, won't it?"

Thea raised her chin. "Has your vision totally cleared?"

Banning ignored her.

"Is your head wound causing you pain?"

No response.

"You'll be better off if you answer me. Aunt Victoria said to give you a powder if you're in pain."

Banning closed his eyes.

Beyond patience, Thea put steel in her voice. "If you think this act you're putting on will distract me from recognizing you, you're mistaken. I recognized you immediately. I know who you are."

Banning's eyes flicked open. "Really? Who am I? *Wade?*"

Thea gasped.

"You really are a bastard!"

"And it seems you're really not the *lady* you pretend to be."

Ignoring his deliberate affront, Thea responded, "You're wasting your time if you think you're fooling me. Just for the record, I know you're not Wade. You look like him, but that's where the resemblance ends. Your personality is sadly lacking—but most importantly, Wade was a *lawman*." Pausing, she then spat, "And you're a *thief!*"

When Banning did not react, she continued hotly, "It's no use pretending. I recognized you the moment I saw you. You were with the gang that robbed the stagecoach I arrived on a few weeks ago."

"I don't know what you're talking about."

"Oh, yes, you do!"

"Do I? If you're so sure I'm a part of that gang, why don't you tell the sheriff and have him arrest me?"

Yes . . . why didn't she?

Banning awaited her response.

"I *will*—when I'm ready."

Banning closed his eyes again. "Anything you say. Just get out."

Thea trembled with anger. So, he thought he could make her doubt herself by pretending he didn't care what she thought. Well, she knew better—and she'd tell the sheriff what

51

she knew, too—when she was ready. The only thing she was uncertain of was why she was hesitating.

"Are you still here?"

Damn him! Why *was* she hesitating?

Frustrated when the answer eluded her, Thea turned abruptly toward the door. Halting just as abruptly, she looked back, then said over her shoulder in the most pleasant voice she could muster, "If you get hungry and feel like eating something a little later, just call me."

Banning slowly opened his eyes.

Her smile saccharine sweet, Thea added, "I'll be only too happy to scoop that mess off the floor and put it back on a plate for you— but for now, I'll leave it right where it is."

Silence.

Thea raised her chin. *Now* she was ready to leave.

Quinn watched as Thea departed the room with a swish of her skirt and a satisfied smile. If his head didn't hurt so much, he might actually have laughed at the smug expression on her face when she'd delivered that parting shot. There was a lot of spirit underneath that woman's crop of fiery locks. Somehow he had felt it the moment he'd looked down into her eyes a few weeks earlier—just before he stole her purse and brooch and rode off with the rest of the gang.

Quinn again closed his eyes. The problem was that he had felt too much that first time he saw the red-haired beauty. As he stood close to her in those few moments beside the stagecoach, the heat of her body had ignited a heat of another kind inside him. Awareness, and something strangely compelling, had quivered through him. The warning bell that had rung in his mind still reverberated, despite his debility.

The danger of such a distraction in his present circumstances did not escape him. He had offered her his most obnoxious best in the hope of avoiding questions. She had responded with anger as he had expected, and with an uncertainty in her gaze that he didn't quite understand.

But she would not give up.

And now it was too late. She had recognized him.

Quinn frowned as he tried to sort the confusion from his thoughts. The angry redhead had said she had recognized him instantly as one of the men who'd robbed the stage; yet, unless he was mistaken, she hadn't shared that knowledge with anyone, including her aunt. She was obviously certain of her identification, yet she hadn't called in the sheriff.

Why?

And who in hell was Wade?

Pain knifed through his head, and Quinn's stomach did a nauseating flip-flop. Damn it all, three days and it still hurt to lift his head from the pillow. The worst part of his present predicament was the realization that it was his own fault. He had known the rules when he joined Max's gang almost a year earlier. If a robbery brought in a big enough haul, they hid out for a few weeks while any posse that might be on their trail wore out its interest. When it was safe, they split the proceeds of the haul and took a holiday until the next job.

Almost three weeks had passed since the stagecoach robbery. Following his usual pattern, Max had taken Ernie with him to watch his back while he checked out the closest town, leaving Boots and him with the contents of the strongbox, and with strict orders to guard it with their lives until he returned. He had known he was taking a chance when he left the cabin, hoping that Boots's drunken stupor would last long enough for him to make it back without anyone realizing he had been gone.

He had known, and he had gone anyway.

That was his first mistake.

As it had turned out, Sheffield hadn't shown up for their meeting. He had waited longer than he should have at the appointed place and was forced to start back at top speed despite the poor trail and encroaching darkness.

That was his second mistake.

The next thing he remembered was waking up with the blurred image of a beauteous redhead leaning over him.

Please tell me . . . is it you, Wade?

Wade.

Quinn cursed aloud as another pain sliced through his temple. Max was probably out looking for him now. He wasn't the kind who took chances. Max would want to know where he'd gone, why and what had happened to him, so he could be sure there was no threat to the rest of the gang. The last thing Quinn wanted was for Max to find him here—in a house where he'd be putting at risk a female doctor who had treated him with the skill of a man and a bossy, bristling redhead who was angry enough not to act wisely if she should happen to recognize Max, too.

Another sharp pain, and Quinn groaned

aloud. Damn it, where was Sheffield? He didn't like being incapacitated—lying here as helpless as a baby. That truth had been made only too clear to him when he had tried to get out of bed by himself only that morning. He had been on his feet for no more than a few seconds before the room had started spinning and his stomach had almost rebelled. Neither his head nor his stomach had stabilized since, and the smell of the food the redhead had delivered had almost sent him over the edge.

You have to eat.

His instinctive reaction to that statement had been to push the tray away from him— and now he was stuck with the smell of food that was also stuck to the floor.

Quinn's stomach squeezed tighter. No, he wouldn't be eating today . . . and he wouldn't be going anywhere, either.

Mercifully, consciousness started drifting away. Strangely, two questions lingered.

Who was Wade?

And why did he care?

"I don't give a damn what you think!"

Max White's angry retort rang in the limited confines of the dank cabin. His stubbled face was flushed a hot red. Daylight was waning; it was the end of another long day spent waiting. He was sick of the place—sick of the smell and the dampness, and sick of hiding; but most of all, he was sick of the two men who looked back at him as he grated, "We need to find Banning."

"We told you, we lost his trail!" Boots Fink replied with uncharacteristic heat that was the product of an empty stomach, too little sleep, and the aftereffects of bad whiskey. "From what Ernie and me could figure out, Banning must've ridden down the stream so's he couldn't be trailed. We covered both sides of the bank for a couple of miles, but we still couldn't pick up his trail again."

"So you gave up."

"Yeah."

Max gave a deprecating snort. "Couldn't pick up his trail . . . Hell, if either of you had to make an honest living, you'd starve to death."

"Yeah, well, if you think it's so easy, go find Banning's trail yourself!"

"Do it myself, huh?"

Boots took an instinctive backward step. He knew he had gone too far the moment the words left his mouth. He'd been riding with Max for almost two years, and there was one thing he knew for sure: What Max lacked in height and muscle, he made up for in sheer ugliness, both inside and out. During that time they'd robbed a few banks and trains, and a couple of stagecoaches, and his share had been more money than he'd seen in his entire life. They had made only one mistake during that time—a robbery that had brought unexpected bounty, bounty that had caused them more trouble than it had been worth. He had played it smart and kept his mouth shut about it, but Pete Bensen hadn't. He remembered that Max's face had flushed the same color that it was now— that purple shade that reminded him of ripe beets—and what happened afterwards hadn't been good. Pete had fallen dead on the spot with Max's bullet in his heart; and Pete's partner, Jeff . . . well, neither Max nor he had waited around to make sure, but he didn't expect that fella had lasted out the hour.

As for Max, he had wasted no time replacing those two with Ernie and Banning—and he'd done it without a word of regret or a backward look.

Boots hastened to amend, "I . . . I mean, Ernie and me was talking, and we thought—"

Ernie interrupted with a placating smile, "Don't go getting yourself upset, boss. Boots didn't mean nothing. You know how he is when he's been drinking and his head's hurting."

Max glared. "Yeah, I know."

"He was just trying to say that we rode them hills for three days without turning up a trace of Banning—and the truth is, we can't see why finding him's so important. Hell, the money from that last robbery ain't been split up yet. Without his share, there's more for us."

"You ain't got the brains you were born with, neither one of you!" Max's apoplectic color heightened. "Banning's been riding with us for almost a year and nothing like this has ever happened before. Don't it make you wonder what happened to him?"

Boots shrugged his beefy shoulders. "I couldn't care less. He never was too friendly."

"Don't it seem strange to you that Banning should disappear *before* the money was split up?"

"Like I said, I couldn't care less. He ain't no kin of mine, and the truth be known, I didn't like him much."

"You didn't like him because he was smarter than you!"

"That ain't true!"

"Ain't it? Would you say he's stupid, then?"

"No."

"Would you say a fella'd have to be stupid to take off without the payoff he waited almost three weeks to get?"

"I guess."

"And that something's funny if he just disappeared without a trace?"

"Maybe, but—"

"Something that might bounce right back in our faces if we don't find out what it is?"

"Wait a minute, boss," wiry brows drawing into a frown, Ernie interrupted. "If Banning got picked up by the sheriff or anything like that and he told them where we were hiding out, they'd have been here by now."

Max drew back a step, his eyes narrowing. "Maybe. Maybe not."

"What're you saying?"

"I'm saying Banning sneaked out of this cabin for a reason."

"Maybe he got tired of taking orders."

"So he left without the money—with Boots drunk as a skunk and no threat to him if he wanted to take it all with him?"

When there was no response, Max shook his head. "No, he intended to come back, and he must have had a damn good reason for leaving or he wouldn't have taken the chance of—"

"—of crossing you, boss." Boots nodded with a half smile. "That's for sure."

"So we finally agree." Max's small eyes were like dark, piercing daggers. "So I guess we're ready to agree on something else, too—that we need to find Banning and hear why he sneaked out like he did." Eyeing the two men coldly when they dared not respond, Max continued. "There are only a couple of towns around here. A few quiet visits should tell us what we want to know."

"Yeah, but—"

"And since I've got a feeling you boys might be needing a reason to come back, we're not going to split that money until we do."

"But I ain't got a penny to my name!" Boots struggled to contain his anger. "I won't even be able to buy myself a drink!"

"Yeah, that's right." Max's thick features hardened. "So I suppose you're going to have to take it easy on the booze, ain't you?"

Noting the resentment that Boots did not allow himself to voice, Max almost smiled. "Let me see, there's Bittersweet, Madison, Willowby and Long Fork. I'll take the towns on the west and you two can take the towns on the east, then we'll meet up here again in a few days."

"Who's going to be watching the money until then?"

"I'll take care of it."

"But—"

"I said, I'll take care of it!"

Angry, Boots pressed, "How do we know that you—" Boots halted. "I mean—"

"I know what you mean. What's the matter? Don't you trust me?"

Ernie nodded. "We trust you, boss."

"Then get going."

A quick exchange of glances their only response, the two men walked out the door, leaving Max and their regrets behind them.

"Well, he thought he got the best of me, but I—"

Thea brought her adamant statement to an abrupt halt as she entered her aunt's kitchen. Her embarrassment at seeing Victoria's guest was obvious.

Larry smiled a brief greeting in the hope of setting Victoria's beautiful niece at ease. He saw the attempt she made to control her anger before she nodded in reply, then continued, "Well, Mr. Banning's morning nap didn't do him much good. He's awake and he's his same, ornery self—but I left him with something to think about."

Thea was obviously seething. Victoria darted a look at Larry, then turned back to Thea with true sympathy and said, "Mr. Banning is difficult—one of the most difficult patients I've ever had—but you shouldn't allow yourself to get so upset, dear. He's ill. He has a serious concussion. He might not be entirely responsible for his behavior."

"He knows exactly what he's doing."

"What did he say that upset you?"

"He said he wasn't hungry."

Appearing momentarily nonplussed, Victoria replied, "Maybe he wasn't."

"Then he pushed the tray off the nightstand onto the floor to emphasize his point."

Larry concealed a sudden rush of anger, remaining silent as Victoria said, "Mr. Banning shouldn't have done that, but—"

"He's purposely rude, Aunt Victoria! And he's deliberately cruel."

"Cruel?" Larry felt Victoria's indignation. "Did he insult you?"

Thea shook her head, refusing to answer.

"I'll speak to him."

"No. You'd be wasting your breath."

"I'll talk to him and make him understand that he—"

"I can handle it."

Victoria glanced at Larry, then said, "He appeared to be a nice enough fellow at first."

Thea's face reddened. "Looks can be deceiving."

"In any case, I need to make it clear to Mr. Banning that the rules of common courtesy are to be observed in this house."

"He's not a nice man, Aunt Victoria. I doubt he knows what 'common courtesy' means."

"It's my duty to explain it to him, then."

"Please don't! He's not the man you think he is, Aunt Victoria. He's a—" Thea glanced at Larry. "He's one of the—"

Thea closed her eyes, then opened them to say, "He'll be better in a few days and then he'll be gone. That's all I want, for him to go away and not come back."

Victoria looked pained. "I don't want you going back into that room, Thea. I'll take care of Mr. Banning myself from here on."

"No."

"Thea . . ."

"I won't let that man get the best of me!" Thea's delicate features tightened. "I've already told Mr. Banning to call me when he decides he's hungry and wants to eat. I'm going back in there when he does, and I'm going to take *very* good care of him."

"Thea . . ."

"When I'm done with him, he'll be so sick of my face, he won't be able to stand the sight of it!"

"Thea!"

Glancing at Larry in silent apology, Thea said, "If you'll both excuse me now, I have some things to do in my room."

Silence followed the sound of Thea's retreating footsteps, and Larry waited. Noting Victoria's rigid posture, he was prepared for the storm that followed when she turned back toward him.

"It's not often that your advice is off the mark, Larry, but it was today. I shouldn't have listened to you. I should've gone in there and taken care of Mr. Banning myself instead of allowing Thea to become so upset that she couldn't even think straight."

"You did the right thing, Victoria. You let Thea handle the situation for herself."

"I allowed that man to abuse her!"

"You let her stand up to him and take control—which she needs to do if she's ever going to feel she's a part of things out here."

"She's extremely upset!"

"She'll get over it. And if she's half the woman her aunt is, she won't let that fella get the best of her."

Victoria stared up at him, the ice in her

gaze melting until her gaze grew unexpectedly moist. A familiar knot of emotion twisted tight inside Larry. Victoria had no idea how that look tore at his heart.

"Oh, Larry, I'm so confused." Victoria absentmindedly brushed a straying wisp of burnished hair from her cheek. "Maybe I should let Thea work things out for herself, but . . . but it hurts to see someone you love so distressed."

"I know."

"What can I do?"

He knew what he could do.

Steeling himself against the emotions churning deep inside him, Larry reached out and drew Victoria against his chest. He had consoled her in that way countless times over the years. He only wished that he—

Forcibly halting the direction of his thoughts, Larry whispered against her hair, "Give Thea a chance to work things out. That's what you wanted for yourself when you first came out here, wasn't it?"

Victoria drew back, her expression sober. "Yes, I did. But I always knew you and Molly were there, standing behind me."

"Thea knows you're standing behind her, too, whatever she decides to do—but you could remind her of that if it would make you feel any better."

The warmth of Victoria's sudden, tremulous smile was almost more than Larry could bear. "That's a good idea," she whispered. "I'll do it right now." Her smile faltered. "You don't mind? I might be a while."

"No, go ahead. I have an errand to take care of myself before I can head home."

Larry watched as Victoria walked down the hallway toward Thea's room, his expression gradually hardening. Victoria had asked his advice and he had given it. Things hadn't gone exactly as he had hoped, but he didn't regret what he had said. Thea needed to work things out for herself while she was adjusting to her new life, but—

When Victoria disappeared from sight, Larry started toward the backroom dispensary. Pausing in the doorway, he scrutinized the man lying asleep on the cot there. He had never set eyes on Banning before, but everything Victoria had said about him was true. He was a big man, broad in the shoulder and deep in the chest. With his dark hair, chiseled features and strong, stubbled chin, he was imposing enough to give anyone second thoughts about going up against him, despite his weakened condition.

A few steps into the room, Larry saw the spilled tray still lying on the floor. His lips tightened. Advancing to the sick man's bedside, he spoke softly, but in a tone that carried forcefully in the silent room.

"Wake up, Banning."

Banning's eyes snapped open. The disorientation revealed in his gaze was gone in a moment. His expression was devoid of fear.

So, the fella wasn't easily intimidated. That was fine with him.

Holding Banning's stare, Larry said in a drawl that brooked no argument, "My name is Larry Hale, friend. I'm thinking that you might be a little confused about things right now, with that bump you had on the head and all, so I'm here to make some things clear. You have two women to thank for saving your life—Doc Sills, who's the best damned doctor this side of the Mississippi; and her niece, Thea, who's been helping to take care of you. Both of these women are *ladies*, and I want you to know that no matter how sick you are, I expect you to treat them with the respect they deserve. If you don't . . . I'll make sure you regret it."

When Banning made no response, Larry nudged, "Do you understand what I'm saying, friend?"

Banning held his gaze coldly. Larry noted that the big man paused deliberately before responding. "I understand, all right."

"I knew you would."

His errand completed with that last statement, Larry left without another word.

Chapter Four

The echoing call of a turtledove beyond the dispensary window awakened Quinn to the dawn. He looked out through the windowpane to see the sun creeping over the horizon, a great ball of blinding gold that portended an unseasonably warm day.

Another sunrise while he lay helpless in bed.

He was determined it would be the last.

Quinn listened intently to the sounds of the household. He heard the muffled clatter of pans in the kitchen and smelled the aroma of coffee and frying bacon. Breakfast would soon be ready. He didn't have much time.

Throwing back the coverlet, Quinn drew

himself gently to a seated position, then waited for the world to right itself. He recalled his unexpected visitor the previous afternoon. The deep drawl that had interrupted his sleep had been laced with steel. The message had been clear. He had briefly wondered if the redhead had sent the fellow in to set him straight, but he had later dismissed that thought. No, that feisty piece didn't need anybody to fight her battles.

He wondered where the fellow fit into the redhead's life.

Quinn stood up gingerly and stretched himself to his full height. He gripped the headboard when a bout of dizziness hit him, forced himself to breathe deeply until it stopped. It occurred to him, not for the first time, that he was naked; and he wondered, not for the first time, how he had gotten that way. The thought that the fiery redhead might have helped in the process raised a surge of heat that did little to stabilize his balance, and he cursed.

Looking down at the floor, Quinn noted that the contents of the spilled tray had been cleaned up while he slept. He remembered the redhead's saccharine-sweet promise and was somehow certain that if it were up to her, the food would still be there.

Breathing deeply, Quinn took a tentative step. Encouraged, he took another. Elated, he could feel his strength returning. Then pain stabbed through his temples with sudden ferocity, and Quinn gasped aloud.

His strength abruptly depleted, Quinn sat down on the edge of the bed. There was no use fooling himself. He couldn't even make it out of town in his present condition, much less back to the cabin. He'd have to wait another day.

Quinn frowned. It had occurred to him as he lay in a disabled semisleep that Max and the others might have decided to take advantage of the opportunity to split his share of the cache from the robbery, but he had discounted that thought, too. Not Max. Max wouldn't be satisfied until he—

Quinn looked up at the sound of light footsteps approaching in the hallway. Lying back, he pulled up the coverlet just as a familiar female figure turned into the room.

It was the redhead—Thea—and her smile looked forced.

Quinn watched as Thea approached the bed. She hesitated beside the nightstand and looked down with surprise at the spot where the spilled tray had lain. So he was right; cleaning it up hadn't been her handiwork.

Thea glanced up at him, the message in her gaze saying more clearly than words that if she had her way, she would dump the tray she was presently holding on to his lap, rather than deliver it to his bedside.

He swept her with his gaze. If he had his way, he knew what he would do.

Quinn halted his straying thoughts. It was the wrong time and place, and the redhead was definitely the wrong woman.

She turned toward him. She was still smiling that stiff smile.

All right. Two could play that game.

Thea stood at her obnoxious patient's bedside, a steaming tray in her hands. She should have realized that Aunt Victoria would have cleaned up the spilled tray, but the thought did not rest easily on her conscience. Well, it wouldn't happen again. She'd take care of her own messes from now on—and she'd handle Mr. Quinn Banning.

Thea placed the tray on the nightstand and turned a forced smile toward her silent patient. She saw Wade's face . . . Quinn Banning's face . . . one and the same. The only true point of difference between them was the love that had shone in Wade's dark eyes—a love meant for her alone.

The same question returned to plague her. Why did she hesitate to tell the sheriff who Quinn Banning was?

The answer still eluded her. The only thing she knew for sure was that Banning was not Wade. She also knew that no matter how fervently she wished it, Banning could never be Wade; that she needed to be rid of the man before she could start her life anew; *and that she could not let him intimidate her.*

That thought was foremost in her mind when Thea addressed Quinn Banning for the first time. Her smile rigid, she managed, "Good morning. I've brought your breakfast."

Banning's dark eyes raked her insolently, and Thea forced herself to smile more brightly. "How do you feel this morning?"

"I'm all right."

Controlling her surprise at his civil response, Thea asked, "Will you be able to eat by yourself?"

"I don't know. I'm still a little shaky."

Oh, he was up to something . . .

"It might be better if you helped me."

He surely was.

"If you don't mind."

If she didn't *mind?*

When she hesitated, he said, "Never mind. I'll manage."

75

Banning reached for the plate of oatmeal, but Thea halted him, forcing herself to say, "I'll be happy to help you."

Was that a smirk on his lips?

Thea's smile approached a grimace. "Can you sit up?"

Banning's reply was to hoist himself up to a seated position with surprising dexterity. His coverlet slipped below his waist in the process, revealing a glimpse of tightly muscled groin. He drew the coverlet back up to his waist without embarrassment as heat rose to Thea's face. He was naked, and he was not the least bit uncomfortable that she should know it.

Well, what did she expect?

Turning back toward the tray, Thea picked up the napkin. She hesitated only briefly before smoothing it across his lap, then glanced up with a shaky breath, her eyes narrowing. Was he laughing at her?

Thea sat abruptly on the chair beside the bed, then reached for the bowl. She could feel Banning's dark eyes burning into her as she raised the spoon to his lips.

He swallowed the first mouthful, then the second.

Refusing to meet his gaze, Thea focused on Banning's mouth, on his full lips as they

parted to accept the food; on the even white
teeth beneath; on the workings of his throat
as he swallowed. A particle of oatmeal clung
to his lip, and Thea took the napkin from his
lap to wipe it away. Her hand brushed the
hard flesh underneath the coverlet as she did,
and her heart began pounding.

Her hand trembling, Thea maintained her
composure with pure strength of will. She fed
him another spoonful, then another.

Looking up abruptly, Thea met Banning's
intent perusal. Those eyes . . . She remembered how loving heat could change them to
black velvet.

The memory quaked through her.

"Is something wrong?"

Thea took a ragged breath, then shook her
head. "No, nothing's wrong."

Tearing her gaze from his, Thea lowered
the spoon back to the bowl.

"Thea . . ."

Thea's head jerked up when Banning spoke
her name. The timbre of his voice was a familiar caress. It was as if Wade had spoken.

Banning's hand closed over hers, and Thea
caught her breath. It was as if Wade was
touching her.

The pain more than she could bear, Thea
closed her eyes. They flew open again at ap-

proaching footsteps in the hallway, and at the sound of Aunt Victoria's voice.

"I asked you to wait in the kitchen, Mr. White. I'll be happy to examine your shoulder, but I have an injured man recuperating in my dispensary. I need to place a screen around him first to afford you both some privacy."

"That's all right, Doc. I ain't shy."

A jolt rocked Banning at the sound of the harsh reply. The jolt shuddered through Thea as well. She turned toward the door, then jumped to her feet at the sight of the fellow who walked into view behind Aunt Victoria.

Obviously annoyed, Aunt Victoria repeated, "Please wait outside, Mr. White."

Ignoring Aunt Victoria, the short, thick-featured fellow brushed past her into the room. His expression cold, he stared at Quinn as he responded, "I told you, I ain't shy."

Inwardly shaking, Thea set the plate down on the tray with a clatter. She knew who that man was!

"Hello, Max," Banning said from the bed behind her. "Fancy meeting you here."

Max was staring at him, his expression sinister. It didn't take much for Quinn to know what he was thinking.

Quinn glanced at Thea, who stood frozen beside the bed. She had recognized Max's voice the moment she'd heard it, but Max had not yet realized that.

"What's going on here, Mr. White?" Victoria asked Max with growing irritation. "Do you want me to look at your shoulder or not?"

"No." Max did not even look her way. "My shoulder don't hurt no more . . . not now that I've found my old friend."

Victoria glanced between the two men, then said, "I've had enough of this."

Max turned on Victoria with a snarl. "Get out of here, Doc, and take that other one with you! This fella and me have some serious talking to do."

"This is my house, Mr. White." Victoria was livid. "I give the orders here, not you. Mr. Banning is my patient. He has a severe concussion and should not be disturbed."

"I don't give a damn about his concussion."

"Please leave!"

"I ain't going nowhere yet."

Quinn glanced again at Thea. She was beginning to shake. He had to get her out of the room before it was too late.

Turning toward the older woman, Quinn grated, "You heard what he said, Doc. Get out and take the redhead with you."

79

Victoria's eyes widened. "Who are you to give me orders? I will not be spoken to that way!"

Max took a threatening step toward her. "You will if you know what's good for you."

Quinn glanced at the chair where his clothes lay neatly folded atop his saddlebags. There was no sign of his gunbelt, but he had to do something quickly. The doc didn't know what she was facing, but Thea did.

Running footsteps in the hall broke into Quinn's thoughts, turning everyone toward the doorway, where a tall brunette dressed in scarlet satin burst unexpectedly into sight. She swept the room with her gaze, her eyes locking with his for a moment before she rushed to his bedside and threw her arms around him. Quinn's arms closed spontaneously around her as she pressed her full breasts against his chest and covered his mouth with hers for a searching kiss.

Still clinging tightly, her face streaked with tears, she drew back far enough to say, "Quinn, I'm so sorry, darling. I tried to meet you as we planned, but my horse came up lame and I had to walk back to town to get another one. When I finally got to the cabin, you were gone. Can you ever forgive me?"

It was Sheffield.

And right now, Quinn knew he could forgive her anything.

"I want an answer, Banning!"

Max glanced at the woman who clung to Banning. He tried to place her. She was taller than most, with thick, upswept black hair; bold, painted features; and a body that filled out her revealing gown to overflowing. She was obviously a saloon woman—one who would leave an impression on any man's mind.

And she couldn't seem to get enough of Banning.

Max squinted at the bold hussy. He couldn't seem to place her. . . .

"What's the matter with *him*, Quinn?" Sheffield glanced at Max, then turned around to look at Thea. "And who's she?"

"Nobody important." Quinn stared pointedly at Thea, his eyes as cold as ice. "She was about to leave, and so was her aunt."

Thea blinked, then moved to her aunt's side and took her arm. "Let's go, Aunt Victoria. These people have some personal matters to discuss. We're obviously not wanted here."

Attempting to pull her arm free of her niece's grip, Victoria responded, "I won't be ordered around in my own house, Thea."

Quinn saw the subtle movement of Max's hand toward his gunbelt. It was a moment before he realized that Thea had seen it, too. Her composure surprising him, she spoke with soft urgency to her agitated aunt, whispering, "Please, Aunt Victoria. Let's leave them alone for a few minutes."

Relenting at last, Victoria turned back to address Max coldly. "All right. I'll give you a few minutes to talk. If I were you, I'd make the most of them."

When the two women left the room, Max turned to Quinn and demanded, "Let's hear it."

"Who is this fella, Quinn?" Sheffield pressed herself closer. Her heavy perfume teased his nostrils as she swept Max with a practiced eye and said, "And what makes him think he's got the right to order anybody around?"

Low on patience, Max grated, "Make her shut up, Banning, or *I* will." Allowing a few seconds for his warning to be absorbed, he spat, "All right, start talking. What's going on?"

"What's he talking about, Quinn?" Interrupting again, Sheffield repeated, "Who is he?"

Quinn shot Sheffield a warning glance,

then responded, "This fella's my . . . boss. He's angry because I was supposed to be watching the . . . herd when he left, but I rode out to meet you, instead. I thought I'd be back before he realized I was gone, but I didn't make it."

"That's how you got hurt, isn't it?" Sheffield's heavily kohled eyes filled with tears. "You waited for me and I didn't come, and when you tried to make up the time—" Sheffield's voice faded into a sob. "This is all my fault."

Becoming more irate by the moment, Max demanded, "What's she talking about, Banning?"

Quinn attempted to pry Sheffield's arms loose from his neck. When she resisted, he ordered coldly, "Get out of here for a few minutes. I need to talk to Max."

"But I—"

"Go on!"

Grunting her displeasure, Sheffield stood up reluctantly, then turned toward the door. She swept Max with another deprecating glance, then said to Quinn, "Don't let this fella bother you, darling. You don't have to work for him. You can ride for anybody you want. This is a big country."

"Bitch!" Following her departing figure

with his gaze, Max turned back toward the bed with a vengeance. "I'm losing patience, Banning. Who is that female, and what's she doing here?"

Never more aware of his vulnerability, Quinn managed a casual shrug. "The week before the stagecoach robbery, when we all took off by ourselves for a while . . . well, I didn't spend that week alone." He smirked. "That Sheffield's some woman."

"So?"

"So, I told her I needed to go back to the 'herd,' that I'd be gone for a few weeks. We set a date to meet at the shack outside Bittersweet where we had spent a few days. I figured I wouldn't have any trouble getting there for a few hours—and I figured Sheffield would make it worth my while—but things didn't work out."

"So?"

"She didn't show up. I waited as long as I could, then I started back, riding like the devil was after me. The next thing I knew, I opened my eyes and here I was."

"How'd she find you here?"

"I don't know; probably the same way you found me." Quinn smirked again. "One thing I do know—Sheffield's pretty good at sniffing out a man. That's her living."

Max glared. "So, you're telling me you took a chance leaving Boots with the cache because of *her?*"

Quinn shrugged again. "Three weeks is a long time. Like I said, I figured at the time that Sheffield would make it worth my while."

"Is she good enough to be worth what you've got coming?"

"I thought she was worth the risk then . . . but I've had a few days to reconsider."

Max's hard gaze did not waver. "What about the other one . . . the redhead? She's the one from the stage, ain't she?"

Aware of Max's intense scrutiny, Quinn grated, "Yeah. She's the doc's niece."

"So?"

"She didn't see our faces when we held up the stage. She didn't recognize me. If she did, I'd be in jail right now."

Quinn held his breath as Max considered that response. Quinn did not blink as Max approached the bed. He scrutinized the neatly stitched cut on Quinn's head and his obvious pallor, then said with slow deliberation, "You're a lucky man, you know that, Banning? If things were different, I wouldn't be wasting time talking to a jackass stupid enough to ignore my orders just so's he could have a few hours alone with a cheap saloon whore. But I got plans, and Boots is too deep in the bottle these days to suit me. I can't afford to lose another man right now." Hesitating a moment longer, Max spat, "How much longer are you going to be laid up here?"

"A few more days . . . until I'm steady on my feet."

"All right." Max nodded. "I'll give you to the end of the week. If you don't make it back to the cabin by then, you can kiss your share of the cache good-bye."

"Don't worry. I'll be there."

"And keep your mouth shut with that cheap piece." He paused. "What's her name?"

"Sheffield . . . Sheffield Turner."

Max started toward the door, then looked back. "Until the end of the week . . ."

"I've had enough of this, Thea." Turning toward Thea the moment they reached the kitchen, Aunt Victoria pinned her niece with her gaze. "You know more about what's going on in that back room than you're saying."

"I don't know anything . . . not for sure." Thea glanced toward the hallway. Lowering her voice, she continued, "But I do know that I was right from the beginning. Quinn Banning isn't a nice man."

"It's more than that."

"That other man—that Mr. White—he's dangerous."

"How do you know that?"

"You just have to look at him, Aunt Victoria!" Thea was beginning to shake. "There's something about him. He wouldn't hesitate to use that gun he's wearing."

"Mr. Banning was wearing a gunbelt, too."

"I know." Thea paused at that thought. "Where is it?" She gasped. "It isn't in his room, is it?"

"I'm not a fool, Thea. I've lived in this country too long not to realize that a woman can't take a man at face value." Thea stiffened at her aunt's unexpected insight. "I put his gun away where he can't find it."

"Where?"

Aunt Victoria looked at her even more sharply. "Why do you want to know?"

"I told you. That man—that Mr. White—he's dangerous."

"If you're so sure he's dangerous, you should tell the sheriff."

"No!"

"Thea . . ."

Gripping her aunt's hand with sudden desperation, Thea glanced again toward the hallway. "Don't bring the sheriff here, please, Aunt Victoria."

"I won't if you'll answer my questions."

Faced with her aunt's tenacity, Thea was about to respond when the brassy woman in red walked unexpectedly into the kitchen.

Thea opened her mouth to speak, but the woman whispered, "Be quiet!"

Leaning back toward the hallway, the woman listened intently to the low rumble of conversation coming from the dispensary. She turned back to face them after a few minutes, then said without any apparent embarrassment, "That ugly bastard threw me out of the room. I just wanted to make sure they weren't talking about me after I left."

Thea withheld a smile of satisfaction.

The woman stared at her, then spat, "But Quinn wants me back in there as soon as they're done talking, so don't get any ideas."

"Any ideas?"

"I saw the way you looked at him."

Thea gasped.

"And I saw the way he looked at you."

Thea's stomach clenched tight.

"Whatever you were thinking before I got here, forget it. He's mine."

Thea controlled her response.

"You got something to say?"

Thea's control was slipping.

The woman advanced a threatening step. "Are you going to answer me or not?"

Something seemed to snap inside her, and Thea heard herself respond in a startlingly feral tone. "Back off!"

"What? Is that a challenge?" The woman almost laughed. " 'Cause if it is, you can take my word for it, dearie, you're no match for me."

"Nor would I want to be."

The woman's smile froze. Recovering, she responded harshly. "You're taking on more than you can handle, girlie. If you're smart, you'll be the one to back off."

"And if I don't?"

"Then you'll get just what you've got coming."

"I'm counting on it."

"And you'd be getting more than you expected. You—"

The woman's angry response halted when Max strode unexpectedly into the kitchen. Striking a deliberately provocative pose when he glowered in her direction, she laughed aloud at his sneering dismissal.

Thea moved a step closer to her aunt when Max addressed the older woman abruptly, saying, "Banning claims you'll have him on his feet in a few days."

Aunt Victoria did not choose to respond.

His face flushing an angry color, Max added with a note of pure menace, "He'd better be right, because if it takes any longer, it just might be too late for both of you."

Thea started toward the hallway the moment the door slammed shut behind Max.

"Stop where you are!" The brassy woman in red grasped her arm. "That's my man in there, not yours, do you understand?"

Thea understood . . . only too well.

Feeling suddenly sick Thea shook off the woman's grip and walked out into the yard.

The sudden silence of his room seemed almost deafening after Max's departure. Quinn strained to hear as the sound of hoofbeats faded into the distance.

Max was gone—for now.

Quinn took a relieved breath, but his relief lasted only until Sheffield strode back into the room. Sitting on the bed, she propped herself intimately close to him, and his lips tightened. When she wound her arms around his neck, he could hold back no longer.

Quinn spat, "What took you so damned long to get here, Sheffield?"

Leaning toward him in an affectionate pose, although her clear skin revealed an angry flush, Sheffield grated against his ear, "You're an unappreciative bastard, aren't you? I saved your hide a few minutes ago, and you've got the nerve to complain!"

"If you'd shown up when and where you were supposed to, there wouldn't have been any need to save my hide."

"I told you what happened. My horse went lame, and I had to walk back to town to get another one."

"That was the truth?"

"Damned right it was."

"Did it ever occur to you that you could've walked to the cabin instead of back to town, and saved us both a lot of trouble?"

"So I could get lost in the dark in that wilderness, and end up like you?"

"You're supposed to be able to handle things like that."

"So are you, and look at the condition you're in."

Sheffield was right. She usually was.

Relenting, Quinn questioned, "How did you find me?"

Sheffield rubbed her cheek lovingly against his, then drew back to grumble, "You need a shave."

"Sheffield . . ."

"I waited at our alternate meeting place. When you didn't show up, I knew something had happened. The rest was just good detective work. I got myself a helluva disguise and figured I'd canvass the towns nearby to see what I could find out." She gave him a shrewd smile. "A fella doesn't get suspicious when a woman like me says her man disappeared and she's trying to find him." She winked. "They just get jealous."

"This isn't the time for jokes, Sheffield."

"All right, let's get down to business." Sheffield leaned warmly against him, then said, "It wouldn't hurt for you to put your arms around me, you know. Hell, if those women came in here right now, there's no way they'd believe you're my man."

"What would Perry have to say about that?"

"Perry knows the kind of work I do. I was already with the department when he transferred in."

"That wouldn't make it any easier."

"Damn it, Quinn! Are you going to put your arms around me or not?"

Sliding his arms around her, Quinn drew her close. He heard her snicker. "You're not wearing much underneath that blanket, are you?"

"Sheffield . . ."

"No wonder that little redhead out there is so shaken up."

"She's shaken up because she was on the stagecoach that we robbed a couple of weeks ago. She knows I was part of the gang."

Sheffield's eyes widened. "Did she recognize Max?"

"Yeah. I'm sure of it."

On her feet in a moment, Sheffield started toward the door. She stopped when he called out, "Where are you going?"

"To stop her from getting the sheriff."

"Don't worry about it." Quinn frowned. "She won't call the sheriff."

"What?" Sheffield stared at him. "Are you sure?"

Quinn nodded.

"Hell . . ." Sheffield shook her head with amazement. "You have a concussion. You can barely stand up, but you still managed to get something going with her."

"I didn't get anything going with her."

Sheffield turned back toward the door.

"Wait a minute." Quinn raised a hand to his forehead. The excitement was taking its toll. The pounding in his head was returning and his stomach was beginning to churn. Hell! He was going to be sick. "Look," he managed through clenched teeth, "don't worry about the redhead. We need to take care of business."

At his side in a moment, Sheffield said, "You don't look so good all of a sudden. Do you want me to call that lady doc back in here?"

"No, not yet." The room started to spin, and Quinn briefly closed his eyes. "Look, contact Perry. Tell him that Max said he has big plans and I think this might be it. He wants me in on it, because Boots has been drinking real heavy and Max can't rely on him anymore. I'm pretty sure he's thinking about making a move."

"Maybe it's just another robbery."

"No, it's too soon. It's something else."

Needles of pain were knifing through Quinn's temples. He spat, "That's all for now. Will you be in town?"

"I'll get a job at the Red Slipper. It's the best saloon on Main Street, and there's no way I'll get turned down looking like this."

"All right." Quinn took a painful breath. "Call that lady doc in here, will you?"

Sheffield hesitated. "About that redhead . . . keep her out of this, Quinn. It could be dangerous for her."

"Sheffield . . ."

"All right, I'm going."

"Drink this. That's right."

Aunt Victoria held the glass to Banning's lips. Thea watched the smooth working of his throat as he emptied it. She saw him wince as he leaned back against the pillow.

"What're you looking at?" demanded the woman called Sheffield.

Thea had come in from the yard in time to see Sheffield run into the kitchen to call Aunt Victoria. She had followed them both into Banning's room and had barely stifled a gasp when she saw their patient. His eyes were closed and his face was colorless. He was obviously in pain. If she didn't miss her guess, he was sick to his stomach, too, and probably wishing the whole world would go away.

"I asked you what you're looking at."

Thea responded curtly, "Mr. Banning's been under my aunt's and my care for four days. It's obvious he's had a setback."

"You weren't thinking about his *setback*, and you know it."

Thea did not deign to reply.

Sheffield's expression hardened. "Look, get something straight: Quinn's going to be better in a couple of days, and then he'll leave here without looking back."

Thea's silence lengthened.

"Get used to the idea."

"Don't tell me what to do!"

"If you're smart, you'll listen."

"Sheffield . . ."

Sheffield turned toward Quinn when he said her name. She went to his side, whispered something inaudible against his lips, then stroked his cheek. Thea saw Banning whisper to the woman in return, and her stomach clenched tight.

The sight of them together succeeded where Sheffield's warnings had not, and Thea left the room.

Chapter Five

Larry Hale straightened up, grunting as he stretched the kinks out of his back. He smiled wryly when Racer snorted, as if in response.

"Don't tell me you're tired." Larry slid a callused hand over the gelding's quivering flank. "I was the one doing the work all night."

Truer words were never spoken. He'd been up half the night with the animal. He'd taken a close look at the gelding's foreleg the previous evening and had been in no doubt that the ragged cut Racer had gotten on a wire fence a week earlier was festering. The look in the horse's eyes had been revealing. Fever. He'd seen that look a few times before, and he'd known in a glance that if he didn't take care of Racer's foreleg pronto, it might be too late.

Larry breathed an unconscious sigh as he stroked Racer's shiny black hide. He could've told Jenkins or Sweets to tend the animal, but he hadn't. Racer had been Molly's horse. Molly had loved the animal and had cared for him like a baby. Racer had stopped eating for a while after Molly died, and it had begun to look like the animal might actually die . . . from no other cause but a broken heart.

Like him.

But he and Racer had both survived. They had each gone on to make the best of the life that was left for them, even though he could somehow read in the gelding's eyes that they both knew life would never be the same.

"That leg's going to be fine now, fella."

Slapping the horse's rump, Larry left the cramped stall behind him and started toward the bright light just beyond the barn doors. He emerged into the yard and squinted up at the sun, making its ascent into the cloudless sky. He watched its brilliant light flow down the hillsides in the distance; listened as a rooster crowed a belated announcement of morning; heard the echo of bawling cattle reverberating from outlying pastures. A light breeze scented with spring touched his face, and he lifted his hat from his head and ran his hand through his graying hair, breathing deeply. He had once believed this particular spot was heaven on earth—only to discover that even heaven could be a lonely place, without Molly.

How long had it been since she had slipped away from him? Larry did not choose to recall. He had been lost without her, unable to derive comfort from life until Victoria had appeared on his doorstep one morning to set him straight. She had been angry. She had reminded him that Molly had loved him with all her heart, and that because she had loved him, she wouldn't want him to live his life in mourning.

Larry smiled. He remembered his reaction that day. Everything Victoria had said rang with truth. He had known Molly would want him to go on, yet after Victoria finished talking, one question still remained.

How?

Victoria had stuck by him—with warmth and understanding, but with patience that was not inexhaustible. She had sympathized with him when he was in need, she had cajoled him when he was uncertain, but she had let him know in no uncertain terms when he went too far in indulging a morbid or occasionally ugly mood.

He came around eventually and picked up the reins of the Bar MH, which he had surrendered to his overburdened foreman. He did it because he had wanted Molly to know, wherever she was, that he wouldn't let her down.

The rattle of a buckboard in the distance interrupted Larry's sober thoughts. He soon recognized the high-stepping mare pulling the conveyance.

What was Victoria doing out here so early in the morning?

Larry's jaw tightened. He had thought the irritable Mr. Banning had gotten his message two days earlier and would change his ways. If the fellow hadn't, he'd settle the matter fast enough!

Larry's jaw was as hard as granite when Victoria reined in beside him at last. Reaching up, he swung her down to the ground, unconsciously noting the difference between the weight of Molly's fragile proportions and Victoria's slender but womanly frame. He studied her sober expression.

Forestalling his inquiry, Victoria said, "I'm out this way because of the Parker baby. James rode into town last night. Little Rose had a high fever for three days, and he and Marianne were beginning to panic. The baby's all right now, though. Her fever broke during the night, and I left some medicine and showed Marianne what to do if the fever starts rising again."

Larry waited.

"Don't look at me like that, Larry. Is there something unusual about a woman paying a friendly visit while passing by?"

"So you just stopped by for a friendly visit."

"Yes."

"Just to have some of Charlie's good coffee, I suppose."

Victoria winced at the thought.

"That's what I figured. What's happened?"

Victoria shook her head with a reluctant smile. "You read me like a book, don't you, Larry Hale?"

He had grown fond of Victoria's smile . . . the way it creased the fair skin of her cheeks and sent little squint lines out from the corners of her eyes. He supposed he had grown especially fond of it because she seldom smiled at anyone else the way she smiled at him.

Victoria's smile faded. "It's Mr. Banning."

He knew it.

"We had a little incident the day after you left—"

"An incident?"

"But that appears to be over with, and Mr. Banning's been behaving himself very well. It's just that his reaction to Thea is strange. It . . . it makes me uneasy, Larry."

"What do you mean?"

"Well, after that man came to see Mr. Banning—"

"What man?"

"Mr. White—but I doubt that's his real name. He looked like an unsavory character. He left and hasn't come back. That woman has come back, though—every day."

"What woman?"

"Her name's Sheffield. She's obviously an . . . *old friend* of Mr. Banning."

Larry cocked his head with a half smile. "A man Banning's age has a right to a past, Victoria."

"I suppose, but—" Victoria halted. She scrutinized his face more closely. "You don't look so good today, Larry. Are you feeling all right?"

"Hell . . ." Larry shook his head. "I guess I've reached an age when I can't hide losing a night's sleep."

"You were up all night?"

"Racer was sick. He needed some attention."

"Molly's horse?"

Larry nodded.

"Let me have a look at him."

"He's all right."

"I'm the doctor, Larry, not you." Victoria was mildly indignant. "Haven't you learned that yet?"

Sliding his arm around her shoulders as she turned toward the barn, Larry drew Victoria against his side. Aware that the gesture afforded him more comfort than it did her, Larry could not quite manage a smile as he said, "All right, but while you're checking on Racer, you can tell me about that 'incident' you passed over so lightly, and why you're so worried about Thea."

"Agreed."

Slipping a comradely arm around his waist in return, Victoria began her soft recitation, unaware that the ache inside Larry had momentarily dulled, and that his heart was briefly lighter.

Quinn looked up at Thea, who had appeared beside his bed. He had been dozing. It had been a difficult two days since Max's visit and Sheffield's appearance on the scene. His damned concussion was taking its time to heal, a reality that had been driven home to him that morning. He had risen at dawn, feeling better than he had in days, and had dressed and started for the kitchen. He hadn't been halfway up the hall when he had staggered for the first time. By the time he had reached the kitchen, he had needed to lean against the wall to steady himself.

The best part of the whole excursion had been when Thea recognized his distress and rushed to his side to support him. She had smelled too damned good for words—not of heavy perfume like Sheffield was fond of wearing—but of a clean, warm fragrance that he had come to realize was Thea's own. The few moments while she had pressed her warmth against him and looked up into his face with true concern had been more heady than he had cared to acknowledge.

Her smile noticeably absent now, Thea brought him back to the present, saying, "You were shaky this morning, but you seemed intent on getting back on your feet. I thought it might be better if I helped when you decided to try again."

When Quinn did not immediately respond, Thea said, "If you'd prefer to have Miss Turner help you . . ."

Sheffield. Quinn mentally winced. Sheffield had visited often since she had located him, and the friction between Thea and her had heightened. He had already spoken to Sheffield about overplaying the part of the jealous lover. Sheffield had reacted with the comment that he should accept the fact that she was doing it for Thea's own good—and if he couldn't, he should examine the reason behind his protests.

He had since done as Sheffield suggested, and he wasn't comfortable with what he had begun to discover. Sheffield was right again.

Taking his extended silence for confirmation, Thea said, "All right, then. I'm sure Miss Turner will be here in an hour or so to help you."

"Thea, wait." Quinn halted her as she turned to leave. Sheffield was right; he needed to put more distance between this fiery redhead and himself, but he wanted to clear up some things first.

Quinn swung his booted feet to the floor and sat up abruptly. Knowing the need for full clarity of mind, he did not stand. He was anxious to get back on his feet, but more important was the need for a conversation between Thea and himself without the outside interference that had dogged his every opportunity—interference in the form of his own debility, of the strong-minded female doctor who watched Thea like a hawk, and of the equally strong-minded female agent intent on keeping Thea out of Department business.

Quinn ventured, "I haven't seen your aunt yet today."

Thea's eyes narrowed.

"Aunt Victoria was called to one of the outlying ranches last night. She's due back any time now."

Quinn began tentatively, "I need to talk to you, about Max."

"I don't want to talk about Mr. White—if that really is his name!" Angry sparks lit Thea's eyes as she hissed, "I recognized his voice the minute I heard it in the hallway. How could I forget it—or the way he held his gun on the passengers of the stagecoach while *you* robbed us?"

Thea took a shuddering breath, then continued with surprising candor, "If you're wondering why I haven't called in the sheriff . . . I don't have an answer for you that you could possibly understand. All I can say is that I don't care about any of it, or why Mr. White is so intent on having you rejoin him by the end of the week. I just want you out of my aunt's house as soon as possible, and out of our lives. If getting you back on your feet will do that, I'll help any way I can."

Thea turned to go, and Quinn stood up spontaneously. He gripped her arms, holding her fast. Her skin was smooth under his palms—disconcertingly so. He could feel her trembling. The tremors touched a chord deep within him that prompted him to whisper, "Don't be afraid of me, Thea. That's the last thing I'd ever want from you."

Thea's eyes widened. "Don't speak to me in that voice!"

"What voice? Thea . . ."

Thea's wide eyes searched his face.

A blue haze of tobacco smoke filled the Red Slipper. The din of harsh laughter, deafening music and boisterous conversation was already mind-numbing—yet it was barely past noon. It occurred to Sheffield that she'd had more trouble dodging groping hands during the past two days of her employment there than she'd had dodging bullets during her entire five illustrious years with the Treasury Department. The Red Slipper might be Willowby's largest and best saloon, but the next time a fella assumed she was his for the asking, she was going to knock him flat on his back!

Unconsciously nodding at the nameless cowpoke beside her as his slurred conversation continued, Sheffield scanned the bar again. She didn't like the delay. Quinn was taking too long to recuperate. If she wasn't sure that he was as anxious as she was to bring this job to an end, she'd already have turned her back on him and walked away.

Sheffield drained the glass in front of her; then, with a pointed smile at the talkative cowboy beside her, she tapped the bar for another.

It was lucky. Max hadn't recognized her. He appeared to have made no connection between Sheffield, the painted floozy, and the hard-eyed female Treasury Department operative who had accompanied the shipment of gold bars that he and his gang had managed to steal over a year earlier.

Sheffield's eyes hardened. She would not forget that day. The shipment of gold bars intended for the U.S. Treasury had been handled with utmost secrecy. No one had been expecting a holdup, yet it was she who had been held responsible when the shipment was stolen.

The gold bars had not been recovered.

Sheffield took an angry breath. Her father had been a legend in the Department before he was killed—shot down in his prime by a second-rate criminal who had gotten off a lucky shot. She had worked hard to live up to her father's image, and she had truly believed that she had overcome the prejudice against her sex—which only showed how wrong she could be.

Determined to erase the mark against her name, she had tracked down the thieves and identified them on her own time, only to discover that the Department would not be satisfied until the gold bars were recovered, and until a suspected inside contact in the Department could be identified and brought to justice.

The final indignity had come, however, when another agent was called in to follow through on *her* case.

Enter Quinn Banning.

Sheffield sniffed. To add insult to injury, it had been Perry who had called Quinn in.

Sheffield's heart gave a spontaneous leap, just as it did every time her department supervisor came to mind. Perry Locke was surprisingly young for the position he held. He was also intelligent, well educated, a confirmed bachelor—and more handsome than a man had a right to be. He had fervently opposed her admission into the Department, but he eventually surrendered to heavy pressure from higher up.

The warmth inside Sheffield expanded. Perry had then surrendered to her charms as well, making his capitulation complete. It was he who had agreed to let her work undercover as Quinn's contact.

A smile teased Sheffield's lips. To give Quinn Banning his due, the fella was all man and muscle, with a penetrating dark-eyed stare and a sharp mind to boot. He was formidable in more ways than one. She suspected that Perry hadn't been keen on pairing her up with Quinn because of Quinn's usual effect on the ladies.

Sheffield's smile deepened. She knew Quinn was uncomfortable pretending to be her lover because Perry was his friend. Angry at having been almost squeezed out of *her* case, she hadn't made it easy on either of them.

However, after two days of delay, the role of Quinn's lover was beginning to wear thin on her, too.

Sheffield unconsciously shook her head. She didn't like the way things were going. Quinn's injury was an unexpected complication; the woman, Thea, was behaving too strangely to anticipate her next move; and Max White was a danger that loomed over everyone concerned—all when it appeared the case was finally drawing to a conclusion.

Sheffield nodded with a dispassionate smile as the wordy cowboy beside her rattled on. She had wired the Department a brief, encrypted report on the case two days earlier. She had yet to receive a reply.

Sheffield struggled to control her annoyance. She didn't like waiting. She wasn't good at it—and she didn't like being forced into doing things at which she didn't excel.

Sheffield's meandering thoughts halted abruptly at first sight of the big man who pushed his way through the Red Slipper's swinging doors. Drawing herself slowly erect, she grabbed the arm of a passing saloon woman and said, "Take care of this cowboy for me, will you, Trixie? I've got something to do."

Trixie slid into her place at the bar with a professional smile, and Sheffield started toward the door. When she saw another woman heading in the same direction, Sheffield cut her off with a few quick steps and grated, "Forget it, Lulu. This fella's mine."

Slipping up to the sober-faced fellow who still stood near the entrance, Sheffield murmured huskily, "Were you waiting for me, handsome?"

A shiver settled somewhere warm and deep inside her when their eyes met.

Oh, yes . . . *this fella was hers.*

Don't be afraid of me, Thea. That's the last thing I'd ever want from you.

Banning's words shuddered through Thea. He'd done it again. He had spoken to her in a voice so closely mimicking Wade's that chills had raced down her spine. And he was looking at her now with a look in his eyes that—

Suddenly desperate to be free of his grasp, Thea ordered, "Let me go."

Banning's grip on her arms tightened.

"I said, let me go!"

Banning's expression hardened. "A minute ago you wanted to help me. Now you're acting like you can't get out of this room fast enough. Just for the record, I'm not going to let you go until you tell me what's going on in that head of yours."

Confronting him squarely, Thea said, "I told you that I won't turn you or Mr. White in to the sheriff—but that's all I'm going to say. My reasons are my own."

"What if I told you that I don't know what you're talking about—that you have no reason to call the sheriff in on either Max or me?"

"Then I'd say you're lying."

"You're sure of that?"

"I've never been more sure of anything in my life."

Banning's expression changed abruptly. It softened, as did his voice when he said, "Thea . . . please believe me. I'd never hurt you."

"Stop it."

"And I wouldn't let anyone else hurt you either."

"I told you to stop talking to me in that tone of voice!" Unable to bear another moment of Wade's gaze looking down into hers, of Wade's voice attempting to soothe her fears, Thea closed her eyes.

"What tone of voice? What are you talking about?"

Didn't he know? Did he really not know?

Banning's arms slid around her. She was unable to resist, incapable of vocal protest when he drew her closer. "I don't know what you're thinking," he whispered, "but I want you to know . . . I need you to know that I appreciate what you've done for me."

Banning's arms felt so good . . . so familiar . . . so *real*.

113

"And I appreciate what your aunt's done for me, too."

She wanted never to leave their warmth.

"I know this has been hard on you."

He'd never know how hard.

"But it's been hard for me, too."

She believed him.

"I just want you to know that whatever you're thinking, you won't be subjected to this situation much longer."

Thea stiffened.

"Whether I'm fully recuperated or not, I'll be out of here by the end of the week."

That was what she wanted, wasn't it?

Banning hesitated. He searched her face, his dark eyes intent. "That's what you want, isn't it . . . for me to leave?"

Thea held her breath. Wasn't it?

"I'm getting tired of waiting."

Boots's angry outburst rang on the silence of the cabin. Too agitated to heed Ernie's warning glance, he faced Max hotly, continuing, "Why do we have to wait for Banning to show up for his cut of the cache? He knew the risk when he sneaked out of here. As far as I'm concerned, he gave up his share the minute he rode off!"

His smile deadly, Max responded, "Did he, now?"

"That's right, and Ernie here agrees with me."

"Hey, wait a minute!" Ernie's smile was feeble. "I ain't complaining, boss. I'm just as anxious as Boots, here, to start having some fun, but a couple of days more or less don't bother me. I figure you got a good reason for waiting for Banning, and that's good enough for me."

"Well, it ain't good enough for me." Boots took an aggressive forward step, his expression tight. "I want my part of that payroll, and I want it now."

"I know what you want right now, Boots," Max sneered, "and it ain't that money I got stashed away. You want a drink . . . maybe a nice tall bottle so you can curl up with it and forget everything else."

"Maybe, but that don't make—"

"No maybes about it!" Max snarled with sudden viciousness. "You're losing control, Boots, and I don't like it. You're not dependable when all you can think about is where your next drink is coming from."

"I was dependable enough to get you the information you needed for that stagecoach robbery."

"Right . . ."

"So now I want what's coming to me."

Max's hand inched toward his holster. The drunken bastard was asking for it. If he didn't need every man he had right now . . .

"Boots don't mean nothing, boss." Stepping nervously between them, Ernie said, "You're right. He needs a drink, is all."

"Is that what you want, Boots . . . a drink?" Max's lips twisted with contempt. " 'Cause if it is, I've got a bottle in my saddlebag that I haven't even opened yet."

Boots's lips twitched revealingly, and Max pinned him with a menacing stare. "That bottle's yours if you want it, but first you're going to listen. If I had my choice right now, I wouldn't be waiting for Banning to return, and I wouldn't be standing here making explanations to a sniveling drunk who can't see past his next drink."

Boots stiffened. "I ain't—"

"Shut up and listen!" Glaring, Max continued, "I got *plans*, I told you. I've been talking to a fella who's going to make us richer than, any one of us ever figured we'd be. But we're going to have to work together on this."

"Together . . ." Boots licked his lips. "What do you mean?"

"I mean it's going to take timing . . . and it's going to take all four of us to handle it."

His eyes narrowing, Boots took a short, backward step. "I'm thinking this has something to do with that robbery we pulled off about a year ago."

Max's gaze tightened. "Maybe."

"Like maybe you finally found a way—"

"I ain't about to tell you nothing else, so don't go guessing."

Appearing to gain strength from his position, Boots pressed, "Maybe I'm tired of waiting. Maybe I'm tired of secrets I ain't supposed to be smart enough to keep. Maybe I'm tired of the whole damned mess!"

"And maybe you're tired of living." Max's smile was ice. " 'Cause the only way you're going out that door right now is feet first."

Boots blinked. He looked at Ernie. Seeing no help there, he gave a nervous shrug. "There's no need for you to get all riled up and make threats." Abruptly backtracking, Boots continued slowly, "All this waiting around sticks in my craw, is all. Maybe Ernie's right. Maybe a drink would settle me down."

Reaching back, Max flipped the buckle on his saddlebag.

"But it don't change what I said about Banning. It's his fault he's laid up the way he is, and I don't like suffering for it."

Max withdrew the unopened bottle of whiskey and held it out in front of him.

Boots snatched the bottle from his hand, adding, "And I'm going to make sure Banning hears what I've got to say, too, when he comes back."

His expression unchanged, Max watched as Boots walked to the corner and broke the seal, then took a long drag from the bottle that left him sputtering.

Max's eyes narrowed into a deadly squint. He didn't like drunks. He didn't trust them and he didn't want them around him. He needed this one . . . temporarily, but when he was done, he wouldn't need anyone at all.

Max smiled.

Yes, he had a plan.

Quinn's unanswered question lingered. *That's what you want, isn't it, for me to leave?*

Quinn held Thea close against him. What had begun as an attempt to halt her departure had somehow become an embrace. He hadn't intended it to be this way, had he?

Looking down into her eyes, Quinn whispered again, "That's what you said you want, Thea . . . for me to leave and not come back."

A response quivered inaudibly on Thea's mouth, and Quinn lowered his head to encourage it with his lips. Her mouth was soft and sweet, and he indulged himself in the taste of it. Bliss unfolded within him unlike any he had experienced before, and he drew her closer. A warning voice nagged in the back of his mind as the kiss deepened, but Thea's lips separated under his and he ignored its nudging.

The warning voice nagged louder, forcing Quinn to draw back and whisper, "I didn't intend this, Thea."

Thea's expression was unreadable.

"It isn't smart for either one of us . . . not right now."

She searched his gaze.

"Not smart . . ."

Quinn kissed her again, slowly, more deliberately, luxuriating in her sweetness as he crushed her closer. He had known somehow that it would be like this to hold Thea in his arms. He had sensed that underneath the strain, the anger and the bickering, there was something deeper . . . something he had hungered for, but which had always eluded him.

Drawing back from her lips, Quinn heard himself say, "You were meant to be in my arms, Thea."

Thea gasped. Suddenly struggling, she pushed herself free of his embrace. She was trembling visibly when she rasped, "Why did you say that?"

Why?

"Tell me!"

"Thea . . ."

"You don't know why you said it, do you?" Thea shook her head, her voice choked as she rasped, "Neither do I. But what I do know is that this is wrong . . . very wrong."

Retreating to the dispensary doorway, she turned back to say, "I'm sorry."

"You did a good job on that foreleg." Releasing Racer's hoof, Victoria looked up at Larry with a smile of approval. "Just keep that cut covered for a while so he doesn't get anything into it and he should be all right."

"I told you his leg was all right, didn't I?"

Victoria straightened up, dusted off her hands, then said with mock severity, "Oh, no, not 'I told you so.' "

But Larry was not amused. He pressed, "This White fellow, you say he threatened you all?"

Victoria frowned. "Indirectly."

"Why didn't you call in the sheriff?"

"Thea begged me not to."

"And you listened to her?"

"I told you, Larry, I'm worried about her."

Victoria stared at him for a silent moment, then turned abruptly toward the barn doors, adding over her shoulder, "I can see you don't understand. I don't think you ever will."

Larry swung her around to face his unexpectedly fierce anger. "I don't understand? What is it that I don't understand, Victoria— that you ignored common sense to listen to a young woman who still isn't thinking straight after a tragic loss? You're supposed to be older . . . more mature. You're supposed to be experienced enough to see the danger in your situation, yet you're reacting almost as childishly as your niece."

"Larry!"

"You're two women alone in that house, Victoria! You don't have a man to protect you from whatever White might intend."

"I've been a woman alone in that house for almost fourteen years, and I've handled things very well."

"Because you used the common sense that you seem to have lost since Thea came to live with you."

"Are you blaming this all on Thea, because if you are—"

"Victoria, listen to me." The depth of concern in Larry's gaze held Victoria fast as he continued, "You have a fellow living in your back room that you don't know anything about."

"A *patient*, Larry . . ." Stiff-jawed, Victoria corrected him. "An *incapacitated* patient."

"From what you've told me, there was nothing incapacitated about that fellow White."

"Mr. White is gone and he won't be coming back."

"You can't be sure of that."

"I can't be sure that the sun won't fall into the horizon tonight, never to rise again, but I have to assume that tomorrow will come."

"That isn't the same thing, and you know it."

"Isn't it?" Victoria stared into Larry's flushed face. "I'm a doctor, Larry. I can't base medical decisions on fear."

"But you can base them on common sense."

"Oh, to hell with common sense!" Suddenly furious and uncertain why she had brought her concerns to Larry in the first place, Victoria said, "I told you I was worried about Thea's reaction to Mr. Banning, and all you can think about is some improbable danger Thea and I are facing at the hands of a man we'll most likely never see again."

Larry started toward a nearby stall. "I'm going back with you. We'll talk to the sheriff together."

"No!"

Standing rigidly still as Larry halted in his tracks, then turned slowly toward her, Victoria continued with unconcealed anger, "I won't go to the sheriff, Larry—with or without you—and if you say anything to him about this, our friendship is over."

Watching the impact of her words on Larry, Victoria continued, "I gave Thea my word that I wouldn't go to the sheriff, and I don't intend to break it. I came here seeking advice about Thea. I wish you could see the way she watches Mr. Banning—not exactly as if she's enamored of him, but almost as if . . . as if . . ."

"As if what?"

Victoria blurted, "I don't know! I can't figure it out. That's why I'm here." After a pause, she continued. "But I can see I made a mistake in coming, so you can forget what I said."

"Forget it, huh?"

"That's right."

"Would you forget it if you thought I was in danger?"

"I'd trust that you knew what you were doing if you disagreed with my advice."

"You expect me to believe that?"

"I hope you will."

"I don't."

Victoria's tenuous control snapped. "You're a damned stubborn jackass, do you know that, Larry Hale?"

"That may be right, but I'm not letting you—"

"Stop right there." Her voice was dangerously soft. "Understand what I'm saying, Larry. If you interfere in this situation without my approval, I will write off the past fourteen years with a snap of my fingers. You'll be a stranger to me . . . a stranger who'll be forever unwelcome in my home."

Larry's throat worked tightly before he responded, "You don't mean that, Victoria."

"I do."

"All right."

"I'm warning you, Larry."

"I said, all right."

Suddenly feeling bereft, and sorrier than she had ever been in her life, Victoria walked out of the barn toward her buckboard. She was swung unexpectedly off her feet when she reached it. She turned toward Larry as he settled her in the seat.

Victoria raised her chin. "I've got other patients to see. Good-bye, Larry."

Setting the buckboard into motion with a flick of the reins, Victoria did not look back to see Larry snap into action as she faded from sight. Nor did she hear him shout as he strode toward the bunkhouse, "Buck . . . Manny . . . Pete, get out here, fast!"

I'm sorry.

Thea had left his room with those two words.

You were meant to be in my arms, Thea.

Why did you say that?

He had not answered.

You don't know why you said it, do you?

No, he didn't.

I'm sorry . . .

Yes, he was sorry, too. Sorry in so many ways.

He should go after her.

No, he shouldn't.

He wanted to.

No, he didn't.

Quinn sat abruptly on the edge of the bed, deeply confused. He rubbed his forehead, telling himself it was his head wound that was causing his turmoil. But did his head wound account for the way he had been drawn to the fiery-haired witch from the first moment he had seen her standing beside the stagecoach, with her hair blazing in the afternoon sun and her eyes looking up into his with more astonishment than fear? His fingers had brushed her breast when he pulled the cameo from her dress, and the brief contact singed even in memory.

You were meant to be in my arms, Thea.

The words had sprung spontaneously to his lips minutes earlier. He had been unable to stop himself from taking her into his arms. Nor had he been able to control his longing to erase caution from her eyes and change fear to—

Quinn forced his rioting thoughts to a premature halt. No, damn it! Thea had been right when she'd said this was wrong, but not for the reason she believed. The truth was that he was exposing both Thea and her aunt to danger with every moment that he remained in this house. Thea had said she wouldn't turn Max and him in to the sheriff, but things were moving too swiftly for him to control. He needed to get out of this house and Thea's life as soon as possible—before his common sense failed him completely, and before Max discovered that Thea had recognized them both.

His head throbbing anew, Quinn lay back abruptly on the bed and closed his eyes. The sweet taste of Thea was still on his lips, and Quinn muttered a soft curse.

One more day and he would put Thea and his confusion behind him.

One more day.

Oh, yes . . . *this fella was hers.*

The din of the Red Slipper faded around her as Sheffield held the tall cowpoke's gaze. Tall and fair-haired, with strong features that contrasted sharply with his light coloring, he was indeed more handsome than any man had a right to be—and he was the only man capable of stealing the breath of the strong-willed, independent woman that Sheffield had trained herself to be.

Pressing herself against him boldly, she whispered, "You couldn't stay away, could you, Perry?"

When Perry did not immediately respond, she prompted with a half-lidded glance, "Cat got your tongue?"

Perry's arm closed abruptly around her waist and Sheffield's breath caught in her throat as he turned her toward an empty table in the corner of the room. She had no explanation for the way this man's touch affected her, leaving her weak in the knees and raising in her a hunger for more than casual contact.

Retaining the presence of mind to signal the bar for a bottle once they were seated, Sheffield turned back toward the blue eyes that burned her. She whispered, "You didn't answer my question, darlin'."

"Maybe I didn't answer you because the question was too absurd."

"Absurd . . ." Her lips only a hairsbreadth from his, Sheffield smiled as she whispered, "You'd better watch that. If you want everyone here to believe you're the itinerant cowboy you're pretending to be, you'll have to forget that words like *absurd* are in your vocabulary."

His clear eyes turned cold as Sheffield pressed closer. "You enjoy playing the whore, don't you, Sheffield?"

Sheffield posed with a deliberate pout. "This disguise is very effective."

"I'm sure it is."

"It got me into Quinn's room and put me between Quinn and Max White—and Max didn't even give me a second look."

"You took too big a chance there, and you know it." Perry's hand clamped over hers. "That bastard is quick with his gun. If he had recognized you—"

"But he didn't recognize me, and I gave him ample opportunity."

"You're taking too many risks, Sheffield."

"I'm following through on your orders, and I'm doing a damned good job of it, if I do say so myself."

"I only put you on this job because you pressured me into it."

"Because you owed it to me, you mean."

"Owed it to you?"

"For giving my case away."

"Your case?"

"That's right, *my* case. I'm the one who was blamed for losing those gold bars, and I'm the one who identified Max as the leader of the gang that stole them."

"But Quinn's the one who's been working undercover on the case for almost a year."

"With me as his contact—the way *you* set it up."

"Yeah . . . the way I set it up."

The look in Perry's eyes said more than words, and Sheffield took a quivering breath. "You've missed me, haven't you?"

Perry's gaze dropped to her lips.

"You were worried about me, too, huh?"

The intensity of Perry's gaze deepened.

"Well, you shouldn't worry. I'm as good as any man in the field."

"Sheffield . . ."

"I'm here to do a job, and I'm doing it as

well or better than any of your other agents could."

"It's not your ability I'm worried about."

"Well, then—"

"It's your judgment."

"My judgment!"

Sheffield drew back in anger, and Perry warned, "Watch it, Sheffield. You're stepping out of character. Remember, you're a saloon whore after my money."

Sheffield gritted her teeth and smiled. "Don't tell me how to do my job."

"I've got a right."

"Why, because you're my boss?"

"Because I'm the man who's going to prove to you just how much he missed you as soon as we get out of here."

Intentionally provocative, Sheffield rubbed against him and purred, "Promises . . ."

His face flushing with sudden heat, Perry growled, "Now you've gone too far." Standing up unexpectedly, Perry pulled Sheffield up beside him and snatched the bottle from the table. He demanded loudly enough to be heard by those at the surrounding tables, "Where's your boss?"

Uncertain, Sheffield pointed an unsteady hand toward a swarthy fellow standing at the end of the bar.

"Tell him you're going out for a while and you'll be back in a few hours." Perry stared down into her eyes. "Tell him I'll pay him for your time."

Her knees suddenly wobbling, Sheffield responded, "This is a saloon, not a—"

"Tell him."

Sheffield glanced toward the end of the bar, and the swarthy proprietor nodded.

She should've known. It was a man's world, all right.

Perry's gaze locked with hers. Its heat scorched her, and Sheffield's heart began pounding.

A man's world . . . but at the moment, that suited her fine.

Breaking the silence that hung over the small contingent riding steadily toward town, Pete said unexpectedly, "Boss, this whole business is crazy, and you know it."

His attention diverted from the sun-drenched trail ahead and private thoughts he had no intention of sharing, Larry turned toward the weathered cowhand and the two other ranch hands who rode beside him. He had been unable to banish from his mind the image of Victoria's buckboard as it had disappeared from view earlier that day. Her departing words still lingered in his mind.

If you interfere without my approval. I'll write off the past fourteen years with a snap of my fingers. You'll be a stranger to me . . . a stranger who'll be forever unwelcome in my home.

He had known Victoria meant every word. After a moment's reflection, he had known he could not allow that to happen. His decision had been automatic.

It had taken only a few minutes for Manny, Pete and Buck to answer his summons, and for them all to saddle up. Brief instructions as to what would be expected of the ranch hands once they reached town had taken only a few minutes longer. Consumed by his own thoughts, he had not considered his men's reaction to the unexpected task he had set for them.

Larry did not immediately respond. Pete had been with the Bar MH for fifteen years. He knew Pete believed his years of service gave him special privileges, and he supposed at times they did.

But this wasn't one of those times.

His temper short, Larry snapped, "I don't remember asking you or anybody else for an opinion."

"Hell, boss . . ." Pete glanced at Manny and

Buck for support. Finding none when they avoided his glance, the whiskered cowhand continued with a frown, "You're needin' every hand out on the range this time of year. We ain't finished roundin' up them cows from the high pasture, and we're way behind in brandin'. With all that's comin' up—"

"What did you call me?"

Momentarily distracted, Pete paused. "What did I call you? I called you 'boss,' like I always do."

"*Boss.*" Larry's gaze was hard. "That means *I* give the orders around here."

"That's right, but—"

"That also means that *I* set the priorities on my ranch. My men don't."

"We wasn't hired for this kind of work, boss," Manny interjected.

Larry glared at the stiff-faced cowhand, then drew his mount to an abrupt halt. Waiting until the others did as well, he rounded on the three men, pinning Pete with his gaze as he said, "Maybe my memory doesn't serve me as well as it should, but didn't Doc ride out almost every day to check on how you were coming along when you got bit by that rattler a couple of years ago?"

At Pete's nod, he added, "Saved your life for you, didn't she?"

Not waiting for Pete's response, Larry turned on Manny. "How about you, when you couldn't shake that fever a while back, and Doc sat right by your bunk until it finally broke? Seems to me you were pretty happy to have her around then."

Larry turned toward Buck, only to have the lanky cowhand offer before he could speak, "I know what you're goin' to say. Doc set my leg when I broke it a couple of years ago, and she fixed it good, so's I don't even limp. Everythin' you said about the doc is true, but what's that got to do with what you're wantin' us to do now?"

Larry did not immediately respond. He was a private man. He had no intention of revealing to these three men that the same woman they were discussing had whispered to him over the frozen body of her intended that she would never allow herself to love again. Neither did he intend to disclose that he had made that same vow in her presence after Molly's death—only to have it become a farce when he was no longer able to deny his love for Victoria.

Instead, Larry stated flatly, "You want to know why I'm setting you up in shifts to watch Victoria's house without her knowing. I figure that's none of your business, but I'll tell you this: A fella threatened Victoria and her niece a few days ago. She doesn't want me to interfere, but I'm not about to take the chance that he'll follow through on his threat."

"What's the bastard's name?" Pete's reply was instantaneous. "I'll set him straight."

"What she ought to do is call in the sheriff and get the bastard arrested."

"Hell, the sheriff would jump at the chance. Willy Knowles always did have a fancy for the doc."

That last comment tightened Larry's mouth into a hard line. "Victoria doesn't want to call the sheriff in."

"Why not?"

Larry's gaze hardened. "I didn't see Victoria asking any questions when that rattler bit you, Pete, or when Buck broke his leg, or when that fever laid Manny out flat on his back."

No reply.

"If you're looking for an answer, you're not going to get one from me. I don't know the whole story. All I can say is that whatever her reasons are, they're good enough for me. What I need to know before we go any farther is whether I can count on you."

The first again to reply, Pete said, "You

know damned well we wouldn't let the doc
down. You should've told us the doc was in
some kind of danger in the first place."

Waiting until that statement was confirmed
by solemn nods all around, Larry stated flatly,
"One more thing: Whatever's got Victoria so
worried is tied up with that fella she's got recuperating in her back room. He should be
back on his feet soon. My guess is that when
he is, he'll shake the dust of this town off his
boots and not look back. With him should go
any trouble the doc might be expecting, but
until then I'm not taking any chances."

"Anythin' you say, boss."

Afternoon was fading, lengthening the shadows in Sheffield's small hotel room as she attempted to draw the straps of her chemise up
onto her shoulders. Standing beside her, the
naked, muscled length of his body pale in
the golden light filtering through the crack
in the window shade, Perry cupped her
breasts with his palms, then bent his head to
suckle the warm flesh briefly.

"Perry, please . . ." Sheffield struggled to regain her composure. They had spent the afternoon in loving solitude, during which few
words had been exchanged between them.
She had been lost for too many hours in the

passion that never failed to ignite when they were together—but it was getting late.

Gathering all her strength, Sheffield pushed Perry away, then drew the straps of her chemise up onto her shoulders. She forced herself to ignore his frown when she said, "Quinn will be wondering where I am. It's time to get down to business."

"Quinn?" Perry's jaw tightened noticeably. "Since when did you begin worrying about Quinn?"

Sheffield grew still. "I don't think I like the way you said that."

"It's a simple question."

"Too simple. You know as well as I do that Quinn has a right to expect me to keep in contact with him while he's incapacitated."

"He should be recuperated by now."

"Since when did you become his doctor?"

"Since when did you become his advocate?"

"Since *you* made me his contact, that's when." Pulling her dress off the nearby chair, Sheffield slipped it over her head, then demanded as she struggled to secure the back, "Are you ready to discuss business or not?"

"And if I'm not?"

"Then you're wasting my time." Exasperated by a button that refused to cooperate with her trembling fingers, Sheffield added, "You wouldn't be behaving this way if I were a *male* agent."

"Damned right I wouldn't!"

Abandoning the recalcitrant button, Sheffield snapped, "You're jealous of Quinn, is that it?"

"No."

"Isn't it?"

"I'm tired of competing for your time with a job that you've made your life's work."

"I made it clear to you what this job means to me the first time we met."

"But I never believed the job would become a rival I couldn't beat."

Sheffield went suddenly still. "What are you trying to say, Perry? Whatever it is, say it now and get it over with."

Slipping his legs into his trousers, Perry waited to secure his own buttons before responding. "I don't like entering a saloon and seeing all the men in the place staring at you like you're a plate of sweets they're waiting in line to devour."

"Perry!"

"And I don't like lying in bed with you and realizing that you're thinking about another man."

"You *are* jealous."

Perry did not respond.

Unflattered by his jealousy, Sheffield asked, "When did you stop trusting me, Perry?"

Still no response.

"Or is it that you never did trust me . . . that you only felt secure while you were able to keep me within view?"

"This disguise you're maintaining is beneath you, and you know it."

"Is it? With this disguise I was able to track down Quinn without suspicion. I was able to maintain contact with him while he was incapacitated, and I was able to learn that he thinks Max is planning something that will make him reveal the location of the gold bars."

"He's that close to discovering where they're hidden? Why didn't you say that before?"

"Because you weren't of a mind to talk."

"What else did Quinn say?"

Reaching for her brush to delay responding, Sheffield swept the straying strands of hair from her neck.

"I asked you a question, Sheffield."

"Tell me . . . is it Perry Locke, my supervisor, or Perry Locke, my damned, distrustful lover, asking me that question?"

"Just answer me!"

"In response to my supervisor, Quinn said that Max might not so easily have accepted the fact that he'd disobeyed orders, except that Max needs him for something *big* he's planning. Max also warned Quinn that if he doesn't get back to the cabin by the end of the week, they're going to go ahead without him."

"By the end of the week. That means Quinn has to be back at the cabin in two days."

"Right."

"Does Quinn expect to make it?"

"You know Quinn as well as I do. He'll make it or die trying."

"Sheffield—"

"And I'm telling you here and now . . . he's not going to die trying if I have anything to say about it."

Perry's light eyes swept Sheffield's determined expression. "As your supervisor, I'm gratified to know that you're such a dedicated agent."

Perry took a step closer, then swept Sheffield unexpectedly into his arms. Holding her motionless despite her protests, he continued against her lips, "As a man, I'm going to make sure you never forget—even for a moment— whom you belong to."

"Belong to?" Sheffield's eyes were suddenly

blazing. "I'm nobody's *possession*—most especially not yours!"

"Shut up, Sheffield."

"What did you s—"

Cutting off her protest, Perry claimed Sheffield's mouth with his. His imprisoning arms crushed her closer. His drugging kiss deepened, and as it did, Sheffield soon forgot that she had any protest at all.

Max's lips curled with disgust as the heavy snoring continued. Glancing into the corner of the cabin where Boots lay sleeping on his bedroll with an empty bottle beside him, he grunted a lewd curse.

His hand flew to his holster when Ernie entered the cabin unexpectedly, then dropped back to his side. He watched in silence as Ernie crossed the cabin, dropped some wood beside the fireplace, looked down into the pot bubbling there and said, "Them beans should be ready soon."

Yeah, beans.

Max stifled a smile. It wouldn't be long before he'd be eating at one of them big restaurants—in San Francisco, maybe. He had always wanted to see San Francisco, and he'd soon have the money to make that trip in style.

Max glanced again at the corner when Boots's snoring grew louder. Damn that Banning and his fancy whore! If waiting for him ended up complicating his plan, he'd make sure Banning spent a short life regretting it.

Yeah . . . a real short life.

Quinn stiffened on his bed at the sound of a woman's footsteps approaching his room. He had dozed again, and his headache had faded. He had spent the time since Thea's departure regretting his unwise behavior, but he wasn't ready to face her yet. He hadn't steeled himself against her appeal. He wasn't sure how he would react if she—

The flash of a crimson skirt in the doorway preceded the entrance of a familiar buxom figure.

"Oh, it's you, Sheffield."

Sheffield glanced behind her before entering the room. Her expression was wry. "I'm glad nobody was around to hear that reception. You're going to have to try a little harder if you want anybody here to believe you're crazy about me."

"I'm not in the mood for games, Sheffield."

Sheffield's expression sobered. "I can see that. Well, the truth is, I'm a little tired, myself."

"Tired?"

"I've been working hard."

Quinn did not respond.

"Perry's here."

"Oh."

Pointedly ignoring his knowing glance, Sheffield sat on the side of his bed and leaned toward him. She slid her arms around his neck and whispered, "Perry wants to know if you'll be back on your feet in time to meet Max like you planned."

Quinn frowned. "I'm leaving here tomorrow."

"Tomorrow? You said you have until the end of the week."

"I'm going back to the cabin tomorrow."

To her credit, Sheffield looked sincerely concerned. "You're still kind of pale."

"I feel well enough."

"You're sure . . ."

"I said, I'm leaving here tomorrow."

Silent, Sheffield scrutinized Quinn more closely. "Trouble with the doc?"

"No."

"With the redhead, then."

No comment.

"I knew it." Sheffield's lips tightened. "Is she threatening to go to the sheriff? We can't let that happen, Quinn."

"Thea's not threatening anything."

"Then why—" Sheffield halted abruptly. "You said you were too sick to get anything going with her." She gave a short laugh. "Damned if I wasn't fool enough to believe you."

Quinn replied pointedly, "Perry's waiting for you, isn't he?"

"Don't change the subject."

Suddenly angry, Quinn said, "You're my contact, not my conscience. How I treat Thea or any other woman is no concern of yours."

Stiffening under his unexpected attack, Sheffield retorted, "All right, if that's the way you want it, but Perry's going to want to know exactly what you're planning."

"Tell Perry I'm going back to the cabin tomorrow. I'm going to play the game the way Max wants it until I learn what his big 'plan' is." Gritting his teeth, Quinn continued, "And it damned well better not be some harebrained scheme."

"Calm down, Quinn."

"Don't tell me to calm down."

"All right. I won't tell you anything. You tell me. When do you want to set up our next contact?"

"Just stay at the Red Slipper and I'll find you."

"Stay at the Red Slipper . . ."

"I thought you liked playing the whore."

Her lips twitching, Sheffield shrugged. "Not when I've got better things to do."

Turning abruptly toward approaching footsteps in the hall, Sheffield announced, "I have to go now, darlin'. I'm a working girl, you know."

Waiting until the footsteps neared, Sheffield leaned forward to press a lingering kiss against Quinn's mouth. Angry at the realization that Sheffield's kiss left him totally cold, Quinn wrapped his arms around her, deliberately deepening the kiss as Thea entered the room.

Though he derived little satisfaction from Thea's sudden flush and her mumbled apology as she backed out of the room, he added loudly, "I'll be missing you while you're gone, Sheffield, darlin'."

Turning toward him when the hallway was silent again, Sheffield spat, "You know, I never realized what a true bastard you are."

"Tell Perry I'll be back on the job tomorrow."

"You didn't have to make that woman feel—"

"Tomorrow, Sheffield."

* * *

Still trembling, Thea stepped into the silent kitchen and halted abruptly. She had walked back into Quinn's room unaware that Sheffield had entered the house. Her lips still tingling from his kiss, she had been determined to speak to Quinn and ask him—

The slam of the front door interrupted Thea's thoughts, announcing Sheffield's exit. Thea raised a trembling hand to her head.

You were meant to be in my arms, Thea.

She could not explain how Wade's words had become Quinn's words, yet when she had walked in on him moments earlier, Quinn had proved more clearly than ever before that he wasn't Wade—that he was simply playing some kind of cruel game. The difference between the two men could never have been more obvious.

The familiar kitchen walls seemed suddenly suffocating. Thea walked out into the yard and breathed deeply. She turned abruptly toward the sound of Aunt Victoria's buckboard.

Struggling to regain control of her emotions as the buckboard neared, Thea forced a smile. When her aunt dismounted and turned to face her, she inquired, "How's the Parker baby?"

"Her fever broke. She'll be all right." Her

gaze discerning, Aunt Victoria asked, "Is something wrong, dear?"

"No, I . . . I just came out for some air."

"Where's Mr. Banning?"

"He's in his room."

Aunt Victoria scrutinized her a moment longer. "You're sure you're all right?"

"Yes."

Hesitating, Aunt Victoria said, "All right. I'm going inside."

Thea held her breath as her aunt disappeared into the house. Then she turned to walk blindly across the yard.

Was she all right?

No.

What was wrong?

Nothing, except that for brief moments she had believed she had seen Wade in Quinn Banning's eyes. She had felt his touch, heard his voice, only to discover that it was all a lie.

Turning the corner of the barn, Thea leaned back against the weathered board and closed her eyes.

Yet when Quinn had kissed her, she had been so sure—

Thea took a shuddering breath.

She had been so sure she felt *love*.

Chapter Six

"I'm leaving. I need to pay what I owe you and collect my gun."

Quinn Banning's statement echoed in the stillness of the small kitchen, leaving Victoria momentarily at a loss for words. Morning had come too quickly after a long night spent twisting and turning while sleep eluded her. Sounds from Thea's bedroom next door, indicating that she was also suffering a restless night, had done nothing to reassure her.

Larry's expression as they had said their good-byes the previous day haunted her. She had reviewed the angry words of their encounter over and again, and she was still uncertain how they had reached such an impasse. Her final warning to him had been harsh and unyielding, and she had meant every word.

Larry, her dear friend and confidant, had been closer to her than any person in her life for more years than she cared to count. How could she manage without him?

That question had nagged her through the silent hours, stirring a myriad of emotions that Victoria even now could not clearly define—except to say that with morning had come a strangely deadening sense of loss.

A subdued clatter in the kitchen—Thea starting breakfast—had awakened her, and she had quickly dressed. She had forced a smile to her lips that faded the moment she realized Thea's smile was forced as well. She had been silently cursing the day Quinn Banning arrived at her door when he walked unexpectedly into the kitchen.

Banning grew impatient. "I want to know how much I owe you, Doc."

Victoria did not reply. Instead, she assessed him with a professional eye. He stood with saddlebags in hand, tall and erect in the flickering morning light. This was a different man from the fellow she had seen after arriving home the previous night. Gone was the incapacitating headache he had obviously been suffering and which he had vigorously denied. His balance appeared to be stable and his eyes were clear. He was paler than she might consider normal beneath the sun-darkened tone of his skin, but that was to be expected under the circumstances. For all intents and purposes, he appeared to have recovered.

Despite herself, Victoria glanced at Thea. Her niece stood in frozen silence near the stove a few feet away. In contrast, Thea's fair complexion had blanched completely of color, her stance was rigid and she was staring at Banning with a look that was somewhere between incredulity and—

Struck by unreasonable anger at her inability to interpret the effect Banning had on her niece, Victoria responded stiffly. "I take it you consider yourself fully recovered and no longer in need of my services?"

Banning's gaze grew cautious. "That's right."

"I hope you'll humor me then by answering a few simple questions." Not allowing him to reply, Victoria pressed, "No more nausea, dizziness or headache? You're steady on your feet and aren't suffering any lapses of memory?"

"I'm fine. How much do I owe you?"

Behind her, Thea moved, knocking a pan to the floor with a clatter that elicited a tightening of Banning's jaw. Irritation soaring, Victoria snapped, "I suppose I'll leave that up to you, Mr. Banning. How much do you feel you owe Thea and me for services rendered?"

Hesitating only a moment, his gaze never straying toward the spot where Thea stood seemingly immobile, Banning advanced aggressively toward Victoria. Halting abruptly beside her, he took some gold coins out of his pocket, slapped them down onto the table and said, "That should cover it."

Incensed, Victoria replied, "No, I don't think so."

Banning looked up sharply.

"I think a polite word in parting is also indicated."

"I was never accused of being polite."

"I can certainly understand that."

"And I don't intend this to be an exception."

Color flooding her face, Victoria raised her chin. Turning toward the pantry, she pulled open the door and stooped down to remove a weathered gunbelt from underneath neatly folded dishcloths on the bottom shelf. She turned back toward him and slapped the gunbelt down on the table, replying, "I agree with you, Mr. Banning. It *is* time for you to leave."

The click of the front door closing behind Banning turned Victoria toward Thea.

Victoria attempted a smile. "Well, I suppose we've seen the last of Mr. Banning."

Wordlessly, Thea walked out into the yard.

Leading his saddled mount, Quinn walked briskly along Willowby's main thoroughfare, leaving the livery stable behind. With the familiar comfort of his gunbelt strapped around his hips, he assessed the town as it awoke to the new day. He glimpsed blinds being raised in windows along the street. He saw the door of the general store opening, a milk wagon making its way down the street, a drunken cowboy stirring in the alleyway beside the saddlery, a woman in a large apron sweeping the walk in front of the town's only restaurant. He heard the crowing of a cock somewhere in the distance, and felt his stomach gurgle at the aromas of strong coffee and frying bacon.

Another average day.

Quinn shook his head. Nothing could be further from the truth. Contempt had been Victoria Sills's reaction when he had left her without a word of thanks, but it was the look in Thea's eyes that was burned into his mind.

Quinn took a shaky breath. He had done

what he must. He had walked away from the
two women in a way calculated to make them
dismiss him forever from their lives. In doing
so, he had removed them from danger. Having accomplished that, he could get back to
business.

Quinn scanned the street again as he approached the Willowby Hotel, then tied up
his mount at the hitching post and walked inside. He glanced at the registration desk,
where the clerk was sleeping soundly, his
head resting on his arms, then started up the
stairs toward the second floor. Sheffield had
said she was staying in Room Twelve.

Quinn gave a wry snort. Yes, his memory
was fine—perhaps too fine to suit him at that
moment. He remembered too clearly for
comfort the day when Perry had called him
into his office to give him his present assignment. Gold bars worth a staggering sum had
been stolen en route to the Treasury Department. The thieves had been identified, but although the location of the bars was unknown,
the Department was certain that it had
blocked all avenues that might possibly be
used by the thieves to profit from their theft.
Perry had actually smiled when he'd said the
thieves were stuck with their haul, and all

Quinn had to do was locate the bars and take them off the bastards' hands.

Quinn's jaw ticked with a familiar frustration. That had been almost a year earlier; and with every day since, he had become more determined to locate those gold bars and get them back to the Treasury Department where they belonged—if only to see the look on Max White's face when he did.

Admittedly, he hadn't appreciated the fact that Perry had assigned a woman to be his contact while working on the case—especially Perry's own woman. But Sheffield had proved herself far superior to many of the men with whom he'd previously worked, even if it did irk him that she had been right again in warning him about the danger of his fascination for Thea.

Stopping as he reached the top of the staircase, Quinn briefly scanned the hallway, then started toward a door near the rear exit. That room would be number twelve. Sheffield always took the room that would afford her the best means of escape in an emergency.

Ignoring the nagging ache in his temple, Quinn knocked lightly on the door. He heard Sheffield say, "Who is it?"

His patience at low ebb, Quinn grated, "Open the door, Sheffield."

The door opened a slit, revealing a glimpse of a female body clad in nightclothes as Sheffield replied, "Oh, it's you, Banning."

Tit for tat.

Sheffield opened the door an inch wider, and Quinn ordered, "Tell Perry to put down his gun. I'm alone."

Sheffield grimaced. "And you surmised correctly that I'm not."

Without bothering to reply, Quinn entered and closed the door behind him, then turned toward Perry. His supervisor stood with his trousers hastily fastened and his gun held limply at his side.

Without preamble, Quinn said flatly, "We're going to have to change our plans."

Concealed in the shadows of the rising sun, Thea stood a few steps off Main Street, staring at the doorway through which Quinn had disappeared minutes earlier. Her throat tight, she struggled for control.

Unable to face Aunt Victoria after Quinn's departure, she had escaped from the kitchen to clear her mind, but solitude had only increased her confusion. Uncertain of her own intentions and hoping Quinn had not already left town, she had started toward the livery stable. She had reached Main Street just as

Quinn tied up his horse in front of the Willowby Hotel and went inside.

Thea took a shuddering breath. Somehow she hadn't expected that Quinn would go directly from his cold farewell to the Willowby Hotel and the warm bed of Sheffield Turner.

But why hadn't she? Quinn had shown only too clearly that those few moments the previous day when he had held her in his arms, when his mouth had claimed hers, were no more than a moment's diversion that he had cast aside the moment Sheffield showed her face at the door.

Sheffield . . . Quinn's woman.

Thea closed her eyes against the images those words evoked.

Forcing her eyes open, Thea took another deep breath. She had been a fool to believe for even a moment that Wade might have found some way to return to her.

Thea stepped back into the shadows—determined to be a fool no longer.

"We'll need time to notify the marshal and organize a posse." Perry's tone held little emotion. "Do you think you'll be able to give it to us?"

"That depends on Max."

"Otherwise, we'll have to handle it without help."

"It won't be the first time."

Perry stared at Quinn, studying his agent's pale face and grim expression. Behind him, Sheffield shrugged into a sheer garment that did little to hide the outline of the womanly curves beneath, but Perry allowed her little thought. Obvious to him for the first time was the fact that Quinn's injury had been more serious than he had realized. The dedicated Treasury agent was not yet fully recovered.

Perry remained silent, and Quinn's frown deepened.

"What's the matter, Perry? I've never seen you hesitate before."

"You're right. It wouldn't be the first time that we've finished up a case without outside help, but—"

"Well?"

"But the truth is, I'm wondering if you're up to it."

"If I'm 'up to it'?"

"You were injured. It's obvious that you haven't fully regained your strength."

"I'm fine."

"Max is a dangerous man."

"I said, I'm fine."

"I heard you, but—"

"I'm fine. You don't have to worry that I'll make a mistake and ruin everything. This role I've been playing for the past year has become second nature to me. I slip into it just like a pair of old boots, and a little bump on the head won't change that."

"A little bump on the head?" Boldly entering the conversation, Sheffield walked unselfconsciously closer. "You forget that I saw the condition you were in a few days ago."

"That was a few days ago. I'm fine now."

"No, you're not. You could've waited another day before going back to the cabin, but you're rushing it, instead." Sheffield's knowing gaze pinned him. "This is all about that redhead, isn't it? You weren't sure what she'd do if you stayed any longer."

"Leave Thea out of this."

"Thea?"

"The doc's niece." Sheffield turned briefly toward Perry. "The woman who was on the stage when Quinn robbed it."

"I told you to leave Thea out of this."

"We need to be sure she won't go to the sheriff."

"She won't."

"Can you guarantee that?" Perry's expression was obdurate. "The outcome of an entire year's work—not to mention your life—might depend on it."

Staring back at Perry with equal firmness, Quinn said flatly, "Yes, I can."

"All right." Halting Sheffield's objection with a glance, Perry continued, "We'll go ahead. You'll return to the cabin, as planned. Instead of waiting in town, Sheffield and I will follow and set up camp as close to the cabin as we can without being detected. As soon as you find out what Max has planned and how he intends to dispose of the gold bars, you'll give us the signal and we'll make sure Max gets some company he isn't expecting."

Quinn paused. "It might not be that easy. Max is smart, and he's cautious. He might not say what he's planning until the last minute."

Perry's even features hardened. "We'll handle it."

Quinn nodded and turned toward the door.

"Quinn . . ." Quinn turned back. "If there's any trouble, the emergency signal remains the same."

"Don't worry. There won't be any trouble."

Buck whistled softly as he followed the trail back to the Bar MH Ranch. The lanky cowhand recalled the boss's insistence that they guard Doc Sills day and night.

Buck unconsciously shook his head. Pete had taken the first watch, and he had taken the second. He had settled himself in for a long siege, only to see that Banning fella leave the house almost at the crack of dawn, with his saddlebags in hand.

Using his discretion, Buck had immediately followed Banning from the doc's place to the livery stable, where Banning had picked up his horse. Banning had stopped off only briefly at the hotel—Buck supposed to visit the saloon woman rumored to have followed him to town—and then like the boss had said, he'd ridden out without giving Willowby a backward look.

Buck smiled. He hadn't wasted any time leaving Willowby, either. With Banning had gone the threat against the doc, and he was anxious to give the boss the good news.

Buck whistled more loudly as he nudged his mount to a faster pace. He was grateful that his watch had ended so quickly, and so well. He was, after all, a cowhand. That was the work he did best, and he was glad to get back to it.

* * *

Her hands trembling and her heart pounding, Thea grunted as she lifted the saddle from the rack and swung it onto the gelding's back. Fumbling as she attempted to tighten the cinch, she stopped to take a breath, aware that her emotions were out of control.

What was she doing?

Thea brushed a fiery strand of hair back from her face and swept Aunt Victoria's barn with a cursory glance, finally admitting to herself that she wasn't sure. All she was certain of at the moment was that she had to speak to Quinn Banning.

"Thea, what are you doing?"

Startled, Thea turned to face Aunt Victoria, who was standing in the doorway.

"You're not going after—I mean, you aren't—" Aunt Victoria trailed off.

"I'm going for a ride, Aunt Victoria. I need to clear my mind." Thea attempted a smile. "I should have asked if I could borrow Brady for an hour or so, but—"

"It's not my horse I'm concerned about," Aunt Victoria said. "I . . . I suppose I should've spoken to you about this sooner, but it's been obvious to me since you came that you've had some difficulty adapting to your new home."

"No, that's not true. I—"

"Please let me finish," Aunt Victoria continued. "It's also been obvious that the situation worsened considerably after Mr. Banning was delivered to our door. I want you to know that I blame myself for much of your discomfort. I obviously failed to provide you the support you needed in acclimating to your new home."

"My discomfort had nothing to do with you, Aunt Victoria."

"But you didn't feel free to talk to me."

"I needed to work things out for myself."

"For yourself . . ." Aunt Victoria looked down. "And have you done that, dear?"

"No, but I soon will."

"Can you at least tell me where you're going?"

Thea responded as truthfully as she was able. "I'm going to confront the past, once and for all."

"But how do you expect to—?"

"Please, Aunt Victoria . . ."

Responding to Thea's unarticulated plea, Aunt Victoria whispered, "All right, no more questions."

Stepping back as Thea threw the reins over the gelding's head, then swung herself up into the saddle, Aunt Victoria added simply, "Take care, dear."

Thea nudged her mount into the rapidly brightening light of morning.

Damn that Boots! His snoring sounded like an old saw.

Shifting on his bedroll, Max grunted with disgust, then turned toward Ernie. The fellow slept, apparently deaf to Boots's maddening nightsong, with drool trailing from the corner of his gaping mouth.

They were a pair, all right.

Throwing back his blanket, Max pulled on his boots and stood up. Glaring a moment longer at his two henchmen, he turned and stomped toward the door. He closed it with a thud behind him and walked to a nearby bush to relieve himself, his mind drifting back to the morning more than a year earlier when he had sat mounted on his horse with gun in hand, hidden in a stand of trees—with Pete, Jeff, and Boots arrayed behind him.

Max remembered that he had almost smiled as the wagon lumbered up the trail toward them. Two male guards and a woman dressed and armed like a man were the only protection the shipment had had. He had reveled in his luck at being in the right place at the right time, when a bank clerk who had drunk one drink too many had related to a friend standing beside him at the bar the particulars of an important shipment that was being secretly transported to the railhead in the next town.

An important shipment.

Snickering, Max recalled the surprised expressions on the faces of the guards when his bullets hit them. He remembered that the female guard had been saved from the same fate when Pete had inadvertently ridden into his line of fire and knocked the woman from her horse with the butt of his gun.

It was over surprisingly fast. The two guards disposed of, the female guard and the driver unconscious, he had thrown back the canvas cover on the rear of the wagon to view his haul.

He had been stunned speechless.

Gold bars. Dozens of them!

He had driven off with a smile on his face and a certainty that his pockets would never be empty again.

Unfortunately, he had never been more wrong.

As it turned out, the gold bars had been intended for the U.S. Treasury, and for a while it had seemed every federal agent in the country was on his trail. Things had gotten hard then. Pete and Jeff had had a lot to say about the cache that had become a millstone around their necks, and when he had gotten tired of hearing them, he had stopped their complaining . . . permanently. Then he had been left with Boots—of all damned people— and a fortune that he was unable to spend.

Max buttoned up his pants and turned back toward the cabin. Yeah, but those days were over. It had taken him a year, but he'd outsmarted all those badge-toting U.S. Government heroes. Now, in a few weeks at most, he'd be rich.

Max glanced toward the trail. He'd wait a day longer for Banning, only because he needed the bastard. Another clear mind and steady hand with a gun would be essential when he retrieved those gold bars from their year-long hiding place and delivered them for his payoff.

Alerted to sounds of movement within the cabin, Max looked in the window and saw Boots and Ernie stirring. His frown deepened. After he cashed in those gold bars for the fortune he had coming, he'd make a fond farewell to the whole lot of them. There would be no loose ends dangling behind him.

* * *

Quinn squinted up at the clear blue of the sky, his mind far from the potential danger of the next few days. The sun had fully risen to shed its brilliant glow on the wilderness terrain surrounding him, but with it had come the dull ache in his temples that he seemed unable to escape.

Sheffield had been right again. Allowing himself another day to recuperate completely might have been wise, but he had been only too aware that another day might be one day too long. Already images of fiery hair and clear skin, of light eyes bright with an emotion he could not quite discern and of warm, full lips sweet to the taste, were too clearly impressed on his mind.

Things had gone poorly that morning. He had entered the kitchen hoping to make a clean break with aunt and niece. But the look on Thea's pale face had almost been his undoing. It had been all he could do not to stride forward and take her into his arms, not to whisper against her lips that Sheffield's kiss had meant nothing to him the previous day, that he had no choice but to leave—an explanation that he had never felt the need or the desire to make to any woman before.

His reaction to his moment of weakness had been anger, and that emotion had lent a harsher tone to his departure than he had originally intended. That moment of weakness had also been a revelation he could not ignore. He had tried to convince himself that he had cut off further contact between the fiery redhead and himself for her sake—because he was a danger to her—but he now knew that the truth was the reverse. He was the one in danger—from Thea, who now dominated his thoughts when he should be concentrating on the job at hand.

Almost grateful for the pain that stabbed sharply in his temple, curtailing his rambling thoughts, Quinn grimaced, then flipped up the buckle on his saddlebag and withdrew one of the packets of headache powder that he had taken from his nightstand before leaving. He muttered a low curse when the image of Thea leaning over his bed with a cup to his lips flashed before his eyes. He remembered the scent of her, the look in her eyes as she watched him intently, almost as if she—

Again halting his wandering thoughts, Quinn drew his horse up beside the trail with a deepening frown. Dismounting, he retrieved a metal cup from his saddlebag and filled it with water from his canteen. He dumped the powder into the lukewarm liquid, then emptied the cup in a few gulps.

His hand sprang to the gun at his hip at the sound of hoofbeats on the trail behind him. Quinn went still as he waited—intent and alert—to identify the mounted figure that came suddenly into view.

"What in hell are you doing back here, Buck?" Larry strode toward the rangy cowhand, who reined his mount to a halt beside the barn. With his harsh encounter with Victoria still fresh in his mind, his disposition was strained at best. The realization that she could so coldly sever the bond that gave his life meaning had been a difficult truth to accept. The knowledge that he was protecting her from danger despite her protests had been his only consolation.

But that consolation was negated by Buck's unexpected return. "You weren't supposed to leave town until Manny came to replace you."

"Take it easy, boss."

"Don't tell me to take it easy. You know how things are and you left the doc alone. If anything happens to her—"

"Nothin's gonna happen to her!" Buck dismounted cautiously. "That Banning fella's gone. He left the doc's house this morning, saddlebags in hand, and headed out of town. You can be sure he don't have no intention of goin' back to the doc's house again, neither."

"What makes you think that?"

"I saw the look on his face. Besides, why would he? He was lyin' in the doc's back room because he couldn't do nothin' else, but he ain't sick no more. He looked fit as a fiddle when he walked out that door." Buck gave a short laugh. "I figure he had to be feelin' pretty good 'cause he went to visit that woman of his at the Willowby Hotel before he left town. You know, the one everybody's talkin' about. It didn't take him long to take care of business there, either."

"What about Doc and her niece?" Larry asked.

"Doc's niece was out in the back yard gettin' some fresh air, and I saw Doc through the window walkin' toward her back room. Everythin' looked fine to me."

Yes, everything *looked* fine.

Turning abruptly toward the men who had filtered out of the barn behind him, Larry ordered, "Take over for me today, Jack. I'm going to town."

"Stop where you are!"

Quinn's deep voice reverberated on the silence of the narrow trail. Startled into spontaneous compliance, Thea drew back sharply on her mount's reins. Her heart pounding, she saw Quinn standing beside his horse on the side of the trail, his hat pulled low on his forehead, his powerful body alert, ready, his hand hovering near the gun at his hip. She noted the angry tightening of his lips when he recognized her.

He spat, "What are you doing out here?"

Suddenly as angry as he, Thea retorted, "What makes you think you have a right to ask me that question?"

"Answer me, Thea."

Foregoing a response, Thea attempted to dismount, only to hear Quinn snap, "No, you don't. Turn that horse around and go back home where you belong. You have no business this far from town."

Aware of the hot flush of color his words provoked Thea retorted, "Yes, I do."

Swinging herself down from the saddle, she saw anger mount to fury in Quinn's eyes. He closed the distance between them in a few rapid steps and ordered, "Get back up on that horse."

"What are you afraid of, Quinn?" Facing him boldly, Thea struggled to ignore his ire as she continued, "Are you afraid I'll interfere with something you have planned—your meeting with Max White perhaps?"

"You'd be smart to forget you ever set eyes on Max."

"Maybe the same could be said for you."

"That's not your concern."

"Isn't it?" Thea's heart pounded harder. Quinn was so close that she could see the agitation in his eyes, and the way his mouth turned down when he was angry. Both were characteristics as familiar to her as the contours of his face, the shape of his lips, and she—

"This is a waste of time, Thea. We've already said good-bye."

"Not to my satisfaction, we haven't."

Quinn's jaw hardened. "You told me you wanted me out of your aunt's house as soon as possible—out of your lives."

"I know, but—"

"Is that what you wanted or not?"

"That's what I said, but I wanted it on my terms, not yours!"

Quinn's short bark of laughter made Thea flush hotter than ever as she went on. "This was all fun and games for you, wasn't it?"

"I don't know what you're talking about."

"Don't you?" Thea's throat squeezed tight as she repeated, " 'You were meant to be in my arms, Thea.' "

Quinn went still.

" 'Don't be afraid of me, Thea. I'd never hurt you.' "

Quinn did not reply.

Suddenly unwilling to abide the conflict between them any longer, Thea whispered, "I couldn't let you leave the way you did, didn't you know that? Talk to me, Quinn. Tell me what this is all about. I have to know."

Thea stared up into the dark-eyed gaze that tore at her heart. She perused Quinn's face, the familiar features of the man she had loved. Her voice became a soft plea.

"Who told you to say those things to me? Why did you speak to me in that tone of voice . . . as tenderly as if you were speaking directly from your heart?" Momentarily unable to continue, Thea rasped, "Who are you, Quinn? What are you? Are you really the thief who robbed me?" Thea paused, her heart pounding like thunder in her ears as she whispered, "Or are you . . . someone else?"

Quinn's dark eyes moved slowly to her lips.

"Quinn, please tell me."

She was pleading with him, her eyes intent. She wanted him to talk to her, to tell her something . . . anything. She would believe anything he told her right now, because she wanted to believe.

Quinn raised a hand to Thea's cheek. It was warm . . . smooth . . . softer than any skin he had touched before. She was beautiful, but she was more than that to him somehow. She was a link to a part of him that he hadn't known before—a part deep inside—and she wanted to believe in him.

"Quinn . . . please."

A single tear slipped from the corner of Thea's eye, and Quinn brushed it away with his thumb. The ache inside him expanded. He heard himself say, "Don't . . . I can't stand to see you cry."

Thea's eyes widened. She was trembling. She was only inches away. And then she was in his arms.

Clasping her close, Quinn rasped, "Tell me what you want me to say, Thea, and I'll say it."

"Quinn . . ."

"Why did I say those things to you? Because I meant them, that's why."

"Quinn, please . . ."

"Why did I speak to you in that tone of voice? Because of the way you made me feel."

"Quinn, wait. I want you to know—"

"What do you want me to know, Thea?" His

emotions were rapidly slipping beyond his control. "That you felt the heat between us the moment we met, just as I did? Because I know it's true. That you fought to ignore your feelings? I know you did because I did, too. That you wanted me to go, to leave your aunt's house and disappear from your life because you weren't sure what was happening, and you knew things were slipping out of control? Because that's the real reason I left.

"Thea . . ." Closing the distance between their lips, Quinn brushed her mouth with his. The taste of her raised a sudden, voracious hunger in him. He crushed her against him, straining to bring her closer as he pressed his kiss deeper.

Finally Quinn tore his mouth from hers. He drew back, but he felt Thea shuddering and could not abandon her. He tasted her fluttering eyelids, the rise of her cheek, the edge of her lips, the curve of her ear, then returned to the compelling comfort of her mouth. He delved deeper, separating her lips, drawing from the warmth within until the last of Thea's restraint vanished and she returned his kiss full measure.

Her throat, the slender column of her neck, the delicate hollows beneath—he consumed them with his kiss.

Frustrated by the narrow strip of flesh revealed in the neckline of her bodice, he fumbled with the buttons at the back of her dress, ignoring her mumbled protests as he freed them at last and pushed her bodice to her waist.

Her breasts were slight and sweet when bared to the warm morning air. The tender crests were a honeyed confection that whetted his appetite for more. He consumed them ravenously, taking the warm flesh into his mouth. He suckled them, laving them with his tongue.

Thea was gasping, pressing him close, holding his lips against her as he worshipped her with growing ardor.

Drawing back from her abruptly, Quinn slid his hands into the fiery hair at her temples, holding her fast under his gaze as he whispered, "You're a part of me, Thea."

Thea stared up at him, overwhelmed by emotion.

Pushed past the bonds of restraint, Quinn swept Thea up into his arms and carried her to a leafy bower a few feet away. He settled her gently there, then crouched over her, kissing her long and deep before raising her skirt and stripping away her flimsy undergarments to settle his mouth against the moist delta between her thighs.

Quinn felt the quaver that shook Thea as he drew from her intimate warmth. He heard a soft word of protest become an impassioned groan as he stroked her with his tongue. He felt her quaking and he reveled in the sounds of her pleasure. He explored her fully, wanting, needing, hungering.

Halting briefly at Thea's first, revealing shudder, Quinn looked up to lock her gaze with his. He saw the telltale flush of her skin. He read a need in her eyes that matched his own, but he saw something else as well that prompted him to whisper, "Don't be afraid, Thea. I'd never hurt you."

A tear slid down her cheek.

Lowering his mouth against her once more, Quinn drew from her deeply, fully, his fervent quest unyielding as Thea shuddered again, as she quivered, then convulsed in ecstatic spasms.

The taste of her still warm in his mouth, Quinn gently freed Thea from the remainder of her clothing, then stripped away his own as well to eliminate the last impediment to the full meeting of their flesh. He paused as she whispered unexpectedly, "Talk to me . . . please."

The words rose spontaneously to his lips, as if waiting to be spoken. "Thea . . . this time between us was meant to be."

"*. . . meant to be . . .*"

Quinn loomed over her. His powerful body dwarfed hers as the familiar words echoed in her mind.

Unwilling to give up the sight of him, Thea watched as Quinn pressed his body to hers, probing her gently. His strong features flushed with passion, he met her gaze briefly before driving full and deep inside her.

Gasping as he filled her, Thea closed her eyes at last, clutching Quinn close as his body met hers with a rhythmic stroking that cast all rational thought from her mind.

Joining him in his thrusts, wondering at the mindless ecstasy of the moment, Thea raised herself to meet Quinn with heedless fervor. She felt the first quaking of his strong frame, and her exhilaration mounted. Meeting him more strongly, taking him into her more deeply, she joined him, gasping her joy as they shuddered to simultaneous release.

Lying moist and replete beneath him, Thea went totally still as Quinn whispered against her lips, "Yes . . . this was meant to be."

*   *   *

The silence of her dispensary seemed deafening, Victoria thought as she went about her work. She had gone there after leaving Thea in the barn, her intention to strip the cot of its linens and scrub the room clean. She wished that she could scrub her mind free of the events of the past few days as well. That was not possible, however. Unable to concentrate, she had spent twice the time and twice the effort needed to accomplish her task. Her work was not yet completed—and Thea had not yet returned.

Four hours! Victoria raised a shaky hand to her head, beside herself with worry. Where could Thea be? The wilderness beyond Willowby was so vast. It was unsafe for her alone out there. If she had wandered off the trail, it would be so easy to become disoriented and totally lost.

Victoria ran a hand through her hair, her concern deepening. Where had Thea gone? Had something happened to her? How long should she wait before alerting the sheriff and setting out in search of her?

Her anxiety approaching panic, Victoria forced back tears. She had been selfish in asking Thea to move to this wilderness country! She had so wanted Margaret's daughter to be near her, but she should have realized the dif-

179

ficulties Thea would have adjusting. She should have realized that Thea would be faced with a different kind of man, a type less polished—less civilized—than the southern gentlemen she had grown up with.

Dropping the instrument she had been cleaning onto a tray with a clatter, Victoria walked again to the window to stare out at the street.

No sign of Thea. What should she do?

Still staring at the street, Victoria gasped aloud as a familiar figure led his horse around the corner into view. She rushed to the front door, a shaky smile on her lips.

Agitated, the journey from his ranch an exercise in pure frustration after his horse stumbled en route and began limping, Larry led the animal down Willowby's main street. He had been more than halfway to town when it happened. His only recourse had been to dismount and lead the injured animal the rest of the way.

Relieved when Willowby finally came into view, he had been comforted by the demeanor of the town as it dozed lazily at midday, without any sign of excitement. Hot, thirsty and footsore, he had turned into view of Victoria's house, immediately noting the movement at the window. He had been prepared for anything—except the sight of Victoria's unsteady smile when she appeared at the door, and her sudden rush toward him.

Reaching his side, Victoria threw her arms around him, shaking as she said, "Larry, I'm so glad you're here." He did not have time for a reply before Victoria drew back unexpectedly, apparently conscious of the inquisitive stares they were attracting. Taking his arm, she urged him back toward the house with a semblance of her usual decorum.

But she was trembling.

Waiting only until the door of the house had closed behind them, Victoria said, "She's gone, Larry! Thea rode out four hours ago. She said she needed to get some fresh air to clear her mind . . . but . . . but I think she rode out after *him*."

"Him?"

"Mr. Banning. He left this morning. He said he had fully recuperated from his fall, but I don't think that was completely true. He was going to meet that man—Max White—I'm sure. He's trouble, Larry. They both are."

"What did Thea have to do with them?"

"I told you there was something about the way Thea looked at Mr. Banning that worried me. She didn't say a word when he announced he was leaving. It was as if she was frozen, unable to speak. He left, and I found Thea saddling Brady a little while later. Then she rode off. That was four hours ago, Larry, and she hasn't returned."

Victoria leaned against him in despair, and Larry slid his arms around her. "You're letting yourself get upset over what might turn out to be nothing at all, Victoria."

Jerking back from his embrace, Victoria faced him with lips tight. "Four hours, Larry! Thea would never stay away that long. She doesn't know anybody outside of a few people in town. She has nowhere to go."

"She said she had some thinking to do."

"Damn it, Larry, haven't you been listening to me at all? She rode out after Mr. Banning, I'm sure of it."

"You're jumping to conclusions."

"Am I? You never did believe me when I said there was something strange in Thea's reaction to that man. I suppose the reason is that you don't really care."

"Do you truly believe that?"

"What am I supposed to believe?" She stared at him a moment longer, then started toward the door.

"Where are you going?"

"I'm going to the livery stable to get a horse.

I'm going to go out looking for her."

"No, you're not!"

"Don't tell me what to do, Larry."

"Victoria, listen to me." Grasping her arm to stay her, Larry continued, "You've been overreacting ever since Thea arrived here in Willowby. Thea's all right, I'm sure of it." That untruth lying heavily on his lips, he continued, "But if you're so worried, I'll ride out and see if I can find her."

"Would you do that?" Victoria's eyes suddenly filled with tears. "Oh, Larry, I'm so sorry about what I said to you. You're the best friend . . . the only true friend I have. I don't know what I'd do without you. Please forgive me."

Closing the distance between them, Victoria reached up impulsively to kiss his cheek. Her mouth grazed his lips and he turned away, unwilling to allow her to see his reaction to the unintended intimacy.

"You're angry at me, aren't you?"

"No, I'm not."

"Then why won't you look at me?"

Forcing himself to turn toward her, Larry said, "I am looking at you."

Victoria's gaze searched his face. He saw her draw back with shock when understanding dawned.

Victoria rasped, "Oh, Larry, I'm sorry."

"Victoria . . ." Larry said softly, "I'm sorry, too."

Attempting to dispel the discomfort of the moment, Larry started toward the door, saying, "I'll have to get a horse at the livery stable first. Mine's gone lame."

"All right."

Outside in the yard, he said, "I'll find her."

"Thank you, Larry."

Friendship.

That was all Victoria would ever want from him.

Thea was still dozing.

Raising himself on his elbow, Quinn looked down at her beautiful, still face. She lay beside him, shadows of the branches above them dancing over her clear skin. Sometime earlier he had drawn her discarded dress across her body to shield her nakedness from the breeze, but one small breast lay exposed to his gaze, tempting his caress. He recalled the taste of that sweet flesh. It had been intoxicating, driving him to depths of passion that were not sated with a single joining of their flesh.

How many times had they made love? He was uncertain. Clear to him, however, was the reality that he had only relented in his intimate ministrations because of Thea's obvious fatigue.

He remembered dozing beside her, then awakening to slide himself inside her as she slept, so he might love her gently once more. He recalled that she had responded to him spontaneously in her semi-sleep, and that the contentment that had welled within him at that moment had been absolute.

Twisting his hand into the fiery curls that had worked loose from her casual coiffure, Quinn clasped them tightly. He had half a mind to wake her even now with his kiss, to taste her again, to reignite the response to the lovemaking that had made him—

Stunned by the direction his thoughts were taking, Quinn released the fiery strands as if his palm had been singed. His next thought was an incredulous question.

What in hell was he doing?

That silent question was still ringing in his mind when Thea's eyelids fluttered, then rose to reveal the glorious gray beneath. He saw her flush as reality dawned. He sensed that she was waiting for him to speak.

What could he tell her, damn it?

Could he explain that something inside him had snapped when he had taken her into his arms a few hours earlier, that the hunger she stirred in him had suddenly surged to a maelstrom that he'd been unable to resist?

How could he tell her that he was at a loss to understand the emotions she raised in him—passions that he had no words to describe?

After the intimacies they had shared, how could he make her understand that he needed to leave her as soon as possible? A year of dedicated work hinged on what would happen in the next few days. Justice demanded to be served.

How could he justify selfishly involving her in a situation that could prove deadly? How could he tell her the truth when that would only involve her more deeply?

He knew the answer to those questions. There was only one thing he could do.

Steeling himself, Quinn said, "Get up, Thea. You have to go back to town. You've been gone too long."

Thea blinked.

Quinn felt the shock his tone elicited as he added more sharply, "If you don't start back soon, someone will come after you. You don't want anybody to find you here like this, do you?"

Thea's breath escaped in a gasp.

"Come on. Hurry up," he insisted.

"What's wrong, Quinn?" Incredulity widened Thea's eyes as she asked, "What happened to make you so angry?"

"I'm not angry."

"But you—"

"It's not safe for you here."

"Not safe?"

"I have things to do—business to finish up. These past few hours . . ." He paused, frowning. "They shouldn't have happened."

"Shouldn't have happened?"

"I have things to do that I can't take care of until you're back in town."

"What things?"

Quinn remained silent. Thea's lips twitched revealingly as she repeated, " 'This time between us was meant to be.' "

His own words echoed between them.

"Why did you say that to me?"

Yes, why did he, when he knew better than to complicate an already tricky situation?

"Answer me, Quinn."

He began to turn away, but stopped when Thea demanded softly, "Look at me. Tell me once and for all—who are you?"

Unaware that she was trembling, Thea waited for Quinn's response. During the intimate hours just past, she had begun to feel that there was no longer any need to ask that question. The handsome man who had lain beside her, loving her with breathtaking tenderness, was Quinn—a man who looked like Wade, who baffled her by speaking with Wade's loving words, but who had demonstrated in the most intimate of ways that he was himself, not the replica of another man as he had first appeared to be.

She had been reassured by that revelation as she lay in his arms. She had surrendered to the emotions he evoked in her, feeling the certainty of being loved—but she had awakened moments earlier in the arms of another man entirely. Now her uncertainty had returned.

Needing an answer, Thea demanded, "Tell me, Quinn!"

His dark eyes growing unfathomable, Quinn replied, "You ask too many questions. I don't have time for the answers."

"You don't have time . . . or you don't want to answer me?"

Quinn's expression hardened. "Both."

"Then I'll answer for you," Thea said coldly. "You're Quinn Banning—except that name might be one you're only using temporarily. You're a thief who lives on other people's hard-earned money. You're the kind of man who has a mistress of his own but who's fast to spot a woman who mistakenly sees in you something she wants to believe is true—the kind of man who takes without any compunctions at all whatever that woman's too weak to deny you."

Pausing, Thea continued determinedly, "You want me out of the way because you're going to meet Max White again—that's right, isn't it? You're going to plan your next robbery, and your next, until the day some decent lawman like Wade will end it all for you with a single gunshot.

"You said I'm in danger here. I know now that's true—but the true danger is believing you."

"If that's what you want to believe."

"What I want to believe?" Thea gasped, "Tell me I'm wrong! Come back to town with me now and show me that everything I've just said isn't true."

Her heart pounding, Thea waited.

She knew what he was going to say before he said it. "It's time for you to go back to town."

On her feet in a moment, Thea dressed as quickly as her trembling fingers would allow. Turning back toward Quinn to find him fully dressed as well, she whispered, "I suppose I should thank you for this last bit of honesty, but all I'm going to say is . . . good-bye."

It occurred to Thea as she mounted her horse and turned the animal back toward the trail that she had thanked Quinn for his honesty—when, in truth, the only person who had finally been honest was herself.

"Hell, here he comes . . ." Boots said with a grunt of disgust.

Max went to the cabin window and glanced outside, then strode to the open doorway. He waited as Quinn reined his horse to a halt and dismounted.

"You're back with a day to spare." Max watched Quinn as he carried his saddlebags inside, his hat pulled down low on his forehead and his shoulders stiff. "I was beginning to think the boys and me would be splitting our haul three ways instead of four."

Quinn responded flatly, "There's no way I'd let that happen."

"Yeah, that's what I figured." Max studied Quinn more closely, then said, "You don't look so good. I need to be able to count on you for this job I'm planning."

"I'm all right."

"You look tired."

"Maybe I am."

"After lying in bed for almost a week?"

Quinn turned back sharply toward him. "Don't worry about me. I'll do what needs to be done, and I'll do it right—like I always do."

Max almost smiled at the bastard's deadly stare. Banning had gall, but his message was clear.

Responding with a simple warning that was just as deadly, Max replied, "You'd better."

His tone openly resentful, Boots interjected, "The boss has been waiting for you, Banning. Seems like he didn't want to make a move without you." He turned back toward Max with a sneer. "So, now that Banning's here, maybe you'll explain these big plans you've been talking about."

Max spat, "That mouth of yours is going to get you in trouble one day, Boots."

"You keep talking about your plan—"

"I'll tell you about it when I'm good and ready, and not a minute sooner. You got that straight?"

"Yeah, but—"

Sick of the sound of Boots's voice, Max growled, "Do yourself a favor and shut up."

"He didn't mean nothing, boss."

"That goes for you, too, Ernie."

An extended silence reigned until Quinn said unexpectedly, "I'm hungry as hell. Are those beans you've got on the fire?"

Noting that Banning didn't wait for an answer, Max watched as the big fellow checked the pot, then pulled a plate from his saddlebag and filled it liberally. No, Banning didn't look too good, but he'd do his job and do it right. He always did.

Her emotions strangely frozen, Thea held her mount steady on the trail back toward town. The coldness in Quinn's eyes when she departed had chilled her so that even the bright sunlight beating down on her shoulders could not warm her.

Forcing Quinn's image from her mind, Thea looked up at the sky and frowned. It was past midday. Aunt Victoria would be worried.

Regretting the anxiety she knew she was causing her aunt, Thea nudged her mount to a faster pace. Her heart jumped a beat at the sound of hoofbeats advancing toward her. She did not smile when a familiar figure came into view.

Drawing her mount to a halt, Thea waited until Larry reined up beside her. "Victoria was worried about you, Thea," he said by way of greeting.

Her shoulders stiffening, Thea prepared herself for questions that did not come as the graying rancher turned his horse and rode beside her. "I told Victoria you'd be on the way back by the time I found you, but I think it would make her feel better if I rode the rest of the way home with you—if you don't mind the company."

She didn't mind.

Willowby came into view before Thea realized that she didn't mind because she was too numb to feel anything at all.

Chapter Seven

"I don't like this." Sheffield lowered the spy-glass through which she had been watching the dilapidated cabin. She turned toward the fair-haired man behind her. "Something's wrong down there, Perry."

"What?" Grasping the glass from her hand, Perry scanned the cabin below for several moments before looking back at her with a frown. "I don't see anything."

"That's the problem. Nothing's going on. Nothing at all."

"Meaning?"

"It's been three days, Perry!" Sheffield pushed back a lock of heavy dark hair that rested against the wash-worn fabric of her shirt. The gaudy red dress that had been her signature garment during her brief stay in Willowby had been replaced by her standard working costume—men's clothing that had brought an expression of mixed relief and regret to Perry's face.

Under other circumstances she would have had no complaint about having to spend several days in isolation with Perry, but their present situation was less than desirable. Living in a makeshift camp on a ridge that overlooked the cabin, with the need to keep their presence secret, they had few luxuries. Long nights sleeping in Perry's arms had done much to make up for the lack of amenities. Nothing, however, negated the frustration they were feeling at this delay in bringing the case to a close.

Sheffield continued tightly, "I want to know what's going on down there."

"You know what's going on down there." Perry's frown deepened. "Nothing—like you said."

"*Why* is nothing going on? What's Max waiting for? He was practically rabid about having Quinn back at the cabin before the end of the week because of his *big plans*. What happened to change things?" Sheffield

196

took a breath. "You don't think he's suspicious of Quinn . . ."

"Max wouldn't waste time being suspicious. He's the kind who settles any uncertainties with his gun."

Sheffield paced the clearing then turned back toward Perry abruptly. "If Quinn doesn't get some kind of a message to us soon, I'm going down there."

"No, you're not."

"Not dressed like this, of course." Indicating the faded men's clothing she wore, Sheffield continued, "I've got that red dress rolled up on the back of my saddle."

"I said, no."

"I'll ride up bold as brass and say I followed Quinn out here because I couldn't stay away from him. Everybody in town knows how I hunted him down when I first found him in Willowby. Max will just figure I'm up to my old tricks."

"No."

"I'm Quinn's contact, Perry! You gave me that assignment, and I intend to follow through on it. I'm telling you now, if Quinn doesn't contact us soon—"

His arms going around her, Perry held Sheffield helpless as he warned, "I'll tie you down if I have to in order to stop you."

"Perry—"

"I mean it, Sheffield."

Sheffield stared up at the tight set of Perry's even features. Despising the familiar twinge deep inside that his hard body never failed to evoke, she said sharply, "You mean it, don't you?"

"Yes."

"But you wouldn't even think of trying that if I were a man."

Avoiding a direct response, Perry said, "Quinn can take care of himself. If he was in trouble, he'd let us know."

"What if he can't let us know?"

"Think what you're saying, Sheffield." Perry's grip gentled. "Quinn's not a prisoner. He goes and comes as he pleases down there. Hell, you just saw him come outside to relieve himself."

Sheffield could not restrain a smirk. "I sure did."

Perry's lips tightened. His gaze held hers with peculiar intensity as he asked, "I need to know, Sheffield. This concern for Quinn . . . is it personal?"

"Personal?" Sheffield paused, then blurted, "Are you asking me if Quinn and I—"

"No, that thought never entered my mind. I know Quinn wouldn't go behind my back."

"Oh, *Quinn* would never go behind your back . . ."

"I'm not saying I don't trust you—"

"You'd better not."

"It's just that you've been increasingly tense since we got here."

"So have you."

"But your concern seems to be focused on Quinn."

"Isn't yours? Because if it isn't, it should be!"

"I trust Quinn to be able to handle the situation. Why can't you?"

"Because . . . because I can sense that something's wrong."

"Nothing's wrong. This kind of work is a waiting game. It always has been. You know that as well as I do." Perry's gaze searched hers. She felt the hardening of his body where it pressed firmly against her. A familiar quiver rolled down her spine as he slid his hand into her hair and said softly, "You need to relax."

"To relax . . ."

"That's right."

"What if I don't feel like relaxing?"

"I could try to convince you."

"And how do you propose to do that?"

Perry's mouth teased hers. Her lips softened under his and his kiss deepened as his hands slipped to the buttons on her blouse. He unfastened them nimbly, whispering, "You always tell me how good I am at relaxing you."

Sliding his hand inside her shirt, Perry caressed her breast, and the quivers traveling Sheffield's spine increased. She was almost at the point of—

Sheffield jerked herself free of Perry's embrace, snatched the spyglass from the ground where he had dropped it and raised it to her eye. "It's Max. He's riding out. You'd better follow him. I'll stay and watch the cabin."

"I'm not leaving you alone here."

"Damn it, Perry. Are you crazy? I can take care of myself!"

"I'm not leaving you alone here."

"Get on that damned horse, Perry!"

Perry did not move.

"All right, *I'll* follow Max and you can wait here."

Perry grabbed Sheffield's arm as she started toward her horse. "It's too dangerous for you."

"Look at me, Perry," Sheffield demanded, "and try to understand. Max White caused a blot on my record when he stole those gold bars under my watch a year ago. I saw Bill Graham and Joe Carter shot down before my eyes by that bastard. I blame myself for letting that happen."

"That wasn't your fault. The shipment was supposed to be a secret. Nobody was expecting trouble."

"I should've been more alert."

"It could've happened to anybody."

"But it happened to me!" Sheffield's delicate jaw hardened. "I've waited a long time to right what went wrong that day, and I'm not about to let the chance slip away from me."

"Sheffield . . ."

"Are you going to follow that bastard or not?"

"All right, I'll follow him."

"Then you'd better hurry or you'll lose him."

"Who's the boss here, Sheffield?"

"Does that make any difference right now?"

"Answer me."

"You're the boss."

"That's right, and right now I'm giving you an order." Perry's gaze drilled into hers. "I don't want you going down to that cabin, do you understand?"

"What?"

"I want your word on it."

"But—"

"Maintain the surveillance. Keep Quinn in

sight, but keep your distance unless there's a dire emergency."

"You're tying my hands, Perry."

"And you're wasting time. I won't leave here until you give me your word."

Her jaw tight, Sheffield said, "All right."

Hesitating only a moment longer to gauge her earnestness, Perry strode toward his horse and mounted.

Looking back briefly, he swept Sheffield with a heated gaze. "And button your damned shirt!" he rapped out.

Thea stood beside the bearded cowpoke sitting on the examination table in Aunt Victoria's dispensary. His forehead was beaded with nervous perspiration as Aunt Victoria worked over the cut on his hand.

Aunt Victoria looked up at him abruptly. "You're going to need stitches, Ira. You should know better than to get in a fight with a man carrying a knife."

"Hell, everybody in these parts carries a knife, Doc."

"Then you should know better than to get into a fight." Aunt Victoria's tone was harsh as she swabbed the open wound.

Ira groaned and jerked back his hand.

"Be still, Ira."

"That stuff burns!"

"Do you want me to fix you up or not?"

"Damn it, Doc, I ain't never seen you so testy."

Aunt Victoria flushed, then looked at Thea and directed, "Hold his arm steady."

It occurred to Thea that what Ira had said was true. Aunt Victoria hadn't been herself the past few days, but she had been so wrapped up in her own concerns that she hadn't really thought about it until that moment.

Guilt nudged Thea as she recalled her return to town three days previously. She had ridden back with Larry in total silence. She had offered her anxious aunt a brief apology that did not include an explanation for her long absence. To her credit, Aunt Victoria had asked no questions about the somewhat disheveled appearance of her hair and clothing. She supposed that her appearance had spoken for itself, but still engrossed in her private thoughts at the time, it had not occurred to her to care.

Questions still plagued her. How could she have been so wrong? How could she have allowed herself to ignore the truth of what Quinn really was, in favor of what she wanted him to be?

Quinn's image appeared unexpectedly before her mind, and Thea reacted with a spontaneous stiffening that caused Ira to yelp, "Hey, ain't you supposed to be holdin' my arm *steady?*"

Thea mumbled an apology, her thoughts returning again to the awkward moment when she had dismounted from her horse, leaving Larry and Aunt Victoria standing silently behind her. She had led Brady back to the barn and unsaddled him. From there she had gone directly to her room, where she had stripped herself bare and had attempted to bathe Quinn's scent from her body. Donning fresh clothing, she had been free of his scent at last, but not free of the memories that had accompanied it.

Those images haunted her. Quinn's gentleness . . . his tenderness . . . the look in his eyes . . . the loving tone of his voice . . . the sense of wonder she had glimpsed in his gaze when he claimed her fully as his own.

No, that was wrong. Quinn *hadn't* claimed her as his own. Unlike Wade, who had loved her deeply, Quinn had merely spent a few hours sating a physical need, after which he had callously sent her home so he could return to a life that she had tried to convince herself didn't exist.

The gnawing ache inside Thea deepened. She had slept each night since then holding Wade's picture. She had talked to him in the darkness. She had asked him to forgive her for acting so foolishly in an attempt to regain what she now knew was lost forever—but the cold, lifeless photograph had granted her little comfort.

It's time for you to go.

You don't want anyone to find you here like this, do you?

The humiliation of that moment returned, and Thea closed her eyes.

"Are you all right, Thea?" Aunt Victoria asked. "I can handle this alone if you feel uncomfortable."

"Yeah . . ." Ira interjected, "The doc don't want you faintin' on her or nothin'."

To his credit, Ira appeared truly concerned.

Thea attempted a smile. "I'm all right. I'm just a little tired."

"Why don't you lie down for a while?" Aunt Victoria scrutinized her more closely. "I'll be done here in a minute."

Nodding, aware that her presence had become a distraction, Thea left the dispensary. She breathed deeply when she reached the backyard, remembering that despite everything that had happened, she had hung on to a faint hope that Quinn would return and make everything right. That hope had died, however, when she had learned the previous day that the whole town was talking about Sheffield, the "shameless hussy" who had tracked Quinn to town, and who had left Willowby shortly after he did to follow him again.

She remembered that Quinn had gone to the Willowby Hotel, where Sheffield had been staying, before he left, and the thought that he had sent her away in order to keep a rendezvous with Sheffield had been too much to bear.

This was meant to be.

Yes, Quinn had said that to her.

But he had lied.

Max frowned and wiped the sweat from his brow with the back of his arm as he rode down Bittersweet's main street. His disposition soured by a long journey in the heat of the day, he scrutinized the bustling traffic of late afternoon, his eye on the lone restaurant among the many saloons that lined the thoroughfare. He had arrived a few days late for his meeting with Whitmore. He hoped the delay wouldn't cause a problem.

Max grunted. He was a cautious man, and

there had been a look in Banning's eyes that nagged at him when Banning finally showed up at the cabin. He had hesitated to make a move until he could figure out what that look meant.

After three days, with Boots whining the entire time until tempers had come close to the breaking point, he had discovered accidentally the reason for Banning's sullen mood. Max had off-handedly mentioned that he wouldn't have minded getting a taste of that doc's red-haired niece, and Banning had almost snapped his head off. Suddenly the look in Banning's eyes wasn't a mystery anymore.

Max's jowled face drew into a sneer. Tough bastard that he was, Banning was pining after a red-haired witch who probably wouldn't let him get near her if he lived a hundred years.

That had happened yesterday, and Max had left the cabin at sunup to finalize his plans.

Unwilling to ignore the nagging growl of his stomach a minute longer, Max urged his mount up to the hitching post in front of the restaurant. He was damned hungry, and he was a man who took first things first. Whitmore would have to wait a little longer.

Dismounting, Max scanned the boardwalk

with a cursory glance before pushing the restaurant door open and walking inside.

He stopped short.

Well, what do you know!

Max's lips parted in an infrequent smile.

"Where do you suppose he went?" Boots had
been grumbling for the past hour and showed
no sign of stopping. "That Max is a bastard,
all right. He thinks we're all stupid, that we
can't do nothing right without him. Hell, I
was doing just fine before I met up with him.
And I didn't have to spend no time sitting
around a cabin, twiddling my thumbs, when
I had better things to do."

"What better things do you have to do,
Boots?" asked Ernie, his patience at an end.
"Something like going into town to find the
nearest saloon, maybe?"

"You're starting to sound like Max," Boots
said in a menacing tone, "and that ain't too
smart."

"Maybe it ain't too smart to keep complaining like you are, either."

Quinn looked up in annoyance. He'd had
his fill of both of them.

Boots's complaints continued unabated
and Ernie warned, "I'm telling you, you're
walking on thin ice with the boss."

"Thin ice?" Boots laughed. "I know too much for the boss to try anything with me."

"Is that right? Ain't you the one who told me about two fellas who used to ride with you and Max, how Max got sick and tired of them and made sure—"

"Whatever I said, I didn't expect you to go spreading it around!"

Ernie glanced at Quinn, then said, "You got something against Banning? I figure he's got as much of a right to know what to expect from Max as any of us do."

Speaking up for the first time, Quinn spat, "I know what to expect from Max, just like you two do, but I'm smart enough to realize that if Max says there's a big payoff coming, it'll be worth the risk."

"Are you saying Ernie and me ain't smart?"

Quinn started toward the door without bothering to reply. The three days past had been some of the hardest he had ever spent. His headaches had stopped, but the image of Thea's white face had given him little rest. He had sensed that Max was watching him, and he had cursed the moment when Max had inadvertently mentioned Thea and he'd almost lost control.

He had seen images of a year's work lost in that flashing second, but strangely enough,

Max had seemed to relax after that, and he had left to "finalize his plans" as soon as the sun was up that morning.

Stepping out into the yard, Quinn resisted the urge to scrutinize the ridge above the cabin. It was the perfect vantage point from which to watch events below. He had no doubt that Perry and Sheffield had set up camp there and were wondering what the delay was all about. He could only hope they had been watching closely enough to see Max leave, and that one of them had followed him so they might be able to get some kind of idea what his plans involved before Max finally put them into motion.

Quinn's eyes narrowed. Ernie and Boots had been too engrossed in their card game the previous night to notice the look on Max's face when Ernie started talking about the amount of time he had spent in Bittersweet with a saloon woman there, and how well known he had become around town because of her.

Max hadn't been pleased.

Bittersweet.

Quinn pondered the thought. If Max was headed there, he'd be gone for a while—at least overnight. That would give him a chance to make contact with Perry and Sheffield.

Quinn nodded. If Max didn't return by sundown, he'd contact them tonight.

"You'd better take care of that cut, Ira. Keep it as clean as you can. I've seen wounds like that fester until amputation was the only thing that could be done."

"Doc . . ." Ira shook his shaggy head. "You tryin' to scare me or somethin'?"

Victoria considered what she had said. Was she trying to scare him?

Victoria pushed a wayward strand of hair back from her face and tried to smile. "I guess you're right. I'm not myself today, but what I said is true. Keep that hand clean or you'll end up back here, one way or another."

Ira was still mumbling when he walked out the door, but Victoria had already canceled his grumbling from her mind. Glancing out into the yard, she saw Thea walking toward the barn. She didn't want to consider why her niece had been detained for so many hours three days earlier. All she knew for sure was that Thea hadn't been happy when she returned, and that her niece hadn't spent a peaceful moment since.

Well, the truth was, Victoria wasn't happy either. Larry was the reason, and an innocent kiss meant to show appreciation had caused it all.

She had been beside herself with worry when Larry appeared three days ago. Thea had been gone for four hours and she had been beset with guilt, knowing that Thea never would have met Quinn Banning if not for her.

All the previous harsh words between Larry and she had been dismissed in that moment, and she had turned to him as she always did, knowing that everything would be right again because he was there. When he said he'd ride out to find Thea, she had been grateful beyond words. The kiss had been a spontaneous expression of her gratitude, but her mouth had brushed his and—

Victoria took a ragged breath. Larry had not wanted to face her afterwards because he had known what she would read in his eyes. How could she have been so blind to his feelings until that moment when the truth became stunningly clear?

"And now the damage is done."

Unaware that she had spoken aloud, Victoria cleared the examination table and began scrubbing it clean with trembling hands.

She loved Larry. She truly did, but it wasn't the wild, heart-thumping excitement of love that had held her breathless in Luke's arms. Instead, it was a warm, deep emotion fed by familiarity and trust.

She loved him *as a friend*.

Larry had found Thea and accompanied her home as he'd promised, but conversation between them had been stilted after Thea went to her room. When Larry left, she had known instinctively that nothing would ever be the same between them again.

Victoria whispered, "I'm sorry, Molly."

Aware that Molly could not hear her words, Victoria allowed herself to take consolation in the fact that she had apologized for having inadvertently compromised one of the most beautiful loves she had ever witnessed between a man and a woman—and for spoiling a friendship that she had believed would never end. She had said the words aloud, somehow sure they would be her only consolation.

Because a precious friendship was now damaged beyond repair.

And her heart was breaking.

Max strode boldly across the restaurant toward the table in the corner. He almost laughed at the look on Whitmore's pockmarked face when the fella saw him coming.

Whitmore sat in his chair, his poorly tailored suit emphasizing his skinny proportions and his thinning hair plastered to his head with oil. Max thought Whitmore had the look of a startled weasel.

Max's tendency to laugh faded when surprise was replaced by tension on Whitmore's sharp features as he cast a quick, furtive glance around the restaurant.

Whitmore looked like a weasel, Max thought, because he *was* a weasel.

Max pulled out a chair and sat down.

"What are you doing here?" Whitmore asked.

Max stared at him coldly. "I'm meeting you in Bittersweet, like we planned."

"We weren't supposed to meet in public."

"Weren't we?"

"We were supposed to make contact in private."

Disgusted with the man's temerity, Max snarled, "So what? Nobody knows me in this town, and you're a stranger here, too."

"I've been waiting here for three days," Whitmore complained. "People start wondering when a person like me hangs around town that long without any obvious reason."

"Not as much as folks would start wondering if I came out to the smelter to finalize our plans. Besides, I warned you that I might be delayed."

"Lower your voice! Nobody in this town knows I manage the smelter in Conrad."

"Good. Then nobody will give us a second thought."

Signaling the aproned woman working the tables, Max barked, "Steak and potatoes, and make it fast."

Turning back to his nervous companion, Max said, "The same goes for you. Make it fast. When can you get things started?"

The nervous blinking of Whitmore's small eyes halted. "I'll need a week to set everything up."

"Good. It'll take me a few days to pick up the gold bars and to bring—"

Whitmore winced and glanced nervously around them.

Amending his statement, Max said, "It'll take me a few days to pick up *the shipment* and bring it to the smelter."

"I'll have the paperwork ready for you when you come."

Max smiled. "And the money."

"The money will take a little longer."

Max's smile faded.

"I don't have that kind of money lying around in a bank account, you know." Whitmore was beginning to perspire. "I thought you understood that I'd have to wait for the paperwork to clear and for a bank draft to be forwarded back to me."

"How long will that take?"

"A few days . . . probably a week."

"A bank draft . . . How long before I can convert it into cash?"

"You can't do that!"

"Who says I can't do that?"

"That would be crazy. You'd draw too much attention to both of us if you did. People would start talking. The Treasury Department has a long memory, you know, and those fraudulent papers won't hold up if somebody starts looking into things too closely."

"Seems to me that would be your problem, not mine."

"Not if your trail is fresh enough for the Treasury Department to follow."

Max was beginning to lose his appetite. "If you think I'm turning those gold bars over to you without some kind of guarantee—"

Whitmore's jaw twitched nervously as he said, "I'd say that gun on your hip is your guarantee that I won't double-cross you. I'm not that greedy. One third of the proceeds from this deal is more money than I'd ever see in my lifetime."

"So?"

"So, I'll deposit the bank draft in an unnamed account. Then I'll make up the necessary papers to transfer it, and I'll put your two thirds of the proceeds into a bank draft in your name to be deposited in whatever bank you pick—anywhere in the country."

"I'll need traveling money."

"I can manage traveling money."

"How long will all this take?"

"Like I said, probably a week for the original bank draft to come back to the smelter, then another week for all the paperwork to be completed on my end."

"Two weeks."

"Not too long to wait to become a rich man."

Max's appetite returned. He said abruptly, "I'll have the . . . *shipment* delivered to the smelter before the week is out."

Whitmore nodded. He withdrew a handkerchief from his pocket and mopped his brow, then said, "Just make sure you deliver it after dark. I'll see to it that I'm there every night, working late, so I can receive the merchandise."

"All right . . . after dark."

"I'm leaving. I'll get the paperwork started as soon as I get back."

"Stay where you are."

Indicating the buxom waitress who was approaching with his plate, Max said under his breath, "Finish your meal and try to look like we're old friends."

Smiling up at the woman as she placed the plate on the table, Max said, "Thanks, darlin'."

Reluctantly, Whitmore picked up his fork.

"Hey, boss, watch what you're doin'!"

Larry snapped back his lariat in time to avoid hooking it on a stand of low-lying brush.

Reining his mount, Larry rolled up the dragging rope, aware that he might have been jerked from the saddle if Pete hadn't warned him in time. He turned without comment toward the calves being herded into temporary branding pens, but halted as Pete drew up his mount beside him and said, "What's the matter with you, boss?"

"Do you see something wrong?"

"Yeah, you might say that."

Larry looked at the frowning wrangler without replying.

"Ain't you gonna answer me?"

"I just did."

"Look, boss . . ." Pete hesitated uncharacteristically, then blurted, "You're gonna get somebody killed if you keep this up."

Larry attempted to turn his mount, but Pete said, "Hear me out, will you? The boys and me are gettin' worried. The day before yesterday you came back from town in a mood like I've never seen you in, and you ain't been the same since. Your body's been here, but your mind sure ain't. Hell, you near killed Manny when you discharged your rifle by accident yesterday, and today things have been even worse. The boys are gettin' so they're afraid to ride with you."

"That right? Well, they can leave whenever they want. Nobody's holding them here."

"They don't want to leave." Pete paused. "Look, boss, the last time I saw you distracted like this was when. . . . well, when the missus passed on."

Larry stiffened.

"Now don't go gettin' mad at me. I'm just tellin' you like it is."

"Years of service on this ranch don't give you the right to butt into my business."

"I guess not, but I figure bein' a friend does." Pete paused again. "Look, boss, rumors travel quicker than truth, you know that. The boys and me heard about the doc's niece takin' off like she did a few days ago, and there wasn't a person in town who didn't hear about how you brought her back, with her lookin' like—well, like she'd had a hard time of it. There's a lot of talk about what happened."

"With people thinking it was me who—?"

"Hell, no! Everybody saw the doc lookin' up at you like you saved the day. But the boys and me have been thinkin' that things ain't right, and you figure you might be needed in town."

"The Bar MH is the only place where I'm needed."

"But like I said, your body's here, but your mind—"

Wheeling his horse unexpectedly, Larry grated, "We're done talking."

Turning his mount toward a runaway calf he spotted in the distance, Larry chased the frenzied animal into a wooded patch, then drew his horse to an abrupt halt as the calf skittered out of sight. He sat stiffly, swearing under his breath.

The boys were right: At the rate he was going, he'd get somebody killed if he didn't sort things out in his mind.

Larry's graying mustache twitched. He had

been unable to concentrate since he had returned from town three days earlier. Over
and over again he had relived the moment
when Victoria's friendly kiss had brushed his
mouth. He cursed himself for betraying his
feelings for her in that fleeting second. But it
had been too long since he had held a woman
he loved in his arms. He ached for the joy of
it, and for the consolation that was unlike any
other. He had truly believed for a while that
Victoria's friendship would be enough, but he
knew now that he had only been fooling himself.

Larry raised a callused hand to his forehead and rubbed it hard. He'd spent two
nights thinking when he should have been
sleeping, but there was no solution. It was
over. The intimacy of having Victoria depend
on him in a way she depended on no one else,
the knowledge that he was the first person she
would turn to, that she *needed* him, was a
thing of the past.

He loved her, but his love had damaged a
precious friendship beyond repair.

And his heart was breaking.

The light of a full moon lit his way as Quinn
guided his mount along the narrow trail that
bordered the ridge above the cabin.

He had been right—Max would not be returning tonight, affording him the opportunity to make contact with Sheffield and Perry. He had waited until Ernie and Boots were snoring noisily before leaving, but the truth was that he would not be worried even if they did wake up and find him gone. A tryst with Sheffield had proved a good excuse before. It would prove a good excuse again, especially now that Max had seen Sheffield in that red dress.

Jerked from his thoughts when his mount stumbled unexpectedly, Quinn muttered under his breath.

"Be careful, Quinn, or you'll find yourself flat on your back in the doc's back room again."

"Damn it, Sheffield!" Quinn scanned the shadows to no avail.

"Did I scare you?"

"Show yourself. I don't have time for games."

Sheffield stepped into sight. "Neither do I. What's going on in that cabin?"

Quinn squinted into the shadows behind her. "Where's Perry?"

"He's following Max."

Quinn dismounted, his expression tense. "I don't have much time. Max went off to finalize his plans. He's still not talking about what his plans include, but as far as I'm concerned, there could be only one reason for that kind of secrecy."

"Those gold bars."

Quinn nodded.

"What's the timetable?"

"That's Max's secret, too."

Sheffield muttered an inaudible curse.

"Unless I miss my guess, he went to Bittersweet. That means he should be back tomorrow sometime. I've got a feeling things will start moving pretty fast after that."

"Not too fast for Perry to get some help here, I hope."

The look in Quinn's eyes caused Sheffield to curse again.

"I have to go." Quinn paused. "Will you be all right up here alone?"

"You're starting to sound like Perry."

"Will you?"

"You forget that I just had the drop on you, not the other way around. Does that tell you anything?"

Right.

"Tell Perry to be ready to move fast when Max returns," Quinn said curtly. "I've got the feeling Max won't be wasting any time."

Sheffield nodded.

Mounting, Quinn turned back with a final word of caution. "Be careful, Sheffield. Max is smart, and he's a killer."

Cracking the door to his room, Perry surveilled the hallway as grunting sounds of animal-like passion reverberated in the night-time silence.

Grimacing, Perry recalled the moment an hour earlier when he had covertly watched Max climb the stairs toward his hotel room with a swaying saloon girl at his side. It hadn't taken them long to get into action, and he had been listening to the grunts and moans that had been issuing from the room ever since.

Perry gave a disgusted snort. The woman had seen better days—plenty of them—but he supposed she was the best Max had been able to find. It was clear that Max wasn't fussy, and that he was celebrating something.

The grunting sounds stopped. Breathing a sigh of relief, Perry turned his thoughts to the man Max had met in the restaurant. The fellow was tall, thin and nervous, his manner of dress indicating that he was a businessman of some kind. Judging from the intensity of their conversation, he was the man Max had come to Bittersweet to see. It had also been obvious that the fellow had been anxious about any attention they might draw, and that he had wanted to terminate their conversation as soon as possible.

Cautious inquiries had garnered Perry the information that the fellow was a stranger in town, that he had arrived three days earlier, that his name was Harry Whitmore and that no one knew anything else about him. In order to stay close to Max, Perry had taken a room across the hall from Max's, where he maintained his present silent vigil.

The grunting sounds began again, and Perry grimaced. The vigil was no longer silent.

Sitting back in his chair, Perry was painfully aware that under other circumstances, he might have proceeded differently with his surveillance of Max. He might have briefly left Max in the saloon earlier that evening, trusting that Max would be there when he returned from conducting a closer investigation into Harry Whitmore's identity . . . but the circumstances of this particular case had made the possibility that Max might slip away from him too risky a chance to take.

The circumstances—Sheffield.

Perry's strong jaw tightened. He had had to make a decision, and he'd made it. He had refused to allow Max out of his sight, know-ing that if Max somehow managed to slip away from him and return to the cabin, Shef-field might be caught unawares. He knew his fears were illogical, knew Sheffield was a su-perior agent capable of handling any situa-tion, but he could not banish them.

The reason was simple: loving Sheffield had compromised his judgement.

That fact was one of the most difficult ad-missions he had ever needed to make. Perry shifted his stiff shoulders and fixed his gaze more intently on the door across the hall. He recalled the first time he'd met Sheffield. Strangely, rather than attraction, instant an-tagonism had flashed between them. He'd been angry to discover that a woman would be in his service simply because his superiors had paid a debt of honor to a fellow agent who had fallen in the line of duty years ear-lier. He had been convinced when he had taken over the command that Sheffield would be nothing but trouble. He'd had no idea, however, the kind of trouble she would be.

It wasn't long before Perry had been forced to admit that Sheffield was a superior oper-ative, and a feisty, intelligent female who was all woman.

And what a woman . . .

In the time since, Sheffield had fought with him, challenged him, tormented him and had eventually made love with him; and when they made love, she swept every other woman he had ever known from his mind. He knew Sheffield also had strong feelings for him. He even believed—except when unreasonable jealousy reared its ugly head—that Sheffield's feelings for him excluded other men from her mind. His competition came from another direction entirely.

He gave a sardonic snort. Perry Locke was considered a confirmed bachelor, the best catch in Washington, D.C. Yet the *confirmed bachelor* wanted nothing more than to marry Sheffield, the woman he loved, so they would be together for the rest of their lives. The *best catch in Washington, D.C.* knew that title was a farce, because Sheffield was a catch he couldn't make—Sheffield, who was content with the status quo, and who had no intention of compromising a career she had struggled to carve for herself out of the hard core of a man's world.

Sheffield had never voiced those convictions, but they rang in every word she had ever spoken.

The time was fast approaching, however, when he would have to tell Sheffield that *he* wasn't satisfied with the status quo—that he wanted more from her—more than he feared she was willing to give.

Perry's thoughts were halted abruptly by the sound of movement behind the door across the hall. He drew back cautiously as the door was opened. The saloon woman stood briefly in the opening before she pulled the door closed behind her.

Her heavy makeup was smeared, her hair disheveled; the harsh lighting of the hallway revealed the deep lines and dark circles that marked her face. The woman hiked the sleeve of her dress back up onto her shoulder, then paused to count the coins in her hand. Slipping them into the bodice of her dress with a satisfied sniff, she started back down the hallway and disappeared from sight.

Perry waited. He heard no further sounds from the room across the hall. He waited longer, then made his way cautiously to listen at the door.

Snoring.

The damned bastard was snoring!

Slipping back to his room, Perry prepared himself for the fitful night's sleep that he knew was to come. He couldn't afford to let Max out of his sight. If he didn't miss his guess, Max's work was done in Bittersweet, and he'd be returning to the cabin at dawn. He needed to be there when Max finally made his move. He needed to be right at Sheffield's side so he could be sure she was safe—even if she did fight him every step of the way.

Quinn glanced up at the full moon shining through the trees overhead as he made his way cautiously back down the ridge trail. The silver light made the landscape almost as bright as day. He had found Sheffield sooner than he had anticipated—or, rather, she had found him. He should have been expecting her to sneak up on him, but he had been distracted—dangerously distracted.

Thea's image returned to his mind, and a nagging regret returned. He had sent Thea away to remove her from danger, but he had wounded her when she was the most vulnerable—after they had made love and she had given herself to him without reservation.

Quinn stared at the fork in the trail as he neared it. He recalled the way Thea had looked up at him that first day. His face had been masked with a bandanna, but she hadn't been afraid of him. The silent chord that had been struck between them at that moment had been impossible to ignore.

Yet the timing had been wrong from the

beginning. Thea shouldn't have been on the stage that day. He shouldn't have gotten close enough to her so that she could recognize him the moment he was carried into her aunt's dispensary. It might have been different otherwise—and Thea might not be back in Willowby now, believing that he had used her.

He had made one mistake after another with Thea. He made his greatest mistake that last day in not sending her back to town the minute she rode up the trail behind him. He made another mistake when he touched her, because once he did, it was too late.

Quinn was suddenly angry. Thea was safe from the danger he had inadvertently exposed her to—but that wasn't enough. He had to explain, to make her understand that she had touched a part of him he had not known existed before, that she had raised feelings in him that he still could not quite comprehend—except to know that he couldn't allow her to continue believing the time she had spent in his arms meant nothing to him.

Quinn glanced up again at the full, silver moon, his heart pounding. He'd have no trouble getting to Willowby and back before Max returned.

Thea had asked him who he was.
She had the right to an answer.

Thea tossed and turned in the bright moonlight that illuminated her room. She struggled to loosen the coverlet tangled around her legs, finally managing to throw back the light covering. She closed her eyes, grateful for the cooling night breeze that filtered through her open window.

Lying motionless, she told herself that daylight would soon come to free her from the tortuous night, but she knew her restlessness would not cease even then. Instead, another day would start, stretching out endlessly while relentless torments plagued her.

Thea slid her hand under her pillow to touch Wade's framed photograph, and the ache inside her increased. Curling on her side, she pressed her palm against the glass, remembering the steady pounding of Wade's heart against her breast as he had held her in his arms. She had felt his love with every beat.

It shamed her to realize that she had felt similarly loved when she had lain in Quinn's arms—that she had allowed herself to believe that a similarity of appearance and coincidental phrases meant that Wade's love had miraculously been restored to her.

Tears overflowed, and Thea brushed them angrily away. She would not allow herself to dishonor Wade's memory by wallowing in self-pity.

"Don't cry, Thea. I can't stand to see you cry."

Wade.

She was dreaming.

"Thea . . ."

But the touch on her shoulder was real. The gentleness with which she was turned to face the shadow hovering over her bed could not be mistaken.

Thea gasped.

"Don't be afraid." The shadow leaned closer, allowing Thea to look up into dark, familiar eyes.

No, it wasn't Wade.

Thea stiffened. "What are you doing here, Quinn?"

"I can't stay long, but I had to come." Quinn searched her face as he continued in a whisper, "I had to tell you that I didn't intend for things to go the way they did the other day. I can't really explain what happened, except to say that the moment I touched you, it was too late to turn back. But reality returned, and I knew that the job I needed to finish had to come first."

"Job?"

Quinn stroked back a fiery wisp of hair that clung to her damp cheek. "I don't expect you to understand right now. I came back tonight to apologize—and to ask you to trust me."

"Trust you?" Thea's response was an incredulous rasp. "I trusted you that day. I trusted the things you said. I believed—" Thea shook her head. "It was a mistake."

"No, it wasn't."

"Who are you, Quinn?" Unable to restrain the question that had gone so long unanswered, Thea whispered, "Please tell me."

"Who do you think I am?"

"I don't know."

"It doesn't really matter, does it? The only thing that's important right now is that I'm the man who sent you away because he had to, and I'm the man who's here tonight because he couldn't stay away."

More words.

"Thea . . ." Quinn caressed her cheek. He leaned down to press his lips against her damp eyelids and the throbbing pulse in her temple. "Something came to life between us that first day at the stagecoach. You know it as well as I do."

"No. I thought—"

"Whatever you thought . . . however you

tried to convince yourself that you imagined what you felt, it was real."

"But I—"

"Thea, listen to me." Unwilling to accept a negative response, Quinn continued, "I can't stay much longer, but I want to make sure you understand why I acted the way I did."

"*Why* can't you stay?" A familiar knot clenched tight inside Thea as she forced herself to ask, "Is someone waiting for you?"

Quinn went still.

"Tell me, Quinn."

"No one's waiting for me."

"Tell me the truth."

"I am."

"Did you send me away because you had a rendezvous with Sheffield?"

"No."

"Why, then? Because you had to meet Max and plan another holdup?"

"Thea . . ."

She was suddenly unwilling to repeat the same questions only to hear the same evasions. "Please go."

"Not yet."

"What are you waiting for?"

"I came to ask you to trust me, Thea . . . to believe that I'm telling you all I can right now."

"Why should I believe you?" she demanded, her voice filled with accusation and despair.

Her pain deepened Quinn's. "Maybe I don't have the right to ask you to trust me, but I *can* ask you to trust the way I make you feel."

Quinn brushed her mouth with his, then whispered, "How can this be wrong when it feels so right?" He pressed his kiss more deeply, then murmured, "All the uncertainties vanish when you're in my arms, Thea. There's no need for questions, or for suspicions or evasions."

"I can't—I *won't* let this happen again."

Quinn pressed his mouth to her cheek, her chin, the fragile shell of her ear. He entreated, "Listen to me, Thea. Nothing will ever be more right than it is when you're in my arms."

"Tell me who you are, Quinn." Thea's resistance was rapidly weakening. Her lips clung to his as she persisted weakly, "I need to know."

"Why?" Quinn's response was a throbbing whisper as Thea's nightgown yielded to his forays. "I came back because I couldn't stay away. That's all that's important right now."

He heard her gasp as he tasted a warm breast. He felt her quivering as he worshipped it with growing fervor, as he slipped her nightgown past her hips and tossed it into the darkness.

"Please . . . stop."

Quinn's hands halted at his belt. His body was quaking so violently that he could hardly speak. "Do you really want me to stop?"

"You don't understand."

"I understand that I need you, Thea." The words left his lips of their own accord. The truth resonated deep inside him as he continued in a voice that he hardly recognized as his own. "I realize now that I wanted you the first moment I saw you. What I didn't expect was that wanting would become such a powerful need. It was the same for you, Thea. I knew it then, and I know it now."

"You don't understand. I thought—"

"What did you think?" Quinn waited. He saw the emotion that welled in her eyes and read the answer there. Stripping away the last impediments of clothing between them, he whispered, "You knew this was meant to be."

Unable to bear the waiting any longer, Quinn lay down beside her. He probed her moistness briefly, then slid himself inside her, reveling at the joy of possessing her even as he rasped, "Tell me you feel the same way I do, darlin'."

"Quinn . . ."

Shifting to lie atop her, Quinn marveled at the beauty that surged to life as he stroked inside her and urged again, "Tell me you believe me."

Quinn thrust harder, his breathing growing ragged. "Tell me you *need* to believe me."

"Quinn, please . . ."

"Tell me now, Thea."

Trembling, she slipped her arms around his neck in wordless response.

As their passion surged to a climax, Quinn clutched Thea close, his elation knowing no bounds as she joined him in rapturous, simultaneous release.

They lay flesh to flesh in the breathless aftermath of their lovemaking, no longer needing words. Rolling to his side, Quinn drew Thea tight against him to whisper, "This is truth, Thea. It's all the truth we need."

But Thea did not reply.

The silence between them lengthened, and Quinn drew back slowly. Concerned when Thea avoided his eyes, he propped himself up to scrutinize her expression more easily. His elbow bumped against something under the pillow. He reached underneath and retrieved a picture frame.

"Give that to me!" Thea demanded.

Thea attempted to snatch the frame from

his hand, but Quinn held it back. The panic in her eyes sent a tremor of apprehension down his spine as he extended his arm out to hold the frame in a shaft of bright moonlight beside the bed.

Incredulous, Quinn blinked, then stared more intently at the photograph of a man whose features were identical to his own.

"Who is this?" Thea's face whitened as he grated, "Where did you get this picture?"

"It belongs to me."

"Who is he?"

"Give it to me!"

Sudden realization struck him. "This is Wade, isn't it?"

Thea was trembling. The hand she extended toward the framed photograph shook wildly. "Give it back to me, I said!"

Sitting up, Quinn pulled Thea up beside him. "Tell me who he is," he demanded.

Thea raised her chin. "His name was Wade Preston. He and I were about to be married."

"To be married . . ."

"He's dead."

Quinn glanced again at the photograph, finding it hard to believe his eyes.

"Aunt Victoria asked me to come out to Wyoming afterwards. There was nothing left for me in Georgia, so I came."

Quinn recalled her anguished words: *Who are you?*

"You look like him."

Is it you, Wade?

"You walk the same way he did. Your voice is the same, and sometimes you even say the same things he said."

Oh, God . . . is it really you, Wade?

Still too stunned to respond, Quinn remembered Thea's expression the first time their gazes met. He had thought she felt the same stirrings that he did, but all she had seen in him was the image of her dead lover.

Suddenly, so many things were clear. Thea wanted to convince herself that he was Wade. She imagined he spoke with Wade's tone of voice, that he walked like Wade, that he thought like Wade, even going so far as to convince herself that he said the same things to her.

She had even tried to convince herself that she wanted *him* the way she had wanted Wade—when all the while she had been responding to the memory of a dead lover, to the ghost of the man she really loved.

A deadening ache expanded inside him. Quinn dropped the picture back onto the bed and stood up. He reached down into the shadows, picked up Thea's nightgown and tossed it on the bed. He dressed himself, then turned back to see Thea again clothed, holding the framed photograph in her hand.

The unanswered question was still in her eyes.

Who are you?

Understanding it fully for the first time, Quinn responded, "I'm not Wade—but you knew that, didn't you? You were only fooling yourself. As it turns out, I was fooling myself, too."

He suddenly felt numb. "I'm sorry, Thea," he said. "I'm sorry . . . for both of us."

Chapter Eight

"I don't give a damn."

Boots's harsh whisper echoed in the morning shadows of the cabin, waking Quinn to a new day. Quinn stirred reluctantly. He had returned to the cabin after leaving Thea two nights previously, prepared to answer any questions Ernie and Boots might pose, only to discover they had both slept so soundly that they hadn't even realized he was gone.

The following day had crawled by interminably while they waited for Max to return. Quinn had slipped into his bedroll that evening with the desperate hope that this would be their last day of waiting.

His visit to Thea's room had played over

and again in his mind during that time, and subtle ironies had emerged.

He had been so concerned about maintaining his own masquerade that it hadn't occurred to him that Thea's question—*Who are you?*—could refer to anything other than the identity he had assumed for the past year.

He had been so disconcerted by his own reaction to Thea that he had never thought to ponder her reaction to him.

He had avoided her questions so skillfully, never realizing that he should have asked some questions of his own.

As for his astounding resemblance to the man in Thea's photograph, he couldn't account for it. He was certain of only one thing—he had no time for the deadening ache that had begun inside him the moment he had turned his back on Thea and walked away.

The low bickering at the other end of the room grew louder, with Boots finally exclaiming, "I don't care, I tell you! If Max don't let us in on his plans when he gets back, I'm gonna tell him that I ain't waitin' around here until he does."

Quinn sat up in his bedroll, surprised to see that the sun was shining brightly. Standing, he walked to the window to look outside.

"I'm glad you're finally awake, Banning." Ernie turned toward him with a frown. "Maybe you can talk some sense into Boots before he does something he'll be sorry for."

"I don't need no advice from Max's *right-hand man.*"

Quinn's eyes narrowed.

"Yeah, that's what I said." Speaking directly to Quinn, Boots snarled, "The boss might be afraid to make a move without knowing you'll be in on whatever he's got in mind, but I ain't."

Ernie glanced between the two men, then turned back toward Boots. "I'm telling you now, Boots," he snapped, "if you mess up whatever the boss has planned, you won't have only him to watch out for."

"Are you threatening me, Ernie?"

"I'm making you a promise." His small eyes pinning Boots with a sudden viciousness that Quinn had not witnessed before, Ernie grated, "I've been waiting for this big payoff just as long as you have, and I'm not gonna let you spoil things now."

"Waiting is all you're good for."

"You think so, huh?"

"Wait a minute." Aware that the heat between the two men was reaching a dangerous level, Quinn interrupted, "Max has taken longer than any of us expected to set up this job, but he should be back soon, and everything will start moving fast then. It would be stupid to buck him now, when we're so close to finding out what he's planning."

Boots glared. "Are you calling me stupid again, Banning?"

"If that's the way you want to hear it."

Boots took an angry step forward that was halted when Ernie glanced out the window and said, "Speak of the devil, here he comes now."

Aware that a crisis had been narrowly averted by Max's arrival, Quinn avoided comment. He turned toward the coffeepot boiling on the fire and picked up his cup. The truth was that he was more anxious to get things settled than either of the two men behind him knew—because he had come to a decision during the night. As soon as this case was closed, he was going to shake the dust of Wyoming from his heels.

And he wasn't coming back.

"Come in, Aunt Victoria."

Struck by her aunt's pallor when she entered the bedroom, Thea was momentarily silent. She had never seen her aunt so ashen. Nor had she ever seen Victoria's eyes so dull, or her mouth so disinclined to smile.

"Is something wrong, Aunt Victoria?" Thea inquired.

Aunt Victoria's lips twitched in an effort at a smile as she responded, "That's what I came here to ask you."

Thea turned back toward her bed, avoiding her aunt's gaze. She supposed she had been acting oddly since Quinn's visit two nights before, but she didn't want to talk about it. Nor did she want to think, because to think was to remember the look on Quinn's face when he left her.

It had occurred to her, during the dark hours following his departure, that Quinn had answered all the questions that had plagued her.

He had said he wasn't Wade. Yes, in her heart, she had known that all along. He had then summed up everything that had passed between them with the simple words, *I'm sorry, Thea. I'm sorry for both of us.*

"Thea, tell me what's bothering you."

Aunt Victoria was waiting for an answer. Thea responded the only way she could manage. "Nothing's bothering me."

Thea turned toward her bed in an effort to avoid her aunt's scrutiny. She fumbled with bedclothes still in disarray after her late awakening, but Aunt Victoria would not be deterred.

Moving to the other side of the bed, her aunt worked along with her, continuing, "I haven't wanted to ask you questions, Thea. I thought if I was patient, you'd eventually tell me what's wrong, but it's obvious that you've been uneasy ever since you arrived in Willowby. I told myself at first that it was a matter of adjustment, but when Mr. Banning arrived at our door—"

"I'd rather not discuss it, Aunt Victoria."

"Let me finish, please, dear." Determined, Aunt Victoria went on. "I saw the way you looked at Mr. Banning."

"I don't know what you mean."

"Yes, you do. If I thought the look said that you were somehow enamored or intrigued by him, I wouldn't have been as concerned, but I knew it was more than that. I waited for you to come to me, but the situation seems to have worsened, somehow, and I can't wait any longer."

Thea could not bear much more.

"My dear . . ." Aunt Victoria's eyes grew moist. "You're suffering. Let me help you. I will . . . any way I can."

Her hands trembling, Thea struggled with

the coverlet a moment longer, then abandoned the effort.

Her expression pained, Aunt Victoria picked up the edge Thea had dropped and tucked it under the pillow. She frowned when her hand struck an object there. She withdrew the framed photograph before Thea could voice a protest.

Rigid, Thea waited.

Aunt Victoria stared at the photo. She said abruptly, "This isn't Mr. Banning. Who is it?"

When Thea did not respond, Aunt Victoria gasped incredulously, "It couldn't be—is this Wade?"

Thea's silence was the only affirmation Victoria needed. Throwing her arms around her niece, she said, "Oh, Thea, I'm so sorry. You must have been shocked beyond belief when you first saw Mr. Banning carried to our door."

Allowing the half-truth to prevail, Thea whispered, "I've made so many mistakes."

"That's understandable, dear."

"No, it isn't. I should've told him, Aunt Victoria. I should've explained. Then Quinn wouldn't have been so angry when he saw the photograph."

Aunt Victoria drew back, confused. "He

saw the photograph? But you kept it here in your room. How did he—?"

Aunt Victoria halted, realization dawning.

"He's not coming back, Aunt Victoria."

"Do you want him to?"

Thea could not reply.

"He'll be back, then. Don't worry."

"No, he won't. I let him leave believing—"

Thea wasn't able to continue.

"You'll get a chance to explain, and if Mr. Banning's the man you hope he is, he'll understand."

"There's more to it than that. That terrible man—Max White—I think Quinn's planning to meet him."

"That's beyond your control, Thea. Mr. Banning's an adult. He makes his own choices. You can only hope he makes the right one."

She could only *hope?* That was all she had been doing, and it wasn't enough.

In a rush of sudden insight, Thea made a decision.

"I have to find him, Aunt Victoria. I have to try to explain."

"But you don't know where he is."

"I found him once. I can find him again."

"You're being unrealistic, Thea."

"I need to use Brady."

"It's too dangerous for you to ride out into unfamiliar territory alone."

"I have to find him."

"But—"

"Please, Aunt Victoria."

"All right, if you must, but let me send for Larry first, so he can—" Aunt Victoria blinked, then stopped in midsentence. "I'll help you saddle Brady."

"Sheffield . . . ?"

Perry stood in the camp that he and Sheffield had set up days earlier. He called out more loudly than before, "Sheffield . . ."

No answer.

Perry glanced at the spot where Sheffield's horse had formerly stood saddled and waiting. It was gone, and Sheffield was gone with it. Perry's heart gave a nervous leap. If she had followed through with her crazy scheme and had ridden down to the cabin in that red dress while he was away—

Perry struggled to maintain control. He had been gone too long. Max's celebrating had gotten out of hand after his meeting with that Whitmore fellow. Max hadn't been able to travel until late morning the following day—and when he finally did start back, he

249

had obviously been nursing a hangover and his progress had been slow.

Anxious to return to Sheffield, Perry had derived little satisfaction from Max's physical distress. He had been frustrated beyond measure when Max made camp for the night, forcing him to do the same.

Back on the trail earlier that morning, he had finally felt safe enough to ride ahead to warn Sheffield of Max's expected arrival, but he had arrived too late.

Perry strode back to his mount and withdrew the spyglass from his saddlebag. He trained it on the cabin below.

"What are you looking at?"

Turning sharply, Perry saw Sheffield standing behind him. Glorious black hair streamed past her narrow shoulders, and her rough clothing did little to hide the full, womanly proportions underneath. She wore an amused smile on her beautiful face that suddenly infuriated him.

Perry snapped, "Where in hell were you?"

Sheffield frowned.

"I asked you where you were."

"I don't like your tone."

"Did you go down to that cabin against my orders?"

Sheffield remained silent.

"Answer me!"

"No."

"No, you didn't go? Or no, you won't answer my question?"

"Take your choice."

"Sheffield . . ."

"I rode down to see if I could get a closer look—maybe overhear what they were talking about in the cabin."

"I told you to stay up here."

"I know what you told me."

Perry's jaw tightened. "Max will be showing up at the cabin any minute."

"I guessed that when I saw you riding up here."

"You saw me?"

Sheffield nodded.

"You heard me calling you and you didn't answer?"

"I suppose I could've shouted back at you so everybody in the cabin would know I was lurking outside, but I thought that might be a bad idea."

Perry didn't reply.

Sheffield turned toward the overlook, then said abruptly, "There he is, right on cue, the ugly bastard." She looked back at Perry. "What did you find out?"

Perry remained silent. What had he found

out? He had found out that he loved Sheffield too much to be able to take much more of this.

"Perry?"

Perry began his report.

Dismounting, Max glanced up at the cabin door. He grimaced as his stomach lurched, then wrapped his mount's reins around the nearest branch and took an uncertain breath.

Bad liquor, that's what that damned bartender had served him. If he hadn't already been delayed too long, he would have gone back to the saloon the next morning and taught that bartender that he couldn't mess with Max White and get away with it—but he had seen the danger in doing that. Drawing attention to himself would have been a mistake. So, instead, he had crawled back to the livery stable and started back, paying heavily for his night of celebration every step of the way.

Max tried another breath. Satisfied that his stomach would not react, he grunted, then snapped at Boots when his henchman appeared in the doorway, "I hope you had a good rest while I was gone, because you won't have much time to put your feet up from here on in."

"Is that right?"

Something about the tone of Boots's voice caused Max to stare at him for a silent second. With a flare of heat, Max realized that the weasel had the gall to be surly. "I'd watch my mouth if I was you," he said in a warning tone.

To his credit, Boots withheld a reply.

Looking past Boots, Max saw Ernie glance nervously at Banning, while Banning had no reaction at all. Max's small eyes narrowed. Two men who weren't worth a damn, and a third who might be too smart for his own good.

But they'd have to do.

Max entered the cabin, then slapped his saddlebags down on the table and said without preamble, "Get your gear packed and make sure we've got enough supplies for a couple of days. We're leaving as soon as we can get ready."

The trail was overgrown, inhibiting her view as Thea held her mount to a steady pace. She glanced up briefly at the position of the sun, realizing that morning had progressed into afternoon, but that for all intents and purposes, she was just as far from finding Quinn as she had been when she'd left Aunt Victoria hours earlier.

I found him once. I can find him again.

Brave words, when she had no idea where to look.

Struggling against encroaching panic, Thea reasoned that Quinn had to be somewhere near. He had said he couldn't stay long when he came to her room—obviously meaning that he needed to be back before he was missed. Steadfastly refusing to speculate who the person missing him might be, she had deduced that wherever Quinn was staying must be close enough so that he expected to reach Aunt Victoria's house and return before morning. With that thought in mind, she had taken the same trail where she had found him once before, hoping that logic and luck would prevail.

Thea glanced again at the position of the sun overhead, then at the foliage thickly lining the trail, and hope waned. Quinn could be anywhere. He could be a short distance ahead, or he could be somewhere miles deep into the heavily wooded area she was now passing. She could ride for hours longer without locating him, or she could find him around the next bend in the trail.

And if she did find him, what would she say?

She could say she was sorry—but Quinn had already said that, in the most final of ways.

She could tell him that she hadn't used him to assuage her grief—but the truth was that, in some ways, she had.

She could confess that she regretted having kept his resemblance to Wade a secret for so long—even though she knew those words were probably too late.

But Quinn had asked her to trust the way he made her feel. She hadn't responded then, and she should have, because she needed to tell Quinn that the way he made her feel was the only thing she'd been unable to deny. She needed to tell him that she had responded to *him* when she had lain in his arms, *to Quinn,* not the man she had once loved and who was now gone forever.

She needed to be sure Quinn understood that—and she'd *make* him listen when she found him.

If she found him.

"They've finished packing the horses. They're leaving."

Sheffield lowered her spyglass and shoved

it into her saddlebag. Without waiting for Perry's response, she mounted and turned her horse toward the ridge trail. Reining back when Perry did not immediately follow, she turned toward him with a frown.

"What are you waiting for, Perry?"

Again that look. It was the same look she had seen in Perry's eyes when she had appeared unexpectedly behind him after he returned. He had given her a detailed report of Max's travels after leaving the cabin, all stated in an emotionless tone that was totally unlike him. He had held himself aloof from her since then, keeping his distance, although she had felt his gaze following her.

Discomfited, Sheffield asked abruptly, "What's wrong?"

Perry mounted and urged his horse to her side. "Nothing's wrong."

"Then what—?"

Reaching out unexpectedly, Perry wrapped his arm around her waist, almost lifting her from the saddle as he kissed her long and deep.

Releasing her abruptly, Perry nudged his mount ahead of her on the trail, then turned back to order sharply, "You follow *my* orders, Sheffield, remember that."

"This is *my* case."

"It's your case because I gave it to you. But I'm here now, and I'll give the orders when the action starts."

"It's my case, Perry."

His expression as unyielding as stone, Perry snapped, "Tell me you'll follow my orders or you're off the case."

"You're crazy!"

"I mean it."

"Get out of the way." Struggling to edge her mount past him on the narrow trail, Sheffield exclaimed, "They're riding out of sight! Now isn't the time for this discussion."

"It isn't a discussion."

"Damn it, Perry!"

Perry remained obdurate.

"All right! You're the boss! I'll follow your orders when the action starts," Sheffield said. "Now, will you get out of the way?"

His expression unchanged, Perry ordered, "Stay behind me. *Behind me*, do you understand, Sheffield?"

Sheffield glared.

Falling resentfully into position at Perry's rear, Sheffield gritted her teeth.

She understood, all right. She understood only too well.

It was a man's world, but she had thought Perry was different.

He wasn't.

*   *   *

Victoria had never felt sicker—but she knew her ailment wasn't physical.

Standing at the edge of town with the sun warming her shoulders and Willowby's lazy afternoon traffic moving at a casual pace around her, Victoria felt her world rocking precariously under her feet.

She stared at the trail that wound into the hillside beyond town, questioning her judgment as she had countless times since Thea first disappeared from sight that morning.

Questions deluged her mind.

Why hadn't she talked Thea out of trying to find Quinn Banning?

Why hadn't she convinced her niece that she was making a mistake chasing after a man who was a virtual stranger?

Why hadn't she told Thea that she needed to put Quinn Banning and everything he had brought into her life behind her, so she could start over?

But what right did she have to tell Thea how to react to her feelings when she had no idea how to deal with her own?

Aware that she had begun to draw curious stares, Victoria turned around abruptly and started back down the street. Questions continued to plague her. When had things started going wrong between Larry and her? She had remained loyal to Luke's memory during the past years because she had loved him with all the vigor and passion of her youthful heart. Having known that kind of love, she had never even considered another man.

She had consoled Larry in the same way that he and Molly had consoled her after Luke was killed. She had shaken him from his despair in the same way they had shaken her. She had indulged the closeness that had grown between them, treasuring the deeper friendship that had evolved.

Then, with a few incautious words, their friendship had ended.

The fierce ache that accompanied the loss of that friendship was consuming her. She missed Larry. She yearned to talk to him, to share with him her fears for Thea. She needed his insight and his composure. She needed the reassurance that he'd be there for her to make everything right, whatever happened.

She needed . . . just to hear the sound of his voice.

Victoria raised a hand to cover her eyes.

"Is something wrong, Doc?"

Victoria's head jerked up at the sound of Sheriff Will Knowles's voice. Forcing a smile for the easygoing lawman, she responded, "No, it's just a little headache."

Will looked at her warmly. "You work too hard, Doc. You ought to take some time for yourself now that your niece is here to help you."

Thea.

Victoria's throat was suddenly tight.

"As a matter of fact, Millie down at the restaurant is cooking up one of her specialties tonight—Virginia ham. It's guaranteed to put that smile back on your face."

Was it so obvious that she was having trouble trying to smile?

Sheriff Knowles took a step closer, his expression sobering. "I'm hoping that if anything was wrong, you'd tell me right out. It's my job, you know, but aside from that, I'd consider it an honor and a privilege to have you confide in me."

Confide in him? This nice man who would never mean anything more to her than he did right now?

"Doc?"

When she had thoughtlessly forced out of her life a man who was truly dear?

Sheriff Knowles took her hand.

Withdrawing her hand gently from his, Victoria said, "I'm fine, Will. All I really need

right now is one of my own headache powders."

"If you say so."

"Thanks for the invitation to supper, but I don't have much of an appetite." Victoria forced an apologetic smile. "It might be nice to get together some time, though, in a group of friends."

Effecting a quick farewell, Victoria kept her eyes fixed on her house at the end of the street. It was her refuge—from all but a truth that was becoming progressively clearer.

His mood foul as they continued their steady progress along the trail, Boots addressed Max with open resentment.

"You still haven't told us where we're going, and I don't like it. Hell, for all we know, we could be following along like lambs to the slaughter while you take us in to collect the rewards on our heads."

"More like *jackasses* to the slaughter, you mean," Max countered, his mood equally foul. "You'll find out where we're going when the time comes for me to tell you."

"Maybe that time is now, boss," Ernie put in, resentment edging his voice as well. "It ain't safe working this way. If something happens, we'll be running around like chickens without heads, wondering which way to go."

"Nothing's going to happen."

Taking his opportunity, Quinn interjected, "The boys are right. You might've had a good reason for keeping everything a secret before, but now that you've counted us in, we need to know what you're planning. There's no way we can watch each other's backs when we don't know where to look or what to expect."

Quinn watched Max's reaction closely. He saw the shift of his gaze and the twitch of his lips that signaled the fact that Max didn't like being taken to task by his subordinates. But he also saw a narrowing of his eyes that said Max was considering what he had said.

"You want to know where we're going?" Max said finally. "We're going to fix things so we can cash in on a haul that's been lying around for more than a year."

"I knew it! It's them gold bars, ain't it?" Excitement flushed Boots's face with color. "You finally found a way to get rid of them."

"Gold bars?" Quinn feigned surprise. "What are you talking about?"

Responding in Max's stead, Boots said, "Gold bars . . . dozens of them! Max was in a saloon a while back when he overhead some bank clerk say that a big shipment was goin' to the railhead the next day. We thought it

was a payroll, but after we held up the wagon and lifted up the tarp, all we saw was gold! We figured we was rich, but the joke was on us. We ended up with more federal marshals on our tail than we could count, and there wasn't no way we could get rid of them gold bars. Me and the boys told Max to dump them, but Max wouldn't do it."

"The boys?"

"Yeah, well"—Boots glanced at Max—"Those fellas uh . . . didn't wait around to collect."

"Yeah, too bad." Max did not smile. "But I got it all worked out this time, and if everything goes right, it won't be long before we have more money in our pockets than any one of us ever dreamed of."

Quinn prodded, "What's the plan?"

Max responded gruffly, "I've got them gold bars hidden in an abandoned mine a little ways from here. All we have to do is pick them up and bring them to a fella named Whitmore. He'll take it from there, and two weeks later, we'll have our money."

Ernie grunted. "Two weeks?"

Boots snapped, "I ain't waiting two weeks!"

Turning venomously on the two men, Max replied, "You'll wait, all right, if you want your share."

Quinn questioned, "Who is this fella we're bringing the gold to? Can we trust him?"

Max's expression tightened. "Yeah, we can trust him, 'cause he knows if he tries anything, he's dead."

"Maybe that's not good enough. Maybe we should—"

The sound of hoofbeats on the trail ahead halted Boots's protest.

Jaw tight, Max signaled for caution as the hoofbeats drew closer.

"It's too late to stop her. She's going to ride right into them."

Watching from a vantage point on the ridge that allowed her a clear view of the trail below, Sheffield held her breath. That red hair was unmistakable. She had recognized the doc's niece the minute she saw her approaching from the opposite direction.

"Damn that Quinn!" she said angrily. "He said he didn't have anything going with the doc's niece. I should've known better than to believe him."

Perry scrutinized her intently. "How do you know she's looking for Quinn?"

"That woman's new to this country. She hasn't been in town long enough to get to know anybody out here. If she's riding out

this way, there's only one person she could be looking for."

"You're jumping to conclusions, Sheffield."

"Am I? I don't think so. And I think she's heading for trouble."

Unwilling to take that thought any further, Sheffield watched as the scene unfolded below.

Her expectations diminishing more with every thud of Brady's hooves, Thea negotiated a bend in the trail, then reined up short at the sight of four horsemen ahead.

One of the men was unmistakable.

Her heart leaping, Thea nudged her horse toward Quinn, only to hear Max snarl, "Stay where you are!"

Reining back at the open menace in his tone, Thea looked at Quinn. Her heart went cold when the eyes of a stranger returned her stare.

"You're a long way from home." Max swept her with an assessing glance before he continued. "What're you doing out here?"

Thea responded, "That's none of your concern."

Max's face reddened. "I asked you what you're doing out here."

"And I said—"

"She came out here to find me." Quinn nudged his mount close enough for Thea to see the ice in his gaze when he demanded, "What do you want, Thea?"

"I want to talk to you . . . alone."

"I said all I had to say to you the last time I saw you."

"But I didn't."

Interrupting, Max grated, "Get rid of her, Banning."

Rounding on him, Thea spat, "Quinn doesn't have to take your orders, and neither do I!"

Max's color deepened to a purple hue. "Get rid of her, Banning, or I will."

"Go home, Thea!"

Incredulous, somehow unable to move, Thea stared at Quinn. Who was he, really? Right now he bore no resemblance at all to the man who had held her in his arms a few nights before, the man who had loved her with tenderness and—

"Did you hear me, Thea? I said, go home."

"I can't leave before I explain—"

"We have nothing to talk about."

"We do! I need to tell you—"

"I already know as much as I want to know." His eyes drilled into hers. "I'm not in-

terested in anything you have to say. We're done, do you understand?"

"But—"

Ignoring her, Quinn looked back at Max. "Leave her here. Let's go."

"I'm warning you one last time. Make her leave," Max ordered.

Quinn spurred his mount to Thea's side. Looking directly into her eyes, he whispered, "It's over. I'm not Wade. I'm Quinn Banning . . . the man who got what he wanted from you, and who doesn't want any more. That should be plain enough even for you to understand."

Thea could not seem to move.

Snatching her reins, Quinn forcibly turned her mount. He shoved the reins back into her hands, then slapped the animal's backside, startling the horse into motion. "Don't come back!" he shouted after her.

Thea was riding hard, back in the direction from which she had come, when she realized with full clarity that she had left a total stranger behind her.

Chapter Nine

The afternoon sun beat down on his shoulders as Quinn scrutinized the surrounding hillside, his rifle cocked and ready. He turned briefly toward the grunting sounds coming from the dilapidated mine entrance behind him where Boots and Ernie were loading a wagon Max had procured a day earlier. He prepared himself for the onslaught to come as Boots shot him a venomous glance, then straightened up and addressed Max hotly.

"How come Ernie and me got to do all the dirty work—digging up them bars down in that mine and pushing them up to the surface on that car, and then loading them onto the wagon—when all Banning has to do is stand guard?"

Max snarled, "You ain't the only one getting his hands dirty. I'm working right beside you, ain't I?"

"Watching us like a hawk is more like it," Boots snarled in response. "You act like Ernie and me are going to take some of them gold bars for ourselves if we get a chance."

His patience expired, Max responded, "Look at it anyway you want—but just remember, I'm the boss here, and you do what I say."

"Yeah . . . how could I forget?"

His eyes narrowing, Quinn turned back to his surveillance of the surrounding terrain. Whatever Max's reason for putting him on guard, it suited him fine. Perry and Sheffield had taken the opportunity to signal their presence nearby while Max and the others were down in the mine retrieving the gold bars. His relief at that communication had been short-lived, however, when he'd realized from their signal that they were alone. Perry obviously hadn't learned enough about Max's plans when he had followed him to be able to alert the federal marshal. It appeared they'd be on their own right up to the end.

Quinn gave a snort. Well, being greatly outnumbered wasn't a big problem. Max was greedy. He would share the cache with as few people as possible in order to get the job done.

Continuing his surveillance of the surrounding terrain, Quinn drifted back to the moment two days earlier when Thea had appeared on the trail in front of them. He had known in an instant that if Max made a move to harm Thea, he would bring the whole thing to a premature end, then and there.

But Max hadn't made a move. Max had left it up to him to handle Thea, and he had said what he needed to say to make sure she was out of harm's way. He had told himself countless times during the tense two days afterwards that it had all happened for the best—but he had yet to make himself believe it.

Thea's fiery hair glinting in the broken shafts of sunlight filtering onto the trail, her fair complexion drained of color, her clear eyes wide with the shock and pain his cruel words had caused—that image continued to haunt him at a time when he was only too aware his attention should be focused on the dangerous hours ahead.

Forcibly ejecting Thea from his mind, Quinn reminded himself that Perry and Sheffield were depending on him, that their safety as well as the success of their mission now depended entirely on his assessment of the situation.

And it would all happen soon.

Sheffield glanced at Perry who was crouching behind a pile of boulders a few yards away, watching the scene below. Perry's hat was pulled down low on his forehead, and his light eyes were trained intently on the gold bars that glinted in the afternoon sunlight as they were loaded onto the back of the wagon.

Sheffield scrutinized the tense set of his broad shoulders and the sober lines of his handsome features. It occurred to Sheffield, she had previously believed Perry and she were so closely attuned that she was able to anticipate his thoughts in tense situations such as this, but too much had changed in the past few days for her to feel secure in that thinking now.

Something was wrong.

Uncertain, Sheffield scrutinized Perry a few moments longer. Perry hadn't been the same since he had returned to their camp after following Max. Aside from that brief, passionate kiss upon leaving the camp, he had held himself aloof from her, snapping orders and maintaining a coldly professional rela-

tionship that clearly defined their positions as supervisor and subordinate.

She didn't like it.

Nor would she accept it.

Turning toward her, Perry said, "They're almost ready to travel. It looks like the end is in sight."

Sheffield nodded, suddenly saddened. Yes, it did.

"Hold his head steady please, dear."

Thea nodded in response to Aunt Victoria's instructions and gripped their patient's ears tighter in an effort to hold him motionless. The effort proved futile when the fellow shook himself free, then swept a hot, moist tongue over her cheek. Thea gave an exasperated grunt.

"Stop that, Barney!" His eight-year-old face anxious, Billy Pace reprimanded the nervous hound occupying Aunt Victoria's examination table. He scolded, "Miss Thea don't want you to kiss her. She just wants you to sit still so the doc can fix you up."

Thea remembered Billy's earlier appearance at the door, with a bloodied and beaten Barney carried by the sympathetic cowpoke standing behind him. The animal had been bleeding profusely from a number of deep gashes inflicted in a fight with another canine, and Billy had been certain the dog was dying. To her surprise, Aunt Victoria had reacted in the same way she would have with any other patient, by ordering the animal to be taken to the dispensary, where she had begun working on him immediately.

In the time since, Aunt Thea had stopped the bleeding, and she was presently attempting to clean a nasty bite on the dog's neck, despite his resistance.

Glancing between the two women, Billy explained with a frown, "It wasn't Barney's fault, you know. He was just walking down the street, minding his own business, when Joe Miller's bear-hound came charging out after him. That dog's a bad one, and he's twice Barney's size. I tried to stop the fight, but I couldn't."

"You did the right thing bringing Barney here, Billy," Aunt Victoria responded in a tone that matched Billy's sobriety. "Barney might not have survived if the bleeding wasn't stopped."

"Yeah, there sure was a lot of blood." Billy's eyes filled, but he angrily shook off the tears, saying, "I'm going to tell old Joe Miller that his dog just ain't no good!"

"I think it might be best if you just took

Barney home when I'm done to make sure he gets some rest. He's had a hard time of things today."

"But that old bear-hound is a bad dog, Doc!"

"Yes, I know, but I think it would be best if you let adults handle it."

"Miss Thea . . ."

Almost smiling when Billy turned to her in wordless appeal, Thea replied, "I think Aunt Victoria is right, Billy. You'd be better off just taking Barney home so you can watch him for a while."

Silent until Aunt Victoria finished working and Barney was placed down on legs that were still wobbly, Billy then said, "I guess you're right. It looks like old Joe Miller will have to wait. Barney's going to need some tending to for a while."

Looking back up at Aunt Victoria, Billy asked, "How much do I owe you, Doc?" Reaching down into the pocket of his trousers, he withdrew three pennies and said, "I was on my way to the store to get myself some of them peppermints, so I've got the money to pay you."

Her expression sober, Aunt Victoria took two pennies from the boy's hand and said, "This will cover the cost quite nicely. Barney

should be feeling better in a few days if you take good care of him."

"I'll do that, ma'am. Come on, Barney."

Turning back toward Thea when Billy and his battered friend had cleared the doorway, Aunt Victoria smiled. "Billy's such a dear boy . . . and so serious. His father's dead, you know. He was killed when he was thrown from a horse a few years ago. Billy considers himself the man of the family now. I couldn't insult him by refusing to accept payment from him." Pausing, Aunt Victoria added, "Thank you for your help. Treating an animal is often hard. It's always facing the unexpected that's difficult."

True words.

Walking down the street as afternoon waned, Thea reviewed those words in her mind. The unexpected was always difficult, and sometimes painful.

I'm the man who got what he wanted from you, and who doesn't want any more. That should be clear enough even for you to understand.

After two days of denial, she had finally accepted the truth of that statement—and everything *was* finally clear.

Entering the post office, Thea forced a smile and handed her letter to the clerk.

The whiskered fellow smiled over the glasses perched at the end of his nose. "Let me see . . . this letter is going to a Miss Maribelle Carter in Georgia. Sending a letter back home, are you? I'm thinking there must be a few fellas back in Georgia who are missing a pretty lady like you."

Thea mumbled a few words in reply. Grateful to be on the street again, she walked back toward her aunt's house, her expression set. Maribelle would be glad to get her letter. Her old friend would be even happier to receive the message it conveyed. It had not been difficult writing the words, but a deep sense of dread grew greater with each step she took at the thought of speaking those same words aloud to her aunt.

It was never easy saying good-bye.

Progress over the uneven terrain with the heavily loaded wagon had been slow and tedious. The sun had begun descending into the horizon. The prospect of another day lost before reaching their destination did not sit well with Max's party, and tensions were high.

Quinn turned toward the wagon as Boots pulled back on the reins and drew it to an unceremonious halt. "I've had enough of this!" Boots burst out. "I want to know where we're going and how much longer it's going to take to get there."

Reining back beside him, Max growled, "I've had enough of you, too, so I'll do you a favor and ignore what you just said."

"I don't want you to ignore it." Boots's jaw firmed. "What I want is an answer. I done all your dirty work, and I got an answer coming."

Quinn saw the effort Max expended to maintain control. It occurred to him that under other circumstances, Max might have drawn his gun and ended the long-standing conflict with Boots then and there, but Max was holding back.

"What if I told you that you opened up your mouth just an hour too soon?" Max said.

"An hour too soon?" Boots shrugged. "I don't know what you're talking about."

"Jackass . . ."

"Jackass, am I?" Boots's hand moved toward his gun.

His own gun drawn before anyone had time to react, Quinn glared at Boots.

"Get your hand away from that gun. I didn't come all this way to have you mess things up at the last minute."

"At the last minute? It's been *the last minute* for days now. Hell, it'll be dark soon. Another day's ending, and for all we know, we ain't any closer to where we're going than we was before!"

"Jackass . . ." Glaring at Boots, Max said, "We'll be there inside an hour."

"An hour? There ain't no town that close around here."

"Who says we're going to a town?"

"Then where are we going?"

"Ain't you figured it out, yet?" Max laughed out loud. "Hell, anybody with half a brain would've."

His own patience waning, Quinn snapped, "Maybe we haven't got half a brain between us, so you might as well explain."

"We're going to the Conrad Smelter."

Silence.

"And we sure as hell ain't going to ride into the yard in broad daylight, with a full load of gold bars that are supposed to be slipped in with the next smelter shipment without anybody being the wiser."

Quinn grunted. So, that was how they expected to do it.

Turning toward Quinn, Max ordered, "Put that gun back in your holster."

Waiting until Quinn complied, Max scrutinized the expressions of the silent men around him. "You want to know the plan? Well, here it is. We deliver the gold to the smelter at night, when nobody's around to see us, and we load the bars in with the next shipment that's going out. Whitmore's the boss there. He's making up duplicate shipping papers, one set to travel with the shipment, the other set for the files at the smelter—so when payment comes back in a bank draft, he can put the amount corresponding to the filed papers in the company account, take out his share and transfer our money to an account in my name with everything matching up on his end." Max paused, then added, "Like I said, inside of two weeks, we'll be rich."

"I still don't like it."

Max turned on Boots with whipcord speed. "You don't like it, huh? Maybe you've got a better idea—like dumping them gold bars the way you wanted to a year ago!" When Boots did not respond, he continued, "Better yet, maybe you'd like to get out now and forfeit your share, just to be safe."

"Two weeks is too long to wait for our money. Too many things can go wrong."

Max cursed, then spat, "All right, let's get everything straight now. Who wants to back out of this deal?"

No response.

"Speak up!"

Ernie glanced at the men around him, then

said, "The plan sounds good to me. I ain't backing out."

Quinn interjected cautiously, "Me neither."

Scanning the faces of the others, Boots said, "Nobody's going to get my share, if that's what you're all thinking."

"Then I don't want to hear no more complaints!" Max snapped. "We'll be there in an hour and Whitmore will be waiting to meet us."

"One more thing," Boots said boldly. "I don't know how many others you cut in on this deal, but I'm telling you now, none of it's coming out of my share."

Quinn held his breath as Max turned slowly back toward Boots. Deadly menace in every word, he replied, "You know as well as I do that we robbed that shipment on our own a year ago. The only fella I cut in outside the four of us here is Whitmore—because we need him."

Quinn's jaw locked tight. It was confirmed. There had never been an inside contact on the robbery.

Thank you, Boots.

Yes, in an hour it would all be over.

"I'm sorry, Aunt Victoria. I need to go back home to Georgia."

Her aunt went abruptly still. "Home . . . but Willowby is your home now."

Thea was momentarily silent. She had returned from the post office only minutes earlier and found her aunt in the kitchen where they now stood. Wanting to get it over with, she had blurted out the words she had so loathed to say without properly preparing her aunt. Aching at the obvious distress she was causing this woman who had treated her with loving generosity, she responded, "I didn't make this decision lightly. I've been thinking about it for a long time."

"Is it something I've said or done?"

"Of course not. You've been wonderful to me . . . generous and helpful in every way."

"Then why?"

"I . . . I just don't think I'm suited to this country, Aunt Victoria."

"Is it because of Mr. Banning?"

Thea stiffened. Halting the spontaneous denial that sprang to her lips, Thea forced herself to explain. "I shouldn't have come here—and I should've realized that it would all turn out badly the day I arrived, when I met up with Quinn the first time."

"Dear . . . you're confused. You didn't meet up with Mr. Banning until later."

"No."

"But—"

"I saw him for the first time when the stage-coach was held up, Aunt Victoria."

Realization abruptly dawning, Aunt Victoria gasped. "Why didn't you tell me?"

"I couldn't."

"But the shock you must've suffered . . . the strain you were under . . . I would have acted differently if I had known. I might have been able to help you."

"That's all in the past now, but even though I've accepted the fact that Quinn isn't the man I wanted him to be, I can't stay. I need to get away—to go back to Georgia where I can put things in proper perspective again."

"Will you be coming back?" Aunt Victoria asked.

"I don't know."

Abruptly closing the distance between them, Aunt Victoria hugged Thea tightly, then drew back. Her smile tremulous, she said, "I'm so sorry that you came all this way to suffer such torment. I understand that you must do what you must, but I hope you'll remember that I'll miss you dreadfully, and that you'll always be welcome here."

"Aunt Victoria . . ."

Releasing her, Aunt Victoria took a steadying breath and attempted a smile. "When do you expect to leave?"

Her smile died when Thea replied, "By the end of the week."

The sun was rapidly setting when Max motioned his tense party to a halt. The shadowy outline of the smelter loomed in the distance as he ordered, "Wait here. I'll go ahead to make sure Whitmore is ready for us."

"I'll go with you," Boots grated. "I've had my fill of waiting."

"I'm going alone."

"Why?" Not bothering to conceal his distrust, Boots pressed, "Ernie and Banning can take care of the wagon. We don't need to leave a third man here."

"I'm going *alone*."

Boots mumbled a curse.

Ignoring him, Max instructed, "I want all of you to stay hidden up here until I signal you to come down."

His mind racing, Quinn glanced at the men beside him. He was uncertain at this point how closely Sheffield and Perry were following, and he needed to be sure they'd see the signal to close in when he gave it.

"Did you hear me, Banning?"

"I heard you."

They all watched intently as Max negotiated the trail down toward the smelter. Then Boots said, "You look nervous, Banning."

"Yeah, I'm nervous," Quinn responded coldly. "I'm about to become a rich man, and I don't want anything going wrong."

"*Maybe* you're about to become a rich man."

"What's that supposed to mean?"

"I know what you and Ernie think about what's been going on between me and Max, but I'm not as crazy as you think I am. I've been traveling with Max a long time, and he's got a look in his eyes that I seen a couple of times before. Each time, there ended up to be one person less to split the cache with."

"You are crazy, Boots." Ernie's objection was heated. "You're just mad because Max has been putting the pressure on you."

"I know what I'm talking about. Max needs us now. He'll need us right up until them bars are loaded and ready to be shipped out—but he won't need us afterwards."

"So?"

"So I'm telling you what that look in his eyes means. He's thinking that splitting the cache two ways is better than splitting it five ways."

"Tell him he's crazy, Banning."

Boots's smile was tight. "You don't think I'm crazy, do you, Banning?"

Quinn did not respond.

"That's what I thought." Boots continued, "I'm telling you now, you all watch my back, and I'll watch yours. Then maybe we'll live to spend that fortune we've got coming."

When neither Quinn nor Ernie responded, Boots grated, "All right, you don't have to say nothing. All you have to do is watch and listen . . . and remember that if Max turns on me, he'll turn on both of you, too."

Still silent, Quinn looked back at Max and saw that he was near the smelter. No, he didn't think Boots was crazy. On the contrary, he had just realized that Boots was a lot smarter than he had ever realized.

And that might be a problem.

Quinn resisted the urge to scan the terrain around him. The timing was going to be close.

Perry . . . Sheffield . . . where are you?

"Can you see them, Perry?" Sheffield called ahead softly.

She didn't like this. The darkness made for too many intangibles.

"Wait a minute. Rein up." Traveling ahead of her, Perry trained his spyglass on the trail below them, straining to see in the darkening twilight. Speaking more softly, he responded, "They're down there with the wagon . . . three of them." He cursed under his breath. "I don't see Max."

"He has to be there somewhere."

Nudging her mount alongside Perry's, Sheffield raised her spyglass to her eye to scan the terrain beyond. She hissed, "There he is. He's riding toward . . . well, I'll be damned! That looks like—"

"It's the Conrad Smelter."

Sheffield lowered her glass and stared at Perry. "The *Conrad Smelter?* You knew where he was heading?"

"I checked the map of this area when Max went to meet Whitmore. After he picked up the gold bars and started heading this way, I remembered there was a smelter somewhere out here."

"Did you?" Sheffield felt a slow heat rising. "But you didn't bother to share your thoughts with me."

Perry did not respond.

"What's the matter, Perry? Did you just want to be sure I kept my place and stayed those few steps behind, so it would be clear you were the *boss?*"

"Don't talk nonsense."

"You explain it to me, then. Why the sudden change in the way you're acting? Why are you keeping secrets from me?"

"You're imagining things."

"Imagining things—I'm acting like a woman—is that what you're saying?"

"This isn't the time or place for this discussion."

Silently agreeing, Sheffield raised her glass back to her eye, then hissed, "Max went into the smelter. It's so damned dark. I can hardly see. We have to get closer."

"I'll go down. You stay here."

"I will not!"

"I'm the boss, remember?"

"So, fire me. I'm going down there with you."

"Sheffield . . ."

"You're wasting precious time. Quinn's depending on us. I'm going down with you and that's the end of it!"

Perry's gaze lingered on her a moment too long, and Sheffield snapped, "I don't know what's going on in that head of yours, but I'm giving you two choices. Either get moving or get out of my way!"

Not waiting for Perry's response, Sheffield spurred her mount into motion.

* * *

"There he is! Max is waving a lantern." Ernie turned back toward Boots. "I guess everything's going like he planned and he wants us to bring the wagon down."

Flicking the reins against the team's backs, Boots started the wagon moving forward, his expression grim.

His expression equally solemn, Quinn flipped up the buckle on his saddlebag and reached furtively inside. His hand closed around the pouch he sought, and he withdrew it and slipped it into his pocket.

On the opposite side of the wagon, Ernie reined back abruptly, "Did you hear something behind us?" Signaling the others to do the same, he hissed, "I thought I heard something in the brush."

Immediately alert, Quinn scrutinized the surrounding foliage, then said, "I don't hear anything, but I'll go back and check."

"No, wait."

A sudden scurrying in the bushes behind them caused Boots to grunt, "If we keep stopping for every animal we hear, we'll have Max on our backs for sure. Come on! I want to get rid of these damned bars."

Dropping back as the wagon moved forward again, Quinn stared into the darkness behind them.

*   *   *

Still shaking after her mount almost lost its footing, Sheffield mumbled, "That was close."

Ahead of her, Perry whispered back, "Are you all right?"

"I'm all right. My horse stumbled, that's all."

But Sheffield knew that *wasn't* all. Her horse had lost its footing because she had lost her concentration, and she was only too aware that her momentary distraction could have proved disastrous. She also knew that agitation over Perry's behavior had caused the momentary lapse—a lapse for which no excuse was adequate when lives hung in the balance.

She could not allow this to continue.

Appearing suddenly beside her, Perry hissed, "You sound strange. Are you sure you're all right?" His arm slid around her waist. "You're shaking."

"Of course I'm shaking! I almost broke my damned neck."

"If you're not up to this—"

"Take your hand off me." Sheffield could feel the heat of Perry's gaze as she shrugged off his arm. "I don't know what you're trying to say—"

"I'm not trying to say anything."

"—but get this through your head. I've been working this case as Quinn's contact for almost a year without any help from you. I've handled every situation that came up without help, and I don't need help now. So just remember, even if you are my boss, stay out of my way."

"Sheffield—"

"Do I make myself clear?"

Tension throbbed in the darkness between them. "Just keep that horse on his feet and your rear end in the saddle, and everything will be fine."

Turning his mount, Perry left Sheffield shaking—with fury now—behind him.

Walking briskly as daylight faded, Victoria stepped out through the doorway of the general store clutching her purchases tightly, only to collide with a figure approaching from the opposite direction. Looking up as strong hands gripped her arms to steady her, she met Larry's startled gaze with her own.

Her stomach tightened when Larry's hands dropped back to his sides as if they had been singed. "I'm sorry." Victoria offered lamely. "I . . . I wasn't watching where I was going. I guess my mind was elsewhere."

The lights of the street lamps illuminated

the lines of strain visible in Larry's features as he said unexpectedly, "Actually, I was looking for you, Victoria." Victoria's heart leaped with hope that was cruelly dashed when he continued, "I wanted to thank you for taking care of my nephew's dog."

"Oh . . ." Struggling against the ache in her heart, Victoria continued, "Yes, well, Billy's a dear boy, and Barney was badly cut. I couldn't turn them away."

"My sister is an independent woman. You know how hard a time of it she's had since Martin was killed. I help her as much as she'll let me, but she's determined to take care of Billy the way his pa would have. Billy told her that you talked him out of going back to face old Joe Miller about his dog, and she's grateful. Joe's a nasty old coot, and she knows Billy would have ended up getting the worst of it,"

Inexplicably at a loss for words, Victoria responded, "Oh . . ."

"I told my sister I'd talk to Joe about his dog, so you won't have to worry about Billy bringing Barney in on a regular basis."

"Oh . . . good."

"I also want to pay you for taking care of Barney."

"Pay me?" Victoria shook her head. "No, Billy paid me." At Larry's raised brow, she explained. "He had pennies for peppermints. It was enough."

"Well"—Larry's gaze briefly lingered—"thanks again."

Tipping his hat, Larry was about to walk away when Victoria blurted, "Thea's going home . . . back to Georgia. She's leaving at the end of the week."

Larry turned back to meet her stricken expression. She felt a spark of the old camaraderie between them as he said, "I'm sorry to hear that. I know how you feel about your niece. Maybe she'll change her mind."

"No, she won't. Too many things have happened. She—"

Larry's gaze dropped toward her lips, and Victoria glanced away. Looking back at him a moment later, she saw an immense sadness flicker across his face before he said abruptly, "I'll try to stop by to see Thea before she leaves. Good-bye, Victoria."

Left standing on the shadowed boardwalk with Larry's polite good-bye echoing in her mind, Victoria swallowed to ease the tightness in her throat, then stiffly turned back toward home.

She had wanted to talk to Larry. She had so much to say. She wanted to confide in him about Thea. She wanted to see that look in his eyes that meant he wanted to make things right for her. She wanted to feel his strong arms around her, holding her comfortingly close. But most of all, she had wanted to apologize for hurting him.

Yet, in the space of an uncertain moment, she had spoiled it all again.

Stepping down off the boardwalk, Victoria turned toward her house at the end of the street, her pace just short of a run. Silently berating herself, she forced herself to admit that if Larry hadn't walked away when he did, she would have blurted out all those things, and would have finished by selfishly telling him she wanted their friendship back the way it had been before.

Selfishly.

Yes, that was the right description when one continued to want something that would only cause another person pain.

Yes, she ought to accept what was painfully clear.

Larry would not be back.

Standing in the shadows of the storefront where he had halted his rapid retreat only moments earlier, Larry watched as Victoria slipped out of sight through her doorway.

He was a damned old fool! He had missed

Victoria and had finally convinced himself that they might be able to overcome the moment that had changed everything between them. He had come to town earlier to speak to her, but he had hesitated, somehow unable to find the words he wanted to say.

With silent chagrin, he remembered seizing the excuse his sister had provided to talk to Victoria—but the result had been a disaster. He had betrayed himself again, and Victoria's reaction had been painfully clear.

Yes, he loved Victoria in a way she could not love him.

Yes, the closeness they had shared was past.

Yet the pain would not die.

The wagon rumbled down the steep trail toward the smelter. Riding ahead to spot pitfalls on the narrow road, Ernie called back with a warning that caused Boots to rein the team to a slower pace. Traveling in the rear, Quinn used the opportunity to scout the edge of the clearing behind him, aware that Perry and Sheffield would remain hidden there until they could emerge without being seen.

When he neared the smelter at last, Quinn looked at Max, who was waiting beside the office doorway. He then scanned the area briefly, noting that the smelter appeared to be deserted, just as Max had said it would be. He looked back toward the office as the door opened and a tall, thin fellow in an ill-fitting suit stepped into sight.

The man had the look of a nervous weasel. It could be no one else but Whitmore.

"Drive the wagon over there."

Max motioned toward a fortified shed nearby as he and Whitmore descended the stairs. His jaw tight, Quinn reined up behind as Boots drew the wagon to a halt.

"The next shipment is already loaded on pallets inside this shed," Max instructed gruffly. "Whitmore has the key, and he fixed it so there ain't any guards on duty. We need to unload the top pallets and put our bars in the middle of the shipment—then reload the pallets so the smelter bars are on top."

"Unload. Reload," Boots's voice boomed. "Hell, I ain't no donkey! What's the problem with putting our bars on top?"

"Lower your voice, jackass."

Boots stiffened as Max grated, "We need to put our bars in the middle of the shipment because we don't want nobody here noticing anything different when those bars go out."

"Sounds like a lot of work for nothing if you ask me."

"Nobody's asking you."

"We have no time to argue," Whitmore said nervously. "Just hurry up. We need to get this done as quickly as possible."

Jumping down from the wagon, Boots looked at Whitmore with open disgust. "I ain't never seen nobody as nervous as you. What's the matter? Afraid your great plans might not be so great after all?"

Glaring at him, Max snapped, "Shut up, Boots, and start moving."

Dismounting, Quinn leaned back against the wagon and withdrew the tobacco pouch from his pocket while the angry exchange continued. He reached into it and rolled a cigarette with a deft hand, then struck it with a match, as the conflict between the three men heightened.

"Just do what you're told and shut up."

The silence after Max's final outburst was broken by the shuffle of Boots's feet as he turned resentfully and followed Whitmore toward the fortified shed. Falling in line, Quinn turned back when Max said, "That cigarette's something new, ain't it? I ain't never seen you smoke before."

Not bothering to reply, Quinn took a last puff, then flicked the cigarette into the darkness and entered the shed.

Halting when Whitmore struck a match to the inside lantern, Quinn remained silent as Ernie stared at the loaded pallets, then said, "All that gold, and there ain't nothing any one of us could do with it if we took it."

"We don't have time for talk, I said." Whitmore was perspiring profusely. "Unload three tiers and stack your gold in between. There are more pallets in the corner."

His senses keenly attuned as they began emptying the pallets, Quinn counted off the minutes. He had smoked that damned cigarette, puffing for all he was worth, hoping that the small pinpoint of light could be seen from the thick foliage in the distance. If his signal hadn't been seen, he would be forced to endure—

Quinn's train of thought was halted by a whisper of sound outside the shed door. Moving to situate himself against the rear wall, he leaned down and grasped his leg.

Obviously agitated, Max snapped, "What's wrong with you, Banning?"

"Charley horse . . ." Quinn gripped his thigh tighter. "It'll be all right in a minute."

"Get back to work!" Flushed with exertion, Max grated, "I ain't standing for no prima donnas here."

"Wait a minute." Whitmore stiffened. "Did you hear that?"

Turning toward the door at the exact moment Perry and Sheffield stepped into sight with guns drawn, Whitmore gasped aloud.

Max's hand flashed to his holster.

"Don't try it." Quinn's gun was leveled and ready.

"Put your hands up!" Perry's command reverberated in the silence. "You're all under arrest."

"What's going on here?" Whitmore's eyes bulged at the sight of the star gleaming on Perry's chest. "I'm just having some of my employees reload this shipment."

"Save your breath, Whitmore" Quinn advised, never taking his eyes off Max. "And, you keep your hands away from your gun."

Stretching his hands high, his gaze shifting between Quinn and Sheffield, Max said, "The whore in the red dress—it's her, ain't it? She's the same one who was riding with them gold bars when we robbed them a year ago. I knew I seen her before."

"Too bad it took you so long to remember me." Sheffield's smile was thin. "Too bad . . . because if you had recognized me that first day in the doc's house, you might not be standing here now with your hands in the air and that stupid look on your face."

"Bitch!"

Casting her a warning glance, Perry ordered, "Get their guns, Sheffield."

"What are you going to do with us?" Whitmore's narrow face was drained of color. "I didn't have anything to do with the robbery, you know. I wouldn't be here right now if Max hadn't threatened me and forced me into this."

"You yellow bastard!" Lunging for Whitmore in sudden fury, Max knocked the taller man against the wall. Pulling his gun from his holster in a lightning-fast movement, he yanked Whitmore around as a shield. "I'm getting out of here. You can shoot if you want, but Whitmore will take the bullet and I'll have enough time to drop at least two of you—and the woman goes first!"

Satisfaction flickering across his thick features when everyone froze, Max looked at Perry and ordered, "Get out of the way."

"I'm going with you!" Boots started toward Max.

"No, you're not."

"Bastard, you ain't leaving without me."

Boots drew his revolver and gunfire rocked the room.

Diving to the floor, Quinn fired in Max's direction. His gun was still smoking when the room went abruptly silent.

Boots and Ernie were lying unmoving nearby. Quinn turned as Perry called out, "Sheffield, are you all right?"

Responding by springing toward the doorway, Sheffield jumped back in time to avoid the gunshots that cracked through the opening.

"Sheffield!"

"Max is getting away!" she shouted.

Charging through the doorway, Quinn stumbled over an obstacle in the shadows. He looked down to see Whitmore's still body, then looked up in time to see Max's mounted figure disappear into the darkness, with their mounts running alongside him.

Chapter Ten

The winding trail was bathed in early morning sunshine.

Glancing at the men riding shotgun on either side of the heavily loaded wagon as she guided it cautiously along the rutted tracks, Sheffield held the reins taut and her back rigid. Two days had passed since the night at the smelter when a blast of gunfire had ended the year-long search for the gold bars they were presently transporting to the nearest railhead. The same unnatural silence that had followed after the smoke cleared now continued.

To her left, Quinn was stone-faced, his eyes cold. It had not set well with him that Max

had escaped. She suspected that he had hated to deliver Whitmore's and Boots's bodies to the nearest town while knowing that the man directly responsible for their deaths was free. It wasn't much better that Ernie had been left with the doctor, narrowly clinging to life.

Max's escape gnawed at her innards too.

Sheffield glanced again at Quinn, her eyes narrowing. But she knew him well enough to be certain something else was bothering him. There was a look about him—all male—that made her think the doctor's niece had not seen the last of him.

Feeling the weight of someone's gaze, Sheffield glanced to her right to see Perry staring at her.

Perry and she had spoken few civil words since the shoot-out. He had turned furiously on her, berating her for charging after Max despite his orders.

Perry had accused her of reckless behavior ill-befitting a federal operative, and failure to follow his orders. He had said his report would contain those words.

She had accused him of glory-seeking and of prejudice against her gender. She had said she would contest his report.

Perry had spent a day seething, and another day boring a glaring hole into her back.

She had spent a day feeling incredulous that Perry could possibly be the same man whom she had charmed, teased and made passionate love with—and another day coming to the realization that that man no longer existed.

Sheffield raised her chin and fixed her eyes on the trail ahead. Whatever Perry decided to write in his report, simple truths could not be denied. Quinn and she had brought their assignment to a positive conclusion. The gold bars had been recovered and would soon be delivered to the railhead, where armed agents would escort them to their final destination. They had positively identified the thieves and established that they'd had no inside help from within the department. With one exception, they had brought to justice the men responsible for the theft.

For all intents and purposes, the black mark on her record had been nullified.

As for Max, she had already decided to request the assignment of bringing him in. She would go over Perry's head if she needed to, in order to have her request approved.

But—

Sheffield shifted uncomfortably.

The past two nights she had lain in her lonely bed with the memory of Perry's hard, warm body tormenting her. She could not banish the image of his deceptively loving gaze; and the thought of the warm lips that knew her body so well had kept her sleepless far longer than she cared to admit.

During those long, dark hours she had forcibly reminded herself that although Perry had managed to find a way into her heart, he was still only a man.

Only a man.

Sheffield tightened the reins.

She'd get over him.

Her bags packed and lying beside her feet, Thea stood on Willowby's dusty main street. She glanced at the early morning traffic as it continued around her, then spoke softly. "I don't want you to accompany me to the railhead, Aunt Victoria. It's unnecessary, and I'm uncomfortable knowing that you'll be traveling back alone."

"I've traveled alone while visiting patients more times than I can count. That doesn't worry me. What does worry me is the thought of making the same mistake I made when you came here, by allowing you to travel in unfamiliar country without an escort."

"I don't need an escort."

"You're going to have one anyway."

"Aunt Victoria . . ."

"Let me do this, dear," Aunt Victoria said simply.

The rattle of the stagecoach rounding the corner interrupted Thea's thoughts, and the knot inside her tightened. Looking up as it drew to a noisy halt nearby, Thea recognized the driver. "Seems like I just brought you to Willowby, Miss Thea. I didn't expect to be taking you back again so soon, but I'm pleased to have you as my passenger." He jumped down from his perch and leaned toward her to whisper, "It'll be a better trip this time. I promise."

Seeming to notice Aunt Victoria's sober traveling clothes for the first time, the driver picked up Thea's bags and asked, "You coming with us, too, Doc?"

"Yes, I am. I intend to keep Thea company until she boards the train for home—even if she protests, Jim."

"You sure you want to do that? It's a long drive."

"In good company." Aunt Victoria smiled. "You can put my bag up there, too."

Tossing the bags up onto the roof of the stagecoach, the driver climbed up to lash them securely before calling down to say, "Looks like you're my only passengers. Climb in, ladies, and we'll be on our way."

Forcing a smile, uncertain if it was for her aunt's benefit or for her own, Thea stepped up into the coach.

Holding himself stiffly erect in the saddle, Perry scrutinized the surrounding terrain as the noon hour approached. His body ached from the extended ride on the rough trail, and his eyes burned from his endless scrutiny of a countryside bathed in relentless sunshine.

Glancing at Sheffield, who maintained a stubborn silence at the reins of the wagon, Perry felt a familiar frustration. She was angry with him—but not as angry as he was with her.

The turbulent scene at the smelter two days earlier flashed before his mind, and Perry's agitation soared anew. He had been determined to protect Sheffield from harm as they trailed Quinn. He had told himself that the estrangement between them was temporary and necessary, that he needed to protect her from herself—all the while knowing that to speak those thoughts to Sheffield would be a death knell for any future between them.

He had truly believed that he was in control when they approached the smelter under cover of darkness, with Sheffield riding a few feet to his rear. He had not for a moment envisioned the horror of seeing her rush heedlessly out the door into the hail of Max's bullets.

Those gunshots had almost stopped his heart—and when Sheffield fell back through the door, miraculously unhurt, a hard truth had flashed before him.

He loved Sheffield too much to be able to face the day when luck would fail her.

He knew that Sheffield's hunger for him was matched only by his unrelenting hunger for her. But he knew something else, as well—that Sheffield's true passion had been committed elsewhere years before they met, to a principle that only she could clearly define.

Perry stared at Sheffield's rigid posture as she drove the wagon at a steady pace.

He loved her, but he was beginning to doubt that his love would be enough.

Standing a short distance away, Larry stared at the stagecoach as it rumbled out of sight on Willowby's main street. Frowning, he stepped up abruptly onto the boardwalk to cover the distance to the stagecoach office in a few impatient steps. Seeing the small, sparsely furnished quarters unmanned, he shouted, "Walter, where are you?"

"I'm here!"

Bumping his head as he popped up from behind the high counter, Walter Burns frowned and rubbed the sore spot on his bald crown. "What's got into you, Larry? You near scared the hell out of me."

"I saw the stage leaving a few minutes ago."

"Right on schedule, too."

"There were two passengers inside," Larry said.

"The doc and Miss Thea."

"Thea was going back to Georgia . . ."

Larry paused, waiting for the clerk to finish his statement. He had not intended to come back to bid Thea farewell because of the tension between Victoria and himself. That decision had been abruptly changed, however, by news that had reached his ranch about a shoot-out at the Conrad Smelter a few days earlier. He had paid little attention to the itinerant wrangler who arrived at the kitchen door until the fellow mentioned the name of the man who had escaped the federal agents involved.

The name was Max White.

Everything had begun falling together in his mind after that—Thea's strange reaction to Banning, which he now assumed was related to the stagecoach robbery the day she arrived; her shock when Max White came to Banning's sick room; Thea's unwillingness to discuss behavior that had confused and worried Victoria from the first. Regret at having dismissed Victoria's concerns had driven him to town in time to witness the women's departure.

Walter broke into Larry's thoughts, saying, "That's right, Miss Thea's going back home. I was sorry to hear it, too. Everybody in town figured she had come to stay, but I was even more surprised that Doc was going with her."

"Did Victoria say why she was leaving?"

"No. Doc bought a round-trip ticket, though. Miss Thea didn't."

Larry pressed, "How long did Victoria say she was staying in Georgia?"

"Oh, she ain't going that far. She's just keeping Miss Thea company as far as the railhead. I told her it seemed like a long trip for her to take when she was just going to turn around and come back again."

"So she's coming back on the next stage?"

"As soon as Miss Thea gets on the train, so she says."

"How long do you think that'll take?"

"Hard to say for sure. A day, maybe two, depending on what happens at the other end."

Larry paused, his frown deepening. "Is Jim carrying his shotgun?"

"What do you want to know that for?"

"Just answer the question."

"Jim always carries a shotgun under his seat—you know that—but that don't mean he's good at using it."

"Did Jim mention hearing anything about a dangerous fella by the name of Max White being on the loose around here?"

"Who in hell is Max White?"

That reply telling him all he needed to know, Larry mumbled a quick good-bye and left the puzzled clerk staring at his back as he strode back out onto the street.

They had stopped the wagon to tend to necessities and eat, but the silence between Sheffield and Perry had destroyed Quinn's already limited appetite.

The look on Perry's face when Sheffield stumbled back through the shed doorway with bullets flying around her had said it all. The fireworks had started between them as soon as the bullets stopped, and knowing both Sheffield and Perry as well as he did, Quinn was uncertain what the final outcome would be.

Remembering his own ill-fated relationship with Thea, Quinn felt regret surge anew.

As if reading his thoughts, Perry said abruptly, "What are your plans after we deliver the bars to the railhead?"

Quinn stiffened. "Why do you ask?"

"Because Max is a dangerous loose end that needs to be tied up. I want you to go back and see if you can pick up his trail."

"Oh, no, you don't!" Sheffield interjected. "You're not giving Quinn that assignment. I'm going after Max as soon as we drop these bars off at the railhead."

"No, you're not."

"Yes, I am."

"I said you're not." Perry stood up abruptly, towering over Sheffield. "You're going to accompany the shipment to their destination like you were supposed to a year ago."

"No."

"What do you mean, no?"

On her feet in an instant, Sheffield trembled with anger. "The word should be simple enough to comprehend. No means *no!* I won't do it!"

"I'm giving you an order, Sheffield."

"Put me on report. Fire me, if that will make you happy."

Perry was suddenly as angry as she. "You've

been begging me to fire you, but you don't think I'll do it."

"No, the trouble is, I think you will."

Perry went suddenly still. "Is that what you think, that I want you out of my service?"

"I don't want to talk about it."

"I do."

Turning her back on him, Sheffield addressed Quinn abruptly. "What about you?"

Quinn shrugged. "I was planning to go after Max whether Perry ordered me to or not."

"You're going to have some company."

Quinn glanced at Perry's tight expression, "The boss, here, has other ideas."

"The *boss* doesn't run my life."

"That's where you're wrong, Sheffield," Perry snapped. "The fact that you've spent a lot of time in my bed doesn't exempt you from following my orders."

"You've got it wrong there, Perry." Sheffield was livid. "You've spent a lot of time in *my* bed—not the other way around."

"You always have to be in control, don't you, Sheffield?"

"I think that statement suits you more than it does me."

Suddenly unwilling to listen to any more of the heated dispute, Quinn wrapped his uneaten food in the wrinkled wrapper and walked back to the wagon. The bickering continued behind him as he raised his face to the sky to study the position of the sun.

It was getting late. He wanted to reach the railhead by nightfall so he could get a good night's sleep before going out after Max.

A vision of fiery red hair and light eyes returned unexpectedly to haunt him. He had one stop to make before beginning his manhunt.

The argument behind him had halted. One look at the faces of the two involved revealed that the outcome had satisfied neither of them.

Quinn stood motionless as they approached.

He was just standing there, still as a statue.

The perfect target.

His heavy features beaded with sweat, Max raised his rifle to his eye and took aim. The star on Banning's chest glinted fittingly in his sights.

Max's finger tensed on the trigger.

Perspiration dripped unexpectedly from his forehead, blurring his vision and Max blinked. In that moment, sudden realization dawned. A bullet was too quick and too painless. A year's worth of deception couldn't be paid back in a fleeting second. Neither could the loss of the biggest haul of his life be avenged with a single bullet.

No, he needed more.

He needed to see Banning's face so he could be sure Banning knew where the bullet was coming from when it hit him. Most of all, he needed to have Banning know that he, Max, had won out in the end.

But the star on Banning's chest glinted so temptingly . . .

"The train's been delayed because of government business?"

Thea stared at the ticket clerk, waiting for his response. They had arrived at the railhead as evening fell, to the loud bawling of cattle in the congested pens, to the arrivals and departures of an endless stream of wagons and conveyances, and to the inevitable din of the saloons and dancehalls that lined the rutted, main thoroughfare.

The journey had been long and difficult, allowing her silent hours to review her encounters with Quinn from the first day onward. Admittedly, she had handled things poorly. There were so many questions she should have asked him that now would never be answered. It had come to her almost in afterthought, that although she now realized Quinn was not the man she had wanted him to be, she knew very little about the man he was.

Where did he come from? Was Banning his true surname? Did he have family in this area of the country? Was his startling resemblance to Wade a coincidence, or possibly—somehow—a matter of relationship? She had not asked any of the questions that under other circumstances might have been spontaneous.

The knowledge that her mistakes were irreversible had sent her straight to the ticket office, where she attempted to purchase a ticket on the first train heading east—only to suffer frustration there as well.

Smiling at her, the clerk replied to her question, "That's right, ma'am. Some kind of government business is holding the train up. It came over the wire a few hours ago."

"Do you know how long it will be delayed?"

"Can't say, ma'am." Appearing to enjoy the opportunity to converse with the red-haired belle standing at his counter, the counterman continued, "It might come through on schedule tomorrow morning at six o'clock, or it might be delayed for days."

"For days!"

"That might not be so bad as it sounds,

ma'am. This is a fine little town." The young fellow ran a hand over his slicked-back hair. "Folks here take pride in saying it's one of the most civilized towns in this part of the country. We have a fine ladies' haberdashery, a general store that ain't lacking in much, a nice restaurant that puts out a real good meal—especially on Saturday night—and countryside that can't be beat for pretty scenery. There's lots of friendly people around for good company, too. As a matter of fact"—the fellow leaned closer—"if you haven't had your supper yet, I'd be happy to escort you to Jessie Carter's place. She serves the best steaks in Wyoming."

"No . . . thank you." Thea turned away, then back to say, "How will I know when the next train is ready to leave?"

"You'll hear it, ma'am." The clerk winked. "I'll make the engineer blow that whistle extra loud for you."

Nodding with a weak smile, Thea walked back to the door, where Aunt Victoria waited.

"The train's been delayed."

"I heard."

"The clerk has no idea when it will arrive."

"I heard that, too."

"There's no need for you to wait with me, Aunt Victoria. You're needed in Willowby."

"I'm needed here, too. I haven't taken a vacation in fourteen years, so Willowby can do without me for a few days."

"But—"

"Thea"—Aunt Victoria's eyes grew moist—"I've realized only recently how much I've come to take important people in my life for granted. You came here, and I just expected that you'd stay. In some ways I neglected my duty to you, just as I've neglected too many other aspects of my life."

"That's not true."

"Yes, it is, but the past is past, and we have an opportunity to make the most of our time here. Let's get a room at the hotel. Then we can try Jessie Carter's place, as that young man suggested."

Aware that she had no recourse, Thea followed her aunt out onto the street.

Walking beside Victoria as they picked their way along the crowded boardwalk, Thea turned to scan the darkening thoroughfare. Spotting the general store across the street, Thea looked down at her ankle and the gaping hole where she had torn her stocking when climbing onto the stage. "I need to stop at the store," she said. "You go ahead to the hotel, Aunt Victoria. I'll join you in a few minutes."

As she waited to cross the flow of traffic, Thea looked toward the far end of the street, where the line of wagons appeared to be thinning.

Her breath caught in her throat when she spotted an approaching wagon and the man who rode beside it. The way he sat his horse, the stretch of his shoulders and his erect carriage, the manner in which he turned his head to scrutinize the crowded street . . .

The fellow twisted in his saddle to respond to the rider opposite him, and the badge pinned to his chest glinted in the rays of the fading sun.

No . . .

Rigid, Thea remained motionless as the wagon rumbled closer.

She could see the man's face clearly . . . the sharply chiseled features . . . the strong set of his jaw.

He was wearing a star.

His eyes met hers . . . dark eyes that she remembered so well.

Thea felt herself sway as Quinn dismounted, then stepped up onto the boardwalk. "What are you doing here, Thea?"

Breathing unsteadily, Thea reached out a shaky, tentative hand toward the badge on his chest.

The metal star was warm from his body heat.

It was real. He was alive.

Reality returned with sudden fury. "Is this some kind of cruel joke?" she demanded.

"What are you talking about?"

"You're not Wade!"

The dark eyes flickered. "No, I'm not Wade, Thea."

"Why are you pretending to be him?"

"I'm not."

"Then why are you wearing a star?"

"The badge is mine."

"No, it isn't! I know who you are, Quinn, and I know *what* you are. The first time I saw you, you were robbing a stage, and the last time I saw you, you were traveling with Max White—and we both know what he is."

Quinn's eyes narrowed.

Thea was trembling violently. "Tell me. Why are you wearing that star?"

Quinn responded slowly, "This badge belongs to me."

"Belongs to you . . ."

"I earned it a long time ago."

"You earned it being a thief?"

"Doing that, too."

"Tell me the truth, Quinn. I need to know."

* * *

The truth.

Quinn's frustration mounted. Thea had been as startled to see him as he had been to see her. Still more shocking to her, however, was the badge he wore—yet another inexplicable similarity between him and the deceased Wade.

But the badge was his, damn it! His badge, *not Wade's*. Law enforcement was a tradition passed on to him by his father, and his father's father before him. Like them, he had earned his badge with the sweat of his brow, and with the shedding of blood—some of it his own—and he'd let no man, living or dead, assume credit for it.

Aware that they were drawing the attention of passersby, Quinn pulled Thea into a nearby alleyway that afforded them privacy from curious stares. When they were no longer visible from the street, he grated, "Maybe you're right, Thea. Maybe everything that's happened between us is some kind of heartless joke—on both of us. Maybe a cruel fate brought us together just so you could pretend that Wade was alive again for a few passionate hours."

Thea gasped.

"But I'm not going to let the joke continue." Pinning her abruptly against the wall with the weight of his body, Quinn held himself hot and hard against her as he demanded, "Look at me, Thea." And when she would not, "Look at me, damn it! I'm alive—and I'm not Wade."

Pressing the revealing swell of his body to the juncture of her thighs, he added, "And this heat you feel is real, not the shadow of a dead man's passion."

"Let me go!"

Restraining her movement when she struggled to escape him, Quinn said, "That badge you feel against your breast is mine, too. I got it the hard way. I've had to do a lot of things that I wouldn't have chosen to do in order to earn it. I had to lie and pretend to be what I wasn't. I had to live with thieves and murderers, and I had to deceive good people along with the bad. I had to deceive you, too. The only difference between us is that my deceit ended when I took you into my arms."

"I didn't deceive you."

Unwilling to accept that answer, Quinn responded with dark eyes drilling into her, "You asked me to tell you the truth just now, and I did. Now it's time for you to tell *me* the truth."

His gaze deepening in intensity, Quinn asked abruptly, "When I rode up on the street just now, who did you think I was?"

Thea did not respond.

"Tell me."

Thea's throat worked convulsively. "I saw the badge. For a minute, I thought it had to be Wade, but . . . but I knew it couldn't be."

A slow ache beginning inside him, Quinn pressed, "The truth, Thea—when you realized it was me, not Wade, were you sorry?"

"No . . . yes . . . I mean—"

"Which is it?"

"For a moment I hoped it was Wade, because that would mean his death had been a terrible dream—but I wasn't sorry it was you."

Quinn's mouth twitched revealingly as he prodded, "Another truth, harder than the last—when I touch you, whose hands do you feel?"

"Please . . ."

"When I kiss you, whose lips do you taste?"

"Quinn . . ."

His mouth brushing hers, Quinn whispered, "Answer me. I need to know."

Covering Thea's mouth with his, Quinn kissed her long and deep, then pulled back abruptly. "Tell me the truth, Thea."

Thea did not respond, and Quinn brushed her mouth with his again. As Thea's arms suddenly curled around his neck, he pressed his kiss deeper, crushing her breathlessly tight against him, melding her to him with the blistering heat of a passion quickly rising out of control.

Sliding his hands into her hair, he held her steady under his kiss, drinking from her with a thirst made more desperate by aching nights of longing. He drew back from her abruptly to savor the matchless contours of her face with his kisses, the curve of her jaw.

Loosening the bodice of her dress with trembling hands, he tasted the warm hollows of her neck, traced the graceful line of her collarbone. He slipped the fine fabric of her bodice down further, baring the warm flesh beneath and suckling greedily. He was lost in a maelstrom of desire that only Thea could appease, a hunger reserved for her alone.

The unexpected sound of a step beside them jerked Quinn's head up. "Hurry up, fella. I'm next," a slurred voice demanded.

Cursing as Thea shuddered, Quinn turned toward the swaying cowboy. Shielding Thea's partial nakedness with his back, he said in a voice throbbing with fury, "Get out of here or you're a dead man."

Facing Thea again as the cowboy staggered back out onto the street, Quinn saw the effort she exerted to control her trembling as she struggled to fasten her dress.

He raised her chin so she was forced to meet his gaze. "You didn't answer me," Quinn pressed relentlessly. "I want the truth. Minutes ago—was it Wade you wanted . . . or was it me?"

Thea's hands halted abruptly at their task. A flicker of some indiscernible emotion moved across her face. Without speaking, she stepped away from him, her head held high, then walked back out onto the street and turned out of view.

Concealed in the darkness at the far end of the alleyway, Max barely controlled his glee as Banning stood motionless, staring at the spot where the red-haired whore had disappeared from view. The horny bastard had put on quite a show for him. Hell, if it hadn't been for the drunk who had wandered in on them, it might've gotten better yet.

Max faded back farther into the shadows as Banning stirred, then started back toward the street. He watched as Banning paused to look in the direction the woman had taken and then walked the other way—like the good peace officer he was, returning to duty.

Max's gleeful smile faded to a sneer. He

should've known that it had all been an act when the whore met them that day on the trail, when Banning told her he was done with her. Banning had brushed her off because he'd had no choice, but he had wasted no time mending the rift between them.

Max nodded. He hadn't been able to hear what they had said to each other, but they had some unfinished business together, those two.

Max pondered that thought.

Yeah, so did he.

Sitting on a hard wooden chair that made dozing impossible, Quinn ran his hand through his hair in a weary gesture, then turned to scan the silent interior of the Citizens First Bank with a professional eye. The gold bars had been delivered to the bank doors after closing, an hour earlier. After much protest and the assurance that he would not be held responsible for their safekeeping, the bank manager, a small man named Howard Forest, whose courage appeared to match his size, had swallowed his protests. With his Adam's apple bobbing, he had reluctantly allowed them to place the gold bars in the bank vault.

Quinn frowned, realizing that under other

circumstances, he might have disliked assuming the first watch while Perry and Sheffield checked the town for potential problems. The promise that he would be relieved of duty in two hours, however, had suited him fine.

Because of Thea.

Quinn stood up and began a slow pacing. Hell, what was wrong with him? Common sense seemed to abandon him every time Thea was within a few feet of him. He had tried to tell himself that there was only one piece of unfinished business between them, that an apology for his treatment of her would satisfy his conscience so he would be able to pursue Max with a clear mind.

His first glimpse of Thea, however, had proved how wrong he was.

Quinn remembered spotting Thea on the crowded walk. Her hair had been a blaze of color, but her face had been as white as chalk. Without conscious intent, he had gone immediately to her side, but conflict had flared the moment she spoke her first word.

Angry accusations . . . his own equally irate responses—the clash had gone from bad to worse. But despite his denials, he had not stopped wanting Thea. He realized now that he never would.

He also knew there could be only one reason for Thea's presence in town. She had decided to return to Georgia.

Frowning, Quinn glanced at the clock on the bank wall. In two hours he would be relieved of duty. Those same two hours would have given Thea time to calm herself.

He had seen Thea walk into the hotel as he had stepped out of the alleyway. He would go there, and they would talk.

Two more hours.

"Are you feeling better, Thea?"

Weaving her way along the crowded main street, Thea avoided responding to her aunt's question. She knew her aunt had noticed her lack of color when she had joined the older woman in the hotel room after her encounter with Quinn. She had forestalled her aunt's questions by claiming a slight nausea. They had gone to eat at her aunt's suggestion, and had visited the railroad ticket office afterwards, only to learn that the train schedule was still uncertain.

Thea fought to suppress the memory of those few revealing minutes in the alleyway. She had accused Quinn of so many things, and he had responded with an explanation that she could hardly believe. Yet when she was in his arms, disbelief became passion, and her humiliation was complete.

Raising her chin, Thea took a stabilizing breath. She needed to be away from this place where emotion assumed control of her senses. She needed to return to a point of safety where she could think clearly again.

Suddenly aware that Aunt Victoria still waited for a response to her question, Thea replied, "I feel fine now, Aunt Victoria."

Relieved to reach the hotel at last, Thea turned into the lobby with her aunt at her side. She nodded at the youthful clerk's greeting and started up the stairs.

Yes, she needed to return to Georgia.

She needed to leave Quinn forever behind her.

Max glanced warily up and down the brightly lit main street, then walked boldly out of the shadows. Stepping up onto the boardwalk, he joined the crowd there, sauntering along as if he hadn't a care in the world. Loud music from the swinging doors of saloons, shouts of laughter, an occasional voice raised in anger— the din of evening grew progressively louder.

Max smiled. The noise pleased him.

He continued his casual pace. He was nearing the entrance to the Horton Hotel where the Radcliffe woman was staying. He paused as he reached the doorway.

Walking beside Perry, the long length of her hair tucked up under her hat and her clothes loosely bloused to conceal her sex, Sheffield matched him stride for stride as she scrutinized the street.

They were approaching a spot across the street from the Horten Hotel, where there was a crowd near the entrance to the Black Steer Saloon, and the noise was especially boisterous. It occurred to her that few people staying in the hotel across the street would sleep soundly this night.

Sheffield glanced at Perry out of the corner of her eye. They had spoken few words during their survey of the town, and Sheffield was grateful. She had little to say to him.

She had thought Perry *believed* in her. She was so disillusioned in—

She tripped over a loose board in the walk, catching herself at the last minute. Her frantic effort to avoid falling drew loud guffaws from the drunken crowd.

"Keep your mind on business, Sheffield." Perry commanded.

Her face flaming, Sheffield spat, "Don't tell me how to do my job."

"If you had been watching where you were going, that wouldn't have happened."

"And if you were doing your job, you'd be watching the street instead of arguing with me now."

"Sheffield . . ."

Turning back to her scrutiny of the street, Sheffield felt as disillusionment expand to pain. *He's only a man*, she reminded herself.

Ignoring the loud guffaws coming from the drunken crowd across the street, Max slipped through the doorway of the Horten Hotel. He did not spare a glance for the pretentious crystal chandelier that dominated the elaborately wainscotted lobby, or the massive mahogany reception desk. "What's the number of Miss Radcliffe's room?" he asked the youthful clerk behind the desk. "She's waiting for me."

The clerk's smile faltered. "You're sure? The ladies just returned from dinner."

Max glared. "What's the number?"

"Number eight." The clerk took a nervous step backwards, then pointed. "To the right at the top of the stairs."

Leaning against the bar of the Black Steer Saloon, Larry turned toward the swinging doors. There was a burst of raucous laughter from the crowd of intoxicated wranglers congregated there. It appeared the cause of their amusement was a slender fellow who had almost fallen—

Larry blinked, then looked more closely. He started toward the door as the slender fellow moved on down the street beside his taller companion. Catching up to them in a few quick strides, Larry grasped the fellow's shoulder and turned him around roughly.

Two hands went to the holsters on their hips as he exclaimed, "I'll be damned! You look different without that red dress, but I knew it was you."

"Who is this fella, Sheffield?"

The taller man kept his hand on the handle of his gun, waiting for a response.

Surprised by the star glinting on Sheffield's chest, Larry noticed that the other man wore a badge as well. Suddenly sober, he questioned, "What's this all about?"

"Sheffield . . ."

Larry's eyes narrowed at the look the two exchanged. Glancing between them he had a sudden realization. "You're part of that group of federal men who were in the shoot-out at the Conrad Smelter, aren't you?"

The taller man's hand tightened on his gun.

"What do you know about the Conrad Smelter?"

"He's all right, Perry." Sheffield turned toward the tall fellow, continuing, "His name's Larry Hale. He's a friend of the doc in Willowby." She turned back to Larry and repeated the tall man's question. "What do you know about the Conrad Smelter?"

"Only that there was a shoot-out there with some federal officers, and that fella Max White got away. I knew White was involved in some way with Quinn Banning. I figured Thea was acting strange because she knew something about it. With Victoria and Thea traveling by stagecoach, I wasn't taking any chances White might show up, so I followed them here."

"Have you talked to them since you arrived?"

"No, not yet, but I intend to stay until Thea gets on that train and Victoria goes back to Willowby."

"To make sure they're all right."

Not bothering to confirm Sheffield's assumption, Larry said, "I need some answers."

Glancing only briefly toward the taller man, Sheffield replied, "The three of us were after a gang that robbed a Treasury Department shipment a year back. We caught up with them at the Conrad Smelter."

"The *three* of you . . ."

"Quinn is the third man."

"Quinn Banning?"

"The shipment's in the bank vault. He's guarding it."

Larry stared at Sheffield a moment longer, then looked at the tall man beside her. Extending his hand abruptly, he said, "Like Sheffield said, my name's Larry Hale. What's yours?"

Hesitating a moment before accepting his hand, the tall man replied, "Perry Locke."

"Now that we all know each other"—Larry looked directly into Locke's eyes—"I want to know the *whole* story."

Thea removed her essentials from her suitcase, avoiding her aunt's eye as she did the same. The thought that Quinn was in town somewhere—perhaps staying at this very hotel—that she might run into him again at any minute, stimulated both hopefulness and dread in her.

Turning toward the bed behind her, Thea struggled to maintain an emotionless facade. Quinn's relentless question haunted her.

Was it Wade you wanted . . . or was it me?

The reply had trembled on her lips, but in

a moment of sudden clarity, she had recognized the futility of response. She had seen the doubt in Quinn's eyes—a doubt that words could not dispel. Doubt that would eventually erode the feelings between them.

Yet . . .

A familiar ache began inside Thea. The ache leaped to hope at the sound of a heavy knock on the door. Her heart pounding, Thea watched as Aunt Victoria walked to the door and pulled it open.

"Hello, ladies . . ."

His gun drawn, Max shoved Victoria backward into the hotel room, then pushed the door shut behind him. A perverted enjoyment deepened his sneer as Thea grasped her aunt's arm to steady her.

"What are you doing here?" Thea demanded. "What do you want?"

Max's fleeting amusement vanished. "I want what's coming to me, that's what. And you're the one who's going to get it for me."

Victoria ordered, "Get out of here or I'll call for help."

"And your niece will be the first to get a bullet."

Victoria paled.

Pulling lengths of cord from his pocket,

Max threw them in Thea's direction. "I don't have time for talk. Tie your aunt up and make it fast."

Thea's jaw clenched stubbornly. "No."

"Do it! If you don't, I'll take care of your aunt myself."

Not doubting the menace in his tone, Thea took a short breath, then picked up the cord and turned stiffly toward her aunt. Max did not miss her sideward glance toward the door.

"Tie her, and hurry up about it. If you're thinking that your boyfriend might come up here any minute, you're wasting your time. The bastard's at the bank, keeping watch over the shipment that was supposed to make me rich. His two friends, that dark-haired bitch and her boyfriend, are out scouting the town—looking for me, no doubt—while I'm here, safe and sound, in your room."

Victoria looked at her niece. "What's he talking about, Thea?"

"I'm not sure."

"Not sure?" Max laughed aloud. "You're trying to tell me you didn't know that bastard Banning is a federal agent—that he rode with us for almost a full year just so's he could find out where I was hiding them gold bars we robbed? He thought he won out, too, but I'm here to prove him wrong."

Thea's hands faltered, and Max commanded with sudden rage, "Tie her tight—hands and feet."

After watching closely as Thea followed his orders, Max pushed her out of his way and leaned over Victoria's chair to check her bonds. Satisfied, he looked up at the older woman, his voice sinister. "The rest is up to you, Doc."

"To me!"

"You're the one who's going to have to carry my message to Banning."

"But—"

"Shut up and listen. Your niece is coming with me." At Victoria's gasp, he sneered, "If you try real hard, you'll be able to work yourself free before too long. Then it's up to you to get over to the bank to tell Banning that if he wants his bitch back, he's going to have to pay for her."

Momentarily amused at the older woman's dismay, Max continued, "Banning knows where to find the bank manager. It won't be hard for him to get the little weasel to open the vault and empty it out, even if Banning has to use his gun to do it. He knows how. He did it often enough while he was riding with me."

"What if he won't do it?" Victoria asked, with a revealing tremor in her voice.

"He will. Tell him he doesn't have time to think it over, that I'll be expecting him to meet me at sun-up, at the abandoned cabin by Winslow Creek, outside town—*with the money.*"

"But—"

"I told you to shut up and listen! Tell him I want him to come *alone* when he brings me the money. Tell him I'll be watching, and if I see any sign of that whore Sheffield or that big fella she's riding with—or anybody else— I'll put a bullet through his girlfriend's heart."

Ignoring Victoria's gasp, Max added, "And tell him not to try anything, like bringing me only a portion of what's in that vault, because if he doesn't bring me enough to make me happy, neither one of them will get out of this alive."

Turning toward Thea when she made a furtive move, Max snapped, "I ain't afraid to pull this trigger, just in case you're wondering."

Satisfied when Thea went still, Max picked up a scarf lying nearby and threw it at her. "Gag her." And when Thea hesitated, "Do it, now!"

When the gag was firmly in place, Max picked up the remaining cord and said to Thea, "Put your hands behind your back."

Thea gasped as the cord cut sharply into the tender skin at her wrists. Perversely pulling the cord tighter, Max jammed his gun against her side, enjoying himself immensely as he whispered against her flaming hair, "We're going down the back staircase and we're going to do it real quiet. I've got horses waiting for us there—and you'd better hope that by the time sun-up comes, Banning decides he cares more about you than he does about that badge he's wearing."

Allowing himself a last look at the woman he left behind, Max checked the hallway, then pushed Thea out the door.

Larry stood hesitantly on the boardwalk outside the Horten Hotel. He looked up at the newly painted facade, at the windows lit by pale lamplight as the raucous sounds of evening continued behind him at the Black Steer Saloon.

Sheffield and Perry Locke had disappeared from sight on the crowded walkway to continue scouting the teeming street. Their conversation had been brief but very informative.

Thea and Victoria were both ignorant of

the true facts; he was sure of it. He also knew they needed to be informed, if only for their own safety.

Entering the hotel lobby, Larry requested the number of Victoria's room. He suffered the youthful clerk's knowing look with little patience as he climbed the stairs to the second floor. Pausing outside the door, Larry hesitated, then knocked with a firm hand.

No response.

Larry waited, then knocked again.

Larry heard a faint thumping sound. The pounding of his heart accelerated. "Victoria?" he called out.

The thumping sound quickened, and Larry waited no longer.

Bursting through the locked door with a well-aimed kick of his boot, Larry uttered a muffled grunt of shock at the sight of Victoria, bound and gagged, her brown eyes frantic.

At her side in a moment, Larry ripped the gag from her mouth. He felt the hot brush of Victoria's breath as she rasped, "Larry . . . thank God you're here!"

The dimly lit office of the Citizens First Bank was no longer silent. The sound of anxious, gasping breaths and shuffling feet preceded

Howard Forest's weak protest as he walked toward the vault door, protesting, "You're supposed to be a lawman . . . a *federal* lawman!"

His jaw hard, his dark eyes icy, Quinn replied with gun drawn, "That's what I am, all right. Now open that damned vault."

Glancing at the gray-haired man standing beside him, then at the woman who stood nearby, Forest pleaded, "Talk to him, will you? Tell him—"

"Open the vault, damn it!" Quinn's patience had expired. "I don't have time to waste."

Forest's knobby Adam's apple bobbed convulsively as he turned toward the vault and began working the dial. Quinn glanced at the night sky outside the window. He looked at the clock on the office wall. Locating Forest's home and arousing the terrified fellow from bed had taken longer than he had anticipated. Sheffield and Perry would be returning soon to relieve him. He needed to have the bags of money carefully strapped to his saddle, and to be far enough away from town so that they would be unable to track him before daylight.

Thea's life depended on it.

Rage permeated Quinn's senses. Max—the bastard—this time he had gone too far.

Quinn fought for control. He needed to be

clearheaded. He needed to be able to think quickly in order to outsmart Max. He needed to see Thea healthy and whole, to hold her in his arms, to feel her warm against him, to taste her breath sweet against his lips. He needed—

He heard the last tumblers click.

He saw Forest pull the vault door open, then step back, perspiration beading his face.

He ordered gruffly, "Get over there, into the corner, and don't move."

Watching Forest's spasmodic movement out of the corner of his eye, Quinn turned toward Larry and directed, "Fill the sacks. Pack up everything that even resembles legal currency, and hurry up!"

Holding his gun on the seemingly paralyzed bank manager as Larry entered the vault, Quinn addressed Victoria tensely. "Max said I need to be at the cabin no later than sunrise?"

"That's right." Victoria was trembling visibly. "At Wi—"

"That's enough." Quinn glanced pointedly at Forest. "Perry and Sheffield will be here soon. I expect to be gone by then, and I don't want them to know where I'm meeting Max."

Stepping back into sight with bags heavily

loaded, Larry said, "You're not going there alone."

"Yes, I am."

"Max will be waiting for you, and we both know he doesn't intend to let you go."

"What he intends and what's going to happen are two different things."

"Quinn . . ." Aware that Victoria had used his given name for the first time, Quinn turned toward the shaken woman. "I'm sorry for all the terrible things I thought about you."

"Don't be sorry." Quinn frowned. "Most of them are probably true."

"You *will* bring her back safely. . . ."

He would . . . or he'd die trying.

"Quinn?"

"I'll bring her back."

Taking the sacks from Larry's hands without another word, Quinn hesitated, holstering his gun only after Larry drew his to level it on the trembling manager.

Mounted, the sacks secured to his saddle, Quinn nudged his mount into motion.

Chapter Eleven

Thea glanced around the dank cabin, her heart pounding as she struggled to loosen the ropes that bound her hands and feet. She winced as the cord cut more deeply into her wrists. She felt the heat of blood flow from the lacerated skin, but her struggles continued. The rough gag covering her mouth rubbed her lips raw as she attempted to pull it free using the corner of the wooden chair where she sat, but her efforts were useless.

Briefly closing her eyes, Thea attempted to rein in emotions rapidly racing out of control. Opening them at a sound outside the window, Thea felt her heart pound. She had no idea who or what it was that had made that sound. Max had brought her to the cabin hours earlier. He had tied her up immediately upon arriving. Saying little, he had regarded her with contempt when she tried to reason with him, and then gagged her with a promise to let her speak all those wasted words to her "boyfriend" one last time before he killed Quinn.

Then he had left the cabin. He had not returned, leaving her alone with the scurrying sounds in the shadows. She had heard him prowling around outside—him, or some other species of animal that used the darkness to its benefit.

Quinn's image flashed before her, and Thea's frustration soared. Everything he had told her was true, but she had refused to believe him.

Quinn moved quietly in the shadows surrounding the cabin. He had not expected it would take so long to locate the isolated cabin in the darkness.

Sunrise was imminent.

Inching closer, Quinn surveyed the cabin with a narrowed gaze. It was dimly lit—no doubt with a single lamp. The shadows could conceal any manner of ambush, inside or out. But he had no fear of a bullet in the darkness.

Max must have been following Sheffield, Perry and him for some time. If Max had wanted to end his life with a bullet from nowhere, his opportunities had been many.

No, Max wanted the satisfaction of facing him and proving that he was the one to win out in the end.

Quinn moved closer to the dilapidated structure. He spotted two horses tied up at the rail outside. One of them was Thea's, further evidence that Max had everything carefully planned.

Quinn silently cursed his stupidity. He should have known that Max would attempt retaliation. He should have realized that Max would look for his weakness—and that he would not have to look far.

But he had not, and Thea's life now hung in the balance.

Quinn used the shadows as his ally as he circled the cabin. Forcing impatience aside, he circled it cautiously a second time.

Satisfied, he inched closer.

Thea glanced at the window, her panic mounting. Dawn had lightened the night sky. The sun would soon be rising. She could not be sure that Aunt Victoria had been able to work herself free in time to find Quinn and tell him the conditions Max had demanded for her release. She almost hoped she had not. She did not fool herself that Max had any intention of allowing either Quinn or herself to leave the cabin alive.

Yet—

Her heart leaped at a rustle of movement outside the cabin's entrance. Thea gasped as the door crashed open wide and Quinn burst into the room, gun drawn. She saw him look at her and felt the control he exerted as he searched the shadows of the room with his gaze. She watched him approach her cautiously, then saw the pained look in his eyes when he crouched beside her, untied her gag and saw her abraded skin.

"Are you all right?"

Momentarily incapable of words Thea nodded.

"Where's Max?"

"I don't know. He left after he tied me up, and he hasn't come back."

Quinn slipped a knife from the sheath at his waist and cut the bonds on her ankles. Moving around her so that he still faced the door, he was leaning down to slash the cords on her wrists when the window crashed open with a startling shower of broken glass and Max shouted with shotgun aimed, "Get away from her, Banning, and throw the knife into the corner."

When Quinn hesitated, he commanded, "Now! Your handgun, too. This shotgun can do a lot of damage to a pretty young thing like your girlfriend."

Quinn tossed the knife and handgun as directed, then pulled himself up slowly to his full height. Looking up at him, Thea was startled to see no sign of anxiety as he responded, "I knew you were lurking somewhere around here."

"So you just walked in."

"Right."

"And you're alone. I made sure of that while I watched you prowling around the cabin." Pushing aside the broken glass, Max stepped through the opening and said, "Did you bring the money?"

"Yes."

"Where is it?"

"I hid it."

"I'm not going to play that game, Banning."

"I figure you don't have much choice if you want to get out of this a rich man, like you planned."

"Arrogant bastard!" Max advanced a threatening step closer. "One shot and your girlfriend's dead."

"Take that shot and you'll never find the money."

"You're trying my patience, Banning.—"

"I emptied the vault and brought every dollar in it with me, like you wanted. You have my word on that. You also have my word that if you let Thea go, I'll take you to where the money's hidden."

"No!" Thea's interjection was harsh. "He's going to kill you the minute he gets the money."

Ignoring her objection, Quinn continued, "Cut her loose and give her a horse. Then the money's yours."

"I won't go!"

Quinn turned toward Thea with a warning glance. Her complexion was drained of color, but her eyes were blazing as she said, "I won't leave here without you."

Max's gaze was deadly. "You'll go if I tell you to go."

"No, I won't. You can't make me."

"But I can make sure you *never* leave this place if you don't shut up!" Max growled and turned back to Quinn. "Once more, Banning . . . where's the money?"

"Let her go, and I'll take you to it."

"Don't do it!"

"Thea!" His angry retort momentarily halted her objection. "You've got nothing to lose, Max. When she's gone, you've still got me. That's what you really want, isn't it?"

"And the money."

"It can be yours, just the way you want it— but I wouldn't wait too long. Sheffield and Perry will be starting out soon."

"I told you—"

"I didn't tell them anything, but they must have discovered that the vault's been emptied by now—and Thea's aunt won't wait forever for her to return. If I don't miss my guess, she's looking out the window right now, waiting for sunrise with her hand on the doorknob, ready to go to Perry and Sheffield and tell them all they want to know if Thea doesn't come back."

His heavy features fiercely drawn, Max remained silent for long moments before saying, "You have the money . . ."

"My word of honor."

"I'm warning you now . . . if I let your woman go and I find out you're lying, you'll die real slow."

"Quinn!"

"I'm not lying."

Max's shifty-eyed gaze darted between the horror on Thea's face and Quinn's emotionless expression. He snapped, "Cut her loose, then toss the knife back into the corner—but remember, a shotgun blast covers more territory than a blade."

Retrieving the knife, Quinn walked back to Thea's chair and cut her free. He tossed the knife aside as Thea stood up abruptly, rubbing the lacerated flesh on her wrists. "I won't leave without you," she said.

"Listen to me, Thea," Quinn said flatly. "I want you to get on that horse and go."

"No."

"You'd better listen to him, girlie."

His gaze locking with hers, Quinn said, "Thea . . ."

Remaining adamant for long moments, Thea said abruptly, "All right."

Max stare at Thea, his gaze venomous. "Your horse is outside."

"I want to see her leave."

"You can hear—"

"I want to see her ride out of sight."

Max laughed. "Out of the range of my gun is what you're thinking."

Quinn did not reply.

"All right, you can watch your girlfriend go, but if either of you makes one false move—"

"Don't worry about that." Quinn turned toward Thea and said, "You heard him."

Thea's eyes burned into his. She did not move.

"Thea . . ."

Thea turned abruptly toward the door. Following behind her, Quinn watched as Thea mounted, then hesitated again.

"Tell her to get out of here before I change my mind," Max snarled.

Thea turned her horse sharply and rode off down the trail. Facing Max when the last flash of her blazing hair had disappeared from sight, Quinn was about to speak when Perry's familiar voice rang unexpectedly from the surrounding shadows.

"Drop your gun, Max."

"Bastard!"

Max emptied his gun in Perry's direction and gave a frenzied laugh when he heard a gasp of pain. In the next moment a rider burst out into the open from behind the cabin. Max could do nothing to save himself from being trampled under the horse's hooves.

Looking up as the clearing fell suddenly silent, Quinn saw Thea seated in the saddle, her face colorless as she looked down at him.

He heard the tremor in her voice as she said, "I couldn't leave you." Then she slid down off her horse into his waiting arms.

*   *   *

"Sheffield's fine." Victoria's voice betrayed her impatience at Perry's adamant concern. "She's young and healthy. I've removed the bullet from her shoulder and given her a powder that will numb the pain. The wound should heal quickly. All she needs now is a little rest."

Perry's worried expression did not change, nor did he reply. He remained looking down at Sheffield lying motionless on the narrow bed.

Victoria glanced at Larry, who was standing near the doorway, then addressed Sheffield directly. "You heard what I said. I don't expect any problems as a result of your wound, but I'll come back in an hour to check on you. Get some rest."

The door clicked closed behind Victoria and Larry. Perry seated himself in the chair beside the bed. Sheffield looked at him, her eyelids heavy as Perry said simply, "I love you, Sheffield."

There, he had said it—words he hadn't dared say before—words freed by the extraordinary circumstances of the day.

He remembered the look in Sheffield's eyes when they had set out from town, with Larry and a determined Victoria Sills riding behind. They had reached the cabin in time to see the shattered window and to overhear the muted conversation inside.

He recalled that there had been no fear in Sheffield's expression while they crouched in the shadows of the yard, waiting for the three inside to emerge.

It had all happened so quickly after that—Max turning unexpectedly toward them to fire blindly in their direction; Sheffield's grunt of pain when she was hit; Thea trampling Max down with her horse.

Strangely, he remembered few details after that, other than seeing Max lying dead beside the cabin as the sun broke through the trees, and Sheffield lying unconscious and bleeding in his arms.

Perry leaned toward Sheffield, emotion choking his throat as he stroked back a strand of heavy, dark hair from her cheek.

"Don't look at me like that, Perry." Sheffield's voice lacked its usual strength, but her gaze was clear. "You heard what the doc said. I'm fine. I just need a little rest."

He repeated softly, "I love you, Sheffield."

Perry had said it again. He loved her.

Sheffield winced as the pain in her shoulder stabbed more sharply. She spoke the only words that came to her lips, "I'm so sorry, Perry."

Reaching for the hand that stroked her cheek, Sheffield clenched it tightly. "I don't know what to say, Perry, except that you've picked the wrong woman to love—because . . . because I don't want to love you back."

She continued quickly, "I know you deserve an explanation. I'm not sure I can make you understand how I feel, but I'll try." She hesitated again, then said, "The truth is, you may love me, but you don't approve of me or my way of life. I've always known that, but I never really cared because I didn't need anybody's approval. It's always been my life and my choice. I've worked to establish my career all my life, since the day my father was killed—because he was my idol. He was dedicated to principles that he never needed to define to me because he lived them. He was the strongest man I ever knew, and he was the ideal I aspired to. I saw the pride in his eyes when I told him that. It didn't matter to him that I was a girl. He never challenged my choice because of my sex. I knew then, just as I know now, that he believed I could accomplish any goal I set my mind to."

Sheffield continued, "He was killed on the

job when I was eleven years old. My mother idolized my father, too, but with her it was different. Without my father, she was lost. She couldn't cope with the life that was left to her, and she just withered away. She died a few years later."

Sheffield took a shaky breath. "I loved my mother, Perry, but I *despised* her surrender. I told myself I'd never let myself be like her. I'd never let my love for a man weaken me to the point that I wasn't a person without him. I told myself that I'd show the world that I wasn't 'only a woman,' and that I was able to live up to the giant shadow my father cast."

Sheffield paused to regain her strength. "It wasn't easy. There weren't many people who believed I could possibly be good enough for the job my father had excelled at—because I was 'only a woman.' Of course, some generous fellas along the way offered to 'help' if I would agree to give a little in return, but I was determined to prove that I didn't need them— that I was as good as any man among them. And I did prove it."

Holding Perry's gaze, Sheffield rasped, "I didn't want to love any man, because I knew what loving a man could cost me. I held true to that resolve and enjoyed men without commitment, as my counterparts did. The life I've led as a result has been productive. It's also been full and satisfying . . . and the woman I am now is the product of that life." Her throat suddenly tight, Sheffield whispered, "It's too late for me to change, Perry, even if I wanted to."

Anger flashed in Perry's eyes.

"I'm so sorry."

Turning his hand, Perry gripped hers as securely as she had held his. He asked abruptly, "Did I ask you to change?"

Taken aback by his unexpected response, Sheffield did not reply.

"Maybe you shouldn't anticipate me, then."

Sheffield pressed, "Did you understand what I said, Perry?"

"You said a lot of things, and I understood most of it—but it's what you avoided saying that's really important." Leaning closer, his handsome features tense, his mouth only inches from hers, Perry whispered, "What you didn't say was whether you love me."

"Perry . . ."

"Answer me, Sheffield."

"How can I answer that question?"

"A yes or no will do."

"Perry . . ."

"Afraid, Sheffield?"

Responding with momentary anger to

Perry's challenge, Sheffield was silent, but the question remained.

Afraid?

Was she?

"I said I love you, Sheffield." Perry's light eyes would not yield. "I love *you*, not the person I thought I wanted you to be. I learned that the hard way, when I thought Max's bullet had robbed me of the chance to say these words."

"Perry . . ."

"Maybe *you're* the person who doesn't understand now, so I'll make myself clearer. I'm saying it doesn't matter to me that you're difficult and determined to prove that the normal boundaries of your sex don't apply to you—"

"Perry . . ."

"—that you're sometimes domineering and abrupt—"

"Like you?"

"—that I want to throttle you almost as often as I want to make love to you—because I realized during those revealing moments this morning that it was too late for me, too. I'm saying that I love you, Sheffield. I want you, *only* you, and it's too late for me to change."

Sheffield closed her eyes.

"I want you to stay the woman you are.

There's only one thing I'll demand in return."

Sheffield's eyes snapped open. *Demand?*

Perry continued, "I want to hear you say the words. I *need* to hear you say them."

No.

"Sheffield . . ."

She couldn't.

"Say it."

Could she?

"Sheffield . . ."

Suddenly unable to restrain the words he waited to hear, Sheffield whispered, "I love you, Perry."

Perry's spontaneous intake of breath reverberated inside Sheffield. She saw him swallow with difficulty. "One other thing," he whispered.

Oh, no . . .

"There's the technicality of marriage."

The coy, male bastard . . .

"Don't answer me now." Sheffield saw the smile that lurked at the corners of Perry's lips as he lowered his mouth to hers and mumbled before claiming it for his own, "We'll save that for another day."

"It's quiet in there all of a sudden." Standing in the hotel hallway outside the door to Sheffield's room, Larry questioned Victoria with iron gray brows drawn into a frown. "Do you think Sheffield finally fell asleep?"

"Probably. She's only a few doors down from my room, in any case. As I said, I'll check on her later. In the meantime, Perry will take good care of her."

Larry looked away as they approached her room. Aware that Thea was not inside, Victoria did not bother to knock. Instead, suddenly sober, she opened the door and said, "I never did thank you for coming to my aid like you did, Larry."

Larry looked back at her, his scowl deepening. "There's never been any need for formalities between us, Victoria." He paused before continuing. "I'd hoped there never would be."

Stepping into the room, Victoria held the door open in silent invitation for Larry to enter, then closed it behind him. "I needed to thank you, but there are other things I need to say, too."

Facing him, Victoria went on. "I suppose I ought to start by telling you that I was frightened after Max left me tied up here last night . . . more afraid than I've ever been in my life. But I wasn't frightened for myself. I was terrified that I wouldn't be able to get loose in time to reach Quinn. Then you were there at the door, and suddenly I knew everything was going to be all right."

Victoria saw a revealing twitch in Larry's jaw as she added more softly, "I was miserable when you kept your distance from me, Larry." She swallowed tightly. "I know why you did, even if you wouldn't say it. I kept telling myself that the dead feeling inside me came from knowing a valued friendship had been damaged beyond repair because I could never feel anything more for you than friendship."

"Victoria, you don't have to say any more."

"But I do!" The knot in Victoria's throat tightened as she continued, "You see, I'm so smart, being a doctor and all. I understand the human body so well. I know what to do when someone's injured, and I know what medicines to use when illness attacks. I comprehend fully the importance of nourishing the body with good food and drink, and an adequate amount of sleep, and I understand the dangers when a person is deprived of any of those important necessities."

"You're an excellent doctor, Victoria. You always have been."

"I am . . . but I never realized how limited my knowledge was when it came to matters of the heart." Victoria took a step closer to him, leaving them only a hairsbreadth apart. "You see, I thought the feeling I had for Luke was a once-in-a-lifetime thing, that I'd never feel that way again. I knew that you and Molly had a marriage that was very special."

Larry's gaze locked with hers as she continued, "I told myself I was satisfied just to remember love, and that you were, too. So, when you looked at me the way you did that day and I realized how you felt, I felt . . . I felt you had almost betrayed Molly and me both."

Larry sighed, then took a backward step. "I have to go."

"No, not yet, please. I haven't finished." Again closing the distance between them, Victoria whispered, "I was stupid, and I was wrong. I realized how wrong I was the moment you burst through that door yesterday, and all the misconceptions burst inside me as well. I knew then that I'd never rely on anyone the way I relied on you; that I'd never value a person's opinion the way I value yours; that I'd never go through the day wanting to share with anyone the way I want to share with you. I realized in that moment how much I had come to depend on your love. You're a part of me, Larry. No, I'll never know a love like I had for Luke again, because I was young and that was my first love. Nothing will ever take its place. The life you and Molly shared was special. Those days will be forever in your heart . . . but Molly's gone, too. And when all my misconceptions burst, Larry, I was left with only one realization—that I wanted to spend the rest of my life in your arms."

Larry did not reply.

Victoria searched his gaze, suddenly uncertain. "You do love me, don't you?"

Larry's lean face twitched with an undefinable emotion.

"Larry Hale, what are you waiting for? An invitation?"

His arms closing abruptly around her, Larry crushed her tight against the lean, tightly muscled length of him. She felt his hand in her hair, saw the revealing twitch of his gray mustache as he drew back to whisper, "Are you telling me you love me, Victoria Sills?"

Embarrassed by the sudden surge of heat his question evoked, Victoria responded, "What do you think?"

"Say it, Victoria . . . so I can hear it before I kiss you and my control is all shot to hell."

"Larry!"

"Say, it, darlin'."

Victoria took a shaky breath. "I love you, Larry."

"Damn it, woman . . ." Larry's voice dropped to a husky murmur. "I love you, too."

Larry kissed her then, and the truth of his desire was rock hard against her.

Larry's arms wound tighter and his kiss pressed deeper. Emotion swept her in an overwhelming swell, and Victoria surrendered to the love she had tried so hard to deny—her control all shot to hell, too.

Quinn stood stiffly at the railside as four sober-faced federal marshals finished their tally of the gold bars that had been loaded onto the train, then signed the shipping papers and handed him back a copy.

"All aboard!"

The blast of the train whistle . . . the harsh grating of metal wheels against rails . . . the labored groan of the engine as it pulled the cars into motion . . . the last, lingering particles of ash floating on the air as the train snaked out of sight in the distance . . .

Quinn folded the shipping receipt and placed it carefully in his pocket. It was over and done. The shipment was on its way. His assignment had been brought to a successful conclusion, but at a price he had not anticipated.

Quinn recounted the price slowly in his mind:

Boots dead.

Harry Whitmore dead.

Ernie lingering between life and death.

Sheffield wounded but recovering.

And, finally, Max, trampled beneath the hooves of Thea's horse.

Quinn recalled the moment when Thea slid down off the horse into his arms, after a reckless act of love that could not be denied.

Turning back toward the ticket office behind him, Quinn stared at Thea, who stood silently, waiting. They had spoken very little after Thea had slid off her horse into his arms. The echo of gunfire had still been reverberating in his mind when he saw Sheffield lying in Perry's arms as Victoria worked over her with silent concentration. Larry had gone to Max's body and nodded coldly, confirming that Max would never pose a threat again.

Words had been superfluous during the activity that followed: Sheffield was carefully conveyed to the hotel; Max's body was delivered without regret to the undertaker; a report was made to the local sheriff and the contents of the Citizens First Bank was returned to a shaken Howard Forest—all only short hours before the federal marshals arrived to transport the shipment of gold bars.

But the time had come for words that could no longer be withheld.

Quinn started toward Thea with long, rapid strides.

Quinn came to her side without speaking a word, gripped her arm firmly and drew her along with him down the street. Startled when he pulled her abruptly into the alleyway that had afforded them privacy once before, Thea gasped as Quinn took her into his arms and crushed her close.

Inhaling the male scent of him, reveling in the warmth of his powerful length—Thea closed her eyes at the pure bliss of the moment.

But Quinn drew back from her unexpectedly. His dark eyes drilled into hers as he said abruptly, "The first time you saw me, you were too startled to talk, Thea. The second time we met, you demanded to know who I was. I didn't answer you."

Thea replied, "I was confused then. I'm not confused anymore."

"You asked me who I was again later, when I thought the answer should've been clear to you, and I refused to answer then, too."

"Quinn . . ."

Quinn's deep voice dropped a note lower. "When I finally did respond, I was angry. I said a lot of things—"

"I said a lot of things, too."

"I want you to ask me that question again, Thea. It's time I gave you an answer."

Thea searched Quinn's strained countenance—the dark eyes burning with intensity, the strong profile that had haunted her dreams, the full lips she knew so well.

No, she didn't need an answer anymore. She knew who he was now.

"Ask me, Thea."

Thea shook her head.

"Are you afraid what my answer might be?"

Thea took a shaken breath. Quinn was right; the time had come for answers to all the questions that had plagued her. Whatever else followed, she needed to face the truth now, before her courage failed her.

Thea raised her chin slowly. Her heart pounding, her eyes locking with his, she forced herself to say, "All right. Tell me, once and for all. Who are you?"

Earnest, Quinn replied, "The answer is simple . . . so simple that you should've known what it was all along."

Searching her gaze for long moments, Quinn whispered in a husky tone that settled the question for all time, "Thea, I'm the man who loves you."

Epilogue

Thea opened her eyes to the first faint light of dawn filtering through the blinds of the silent room. Glancing at the bed beside her, she saw Quinn sleeping soundly, his lips lightly parted as he breathed evenly in peaceful slumber. She allowed herself to dwell for long moments on the image he presented in sleep. She studied his chiseled countenance, his dark hair and brows, his strong profile, his smooth skin tinted by the sun, his broad stretch of shoulder and depth of chest, his muscular arm slung across her waist.

She resisted the urge to touch his cheek, to press her lips to his as the memory of the tender night of passion swept her senses—

one of so many passionate nights since that day two years earlier when the whistle of a departing train had preceded his earnest declaration of love.

The soft cooing of a turtledove drew her attention to the window. Thea carefully inched herself out from under her husband's heavy arm. She stood briefly beside the bed, looking at him a moment longer before walking silently to the dresser.

She hesitated a moment before pulling out the drawer and withdrawing the documents lying there. She walked to the window, her mind unconsciously registering the scents of sage and cedar heavy on the morning air. She had become accustomed to those scents since Quinn and she had made Wyoming their home. Quinn had been assigned to duty there, and they had established a ranch a short distance from the place where Larry and Aunt Victoria now resided in wedded harmony.

She and Quinn had left Wyoming only once since then, to attend Sheffield and Perry's wedding in Washington, a long-awaited affair that had been too elaborate for Sheffield's tastes and too austere for Perry's well-connected family. She had remarked to Quinn's amused agreement, however, that the conflict appeared to have had little effect on the happiness of the bride and groom. She suspected they would continue to battle their respective viewpoints with loving fervor wherever their future took them.

As for Quinn and herself, she had come to the realization that destiny had had a hand in placing her on that stagecoach in the middle of the Wyoming wilderness two years earlier. Thea looked down at the sheets in her hand—official documents she had formally requested. The pages contained startling facts that were indisputable.

She perused the first birth certificate as she had countless times since receiving it:

"Quinn Robert Banning, born at the midnight hour, the first day of June 1853, in Dallas, Texas. Parents—Willis Quinn Banning and Janet Martin Banning."

Thea shifted the papers to reread the second:

"Wade Randolph Preston, born at midnight, the first day of June 1853, in Atlanta, Georgia. Parents—Samuel James Preston and Mary Holmes Preston."

The facts had left her trembling.

Two men, identical in appearance and alike in so many ways as to test credibility—born thousands of miles apart, on the same day and the same hour, to different parents who were related in no way.

She had pondered the information in secret, unwilling to allow Quinn to see the birth certificates until she could find a logical explanation for a phenomenon that seemed inexplicable. Distressed when she was able to find none, she had finally shown the documents to Quinn. She recalled the look in his dark eyes as he studied the elaborately penned sheets.

To her astonishment, Quinn had responded instinctively and without hesitation, saying that the birth certificates proved what he had already come to accept, that Wade and he had been born akin in spirit—destined to love only one woman.

He had taken her into his arms and whispered, "It's just sad that only one of us can have you."

Don't cry, Thea. We'll meet again.

With the loving comfort of those words echoing in her heart, Thea replaced the documents in the drawer and slipped back into bed. Sliding herself up warm and close against Quinn, she pressed her mouth to his. She had learned another indisputable fact from those legal documents. Like Quinn and Wade, she had been destined to love only one man.

Or was it two?

That question faded as Quinn's warm arms closed around her, and Thea's world was complete.

NIGHT RAVEN
Elaine Barbieri

With his fierce golden eyes, Night Raven sees a vision of the future that torments him, drives him to seek vengeance against the white man. Famed for his fearless exploits, sought after by the women of his tribe, he has sworn to show no mercy to the enemies of the Apache.

He sees her first in a dream, a woman with hair of shimmering gold and eyes of brilliant blue. Captured in battle, he is stunned when she appears to doctor his wounds, even more shocked by the traitorous longing she rouses in him. But when he manages to escape the fort, sweeping her onto his horse as hostage, he refuses to give in to his wildfire yearning. She, too, will know the torment of unfulfilled passion, he vows, for she is his enemy. But with each tender touch of her lips to his, Night Raven finds his resolve slipping, until captor becomes hostage and vengeance changes to mercy with the triumph of love.

WISHES ON THE WIND
ELAINE BARBIERI

Born of Irish immigrant parents, Meghan O'Connor's background dictates her hatred of the affluent Lang family. When a mining accident devastates her family, she realizes her friendship with David Lang places them both in peril. But as friendship blossoms into love Meghan will have to listen to her own conscience and follow her heart. . . .

Pampered heir David Lang lives in a world of opulence and luxury. But in Meghan O'Connor he finds the one person to whom he can entrust his heart and soul. Torn between loyalty to his family and love for the wrong woman, David knows his dreams of sharing the passion of a lifetime with Meghan are more than wishes on the wind.

___52348-5　　　　　　　　　　　　　$5.50 US/$6.50 CAN

Dorchester Publishing Co., Inc.
P.O. Box 6640
Wayne, PA 19087-8640

Please add $1.75 for shipping and handling for the first book and $.50 for each book thereafter. NY, NYC, and PA residents, please add appropriate sales tax. No cash, stamps, or C.O.D.s. All orders shipped within 6 weeks via postal service book rate. Canadian orders require $2.00 extra postage and must be paid in U.S. dollars through a U.S. banking facility.

Name_____
Address_____
City_____ State_____ Zip_____
I have enclosed $_____ in payment for the checked book(s).
Payment <u>must</u> accompany all orders. ❑ Please send a free catalog.
CHECK OUT OUR WEBSITE! www.dorchesterpub.com

AMBER FIRE

ELAINE BARBIERI

Melanie Morganfield has grown from a precocious child to a beautiful woman in Asa Parker's lavish home. Melanie is grateful to Asa for all he has done for her, and in her devotion, she longs to make happy the final years of the man who has cared for her in every way that he could. But when she meets Stephen Hull, his dark and youthful sensuality heats her blood in a way which she can neither ignore or deny. She knows instinctively that she must not ever see Stephen again, or she will be fanning the flames which are destined to lead to amber fire.

___52290-X $5.50 US/$6.50 CAN

Dorchester Publishing Co., Inc.
P.O. Box 6640
Wayne, PA 19087-8640

WINGS OF A DOVE
ELAINE BARBIERI

On the harrowing train ride from the slums and tenements of New York City to the wide open farmland of Michigan, Allie Pierce and Delaney Marsh form a bond that no one can break. Traveling to find a new life of opportunity and adventure in the heartland, the two orphans uncover their hearts' only desire. From childhood to adulthood, their friendship grows into something neither have planned or expected. For without Allie, Delaney is nothing more than a street tough, striving to prove his mettle. And without Delaney, Allie is little more than a sad wisp of a girl, frightened and alone. But together, the two will be able to carve opportunity from misfortune, understanding from discord, and ultimately find a passion that will last a lifetime.

___52323-X $5.99 US/$6.99 CAN

EAGLE
Elaine Barbieri

Cheyenne leader Gold Eagle's chiseled face and powerfully muscled body belie his wounded heart. Yet in an ambitious newspaperwoman named Mallory Tompkins, he finds the one thing that can soothe his tormented soul. But where fate has united them, deceit will destroy their bliss, unless they can forever join their love, their souls, their destinies.

___4469-2 $5.99 US/$6.99 CAN

Dorchester Publishing Co., Inc.
P.O. Box 6640
Wayne, PA 19087-8640

Please add $1.75 for shipping and handling for the first book and $.50 for each book thereafter. NY, NYC, and PA residents, please add appropriate sales tax. No cash, stamps, or C.O.D.s. All orders shipped within 6 weeks via postal service book rate. Canadian orders require $2.00 extra postage and must be paid in U.S. dollars through a U.S. banking facility.

Name_____
Address_____
City_____State_____Zip_____
I have enclosed $_____ in payment for the checked book(s).
Payment <u>must</u> accompany all orders. ☐ Please send a free catalog.
CHECK OUT OUR WEBSITE! www.dorchesterpub.com

HAWK

ELAINE BARBIERI

"How can you stand to let him touch you, Eden? He's an *injun!*" Young and idealistic, Eden believes passion will overcome the obstacle of her lover's Kiowa heritage; instead, the hatred and prejudice of two cultures at war force them apart. "Her arms cling to you and your heart answers, but the woman will never by yours." Such is the shaman's prediction about the beautiful girl he once adored, but Iron Hawk refuses to believe it. Eden's betrayal might have sent him to the white man's jail, but her smooth, pale body will still be his. A hardened warrior now, he believes her capture will satisfy his need for revenge; instead, her love will heal their hearts and bring a lasting peace to their people.

___4646-6 $5.99 US/$6.99 CAN

SOMETHING SOMETHING BORROWED, BLUE

ELAINE BARBIERI, CONSTANCE O'BANYON, EVELYN ROGERS, BOBBI SMITH

Here to capture that shimmering excitement, to bring to life the matrimonial mantra of "Something old, something new," are four spellbinding novellas by four historical-romance stars. In "Something Old," Elaine Barbieri crafts a suspenseful tale of an old grudge—and an old flame—that flare passionately—and dangerously—anew. In "Something New," can Constance O'Banyon arrange an arrogant bachelor father, a mysterious baby nurse, and a motherless newborn into the portrait of a proper South Carolina clan? In Evelyn Rogers's "Something Borrowed," a pretty widow and a gambler on the lam borrow identities—and each other—to board a wagon train West to freedom—and bliss. In "Something Blue," Bobbi Smith deftly engages a debonair cavalry officer and a feisty saloon girl in a moving tale of sexy steel and heartmelting magnolias.